FINAL DRAFT

FINAL DRAFT

An Olivia Lively Mystery

SHELLEY BURBANK

Encircle Publications
Farmington, Maine, U.S.A.

FINAL DRAFT Copyright © 2023 Shelley Burbank

Paperback ISBN 13: 978-1-64599-442-8
E-book ISBN 13: 978-1-64599-443-5

Library of Congress Control Number: 2023932971

Cover design by Deirdre Wait
Cover images © Getty Images

Edited by Cynthia Brackett-Vincent

Published by:

Encircle Publications
PO Box 187
Farmington, ME 04938

info@encirclepub.com
http://encirclepub.com

To Craig Burbank,
I couldn't have done this without you, babe.

Prologue

• • • • • • • • • • • • •

In her line of work, private investigator Olivia Lively often found it easiest to hide in plain sight.

Tonight she chose a shoulder-length, ash-blonde wig to cover her dark-brunette pixie cut, lightened her olive skin with foundation, and slicked on some sheer pink gloss rather than her signature classic red lipstick. A pink mini skirt, striped sweater, and black combat boots dropped her age by ten years, from thirty to twenty. Just before leaving her Munjoy Hill apartment, she slid into a tattered black raincoat she'd picked up at Goodwill the previous week.

A short cab ride to the Old Port later, Liv slouched over the bar at El Gordito Burrito and nursed a disgustingly-sweet strawberry margarita. Next to her, a group of art-school students carried on a boisterous conversation. She smiled when the kids laughed, leaned closer to them whenever the door opened. Anyone glancing her way would think she was part of the crowd.

Sure enough, at 7:13 p.m., he entered the restaurant. Robert Mickelson. Her target.

Also, her former client.

And, even worse, her not-quite-divorced boyfriend.

He'd called that afternoon to tell her he was going out of town for work, so he couldn't meet for their regular Wednesday evening rendevouz. "Sorry, babe," he said. "I have a seven o'clock flight from the Jetport. You know how it is."

She'd heard the lie in his voice and known he wasn't embarking on one of his frequent business trips. He was spending the evening with someone else. His soon-to-be ex-wife, Gina, maybe, or more likely, *another* other woman.

Following a hunch, Liv figured he'd show up at El Gordito. He liked the mezcal drinks they served and the dark table in the corner perfect for shadowy kisses, warm hands sliding up short skirts, and naughty whispers.

She ought to know. She'd been there with him often enough.

Her intuition proved accurate. Liv sipped her drink as Rob guided a pretty, young blonde to the expected back table. She made a face as the sweetness hit the back of her throat and Rob bent to kiss the woman's cheek in a practiced move Liv knew all too well.

The blonde looked to be twenty-two, twenty-five at the most. Liv's dark mood deepened. She had the worst taste in men. Always had. Rob Mickelson was just the latest in a long series of mistakes. Any guy who cheated on his wife would also cheat on his girlfriend. At her age, she should have known better than to be that girlfriend.

That he was a client made it even worse. He'd told her he was filing for divorce, but still. Mixing business and pleasure was dumb, not to mention borderline unethical.

The worst part was she'd developed actual feelings for the jerk. Maybe not love, but something close. When weeks turned into months and Rob still didn't leave Gina, Liv should have ended it. She'd held out, though, hoping his divorce would make it all "okay" in the end.

She'd been fooling herself. The realization hit her like a salty, bone-chilling Atlantic wave. Whatever Rob had wanted from her, it wasn't meaningful or exclusive or special. It was simply sleazy.

She needed to end it.

Tonight.

Liv pulled out her phone, snapped a few photos of the couple snuggling close together in the booth. She ordered another marg, regular this time with a salted edge, and waited. When they left, she followed them at a discreet distance to The Cormorant on Congress Street, the elegant hotel where she and Rob had spent so many clandestine evenings. In the lobby, all spiky gold and crystal chandeliers overhead, muted gray and mauve banquette seats, and Scalamandre wall-coverings, Liv took more photos of Rob and the blonde kissing in front of the elevators.

Liv allowed herself a grim smile. Gina might find the pics interesting. She'd send them tomorrow. At least then Rob's wife would have some ammunition with which to fight back if—*big if*—Rob filed for divorce. As far as revenge schemes went, it was pretty weak, but Liv wouldn't lower herself to something like slashing his tires.

Anything else she could think of would land her in prison.

When Rob and the girl stepped into the elevator and the doors slid shut, Liv watched the indicator light. Third floor. *Their* floor.

Liv's eyebrows drew together beneath the short bangs of her wig. Probably booked their usual room, too, she thought. She'd expected him to be a bit more original, but so far, everything about this evening made her feel interchangeable, unremarkable, and cheap.

She despised him for it, yes, but at the moment, she despised herself even more.

Stalking to the front desk, Liv disguised her feelings with an impersonal smile. "Good evening. I'd like a bottle of Veuve Clicquot sent to room 312, please." She dug into her handbag and held out a credit card. "Can you include a note? Have it say, 'Enjoy your evening. We're done.' Sign it Liv. L.I.V. Okay?"

The woman behind the desk tapped her computer keyboard, inspected the card, ran it, and handed it back. "There you are, Ms. Lively. I'll have that sent right up."

"Thank you. Have a good night." Liv stepped out onto a drizzle-soaked sidewalk and decided to walk home despite the fog that had rolled in off Casco Bay. The cold, damp air would help clear her head. God knew she needed it.

Halfway home, her phone vibrated in her hand. She looked down at the screen. Rob.

She reached up to adjust her wig and let the call go to voicemail. When the screen went dark, she slipped the phone into her handbag. She shoved her hands into the deep pockets of her raincoat, walked the cold, wet streets past the Longfellow statue in Monument Square, the hulking edifice of the downtown Portland Fire Station, shadowy Lincoln Park, and the Observatory not far from her apartment overlooking the city. Reaching home, she vowed never to see or speak to Robert Mickelson again. *So. Totally. Done.*

Chapter One

• • • • • • • • • • • • • •

"What's a private detective doing at a shindig like this?" The white-haired gentleman with the goatee and sequined bow tie nudged Olivia Lively's arm, sloshing her glass of sparkling white and earning himself a glare that could refreeze the melting ice cubes in his glass of scotch.

"Oh, I don't know." Liv drained what was left of the wine and signaled to the bartender for another. "Maybe I got tired of spying on gangsters, hanging out on the docks with smugglers, and tailing Mexican drug lords through the streets of Portland." She gave him a mocking smile.

The short, Colonel Sanders look-alike—who happened to be one of Maine's most celebrated poets—honked out a drunken laugh and wagged a finger at her. "Funny girl," he said, slurring his words.

The bartender set a flute in front of her and gave her a sympathetic smile.

"Excuse me." Liv slid from her bar stool. So much for socializing.

She smoothed the green fabric of her Halston gown, a second-hand find bought online for a song, and looked around. She spotted her best friend, Ashleigh, near one of the silent-auction tables where a playful, modern painting was on display.

Mindful of her champagne flute, Liv wove through the well-heeled crowd toward Ashleigh. She'd had her eye on that Rick Hamilton piece all night. Time to put in her bid.

The Telling Room event planners had outdone themselves.

Glittery decor transformed the venue into an Art Deco fantasy. Twinkle-lights looped in long strands across the ceiling. Slim, gold bud vases held single white roses on tables draped in black and white linen. Several young couples, dressed in Roaring Twenties finery, jitterbugged on the parquet dance floor in the corner.

Unlike the stuffy social affairs of her parents' circle, the Glitterati Ball attracted a much more laid-back, affable crowd.

Swaying through the room in the Halston, her grandmother's emerald earrings swinging from her ears, Liv caught several admiring glances. A few people, recognizing her, nodded and smiled. She waved acknowledgment but didn't stop to chat. That Hamilton painting would look perfect hanging above her bed, and she wasn't about to let anyone, not even her best friend, outbid her.

She'd almost reached the painting when someone grabbed her arm.

She tensed, turned.

She was surprised to see the bartender. He was in his mid-twenties, kind of cute with curly brown hair and a dimple in his chin. He glanced past her shoulder and dropped her arm. "I need to talk to you," he said. "It's about, um, a private detective thing. A job."

Liv narrowed her eyes. "Seriously?"

The guy glanced around again. He seemed nervous. Maybe a little desperate. "Yeah. Can we just, you know, go somewhere a little less crowded?"

"All right. Hold on." Liv pressed her lips together for a moment. "Blame it on the champagne, but the only place I can think of at the moment is the coatroom. Let's go."

Giving up on the painting for the time being, she headed for the coat-check area which had been decorated with potted plants and more white twinkle lights and a beautiful Art Deco mirror. She felt a slight prickle of excitement. The evening had taken an unexpected, somewhat delightful, turn.

"Hi there. We need a moment." She flashed a smile and a twenty at the attendant who gave her a suspicious look but accepted the money and stepped aside. Liv and the bartender slipped into the narrow space filled with down puffer coats, capes, and woolens.

"Okay," Liv said, crossing her arms. "Who are you and what's this all about?"

•   •   •   •   •

"Mason Falwell stole my novel!"

With no preamble, the words burst from the cute bartender's mouth. He leaned closer to her, crowding her in the already close confines of the space. "I heard you tell that guy you're a detective. My name's Cooper Tedeschi. I'm a writing student. In the MFA program at Longfellow College." Cooper's mouth twisted. "At least, I used to be a student there."

"Okay." Liv put up a hand. No need for him to get any closer. "So?"

"So, Falwell, that washed-up, old coot, took my manuscript, sent it to his agent, and got a publishing contract." Cooper's nostrils flared. "There's even talk of a movie deal. He's going to make a fortune. With *my* story. I need you to help me prove it."

Mason Falwell.

Liv knew the name. Everyone knew the name. He'd won lots of prizes for fiction back in the '80s and '90s and was Maine's most famous writer... after Stephen King, of course.

Falwell's work had been translated around the world. His short stories and essays had appeared in prominent magazines. A popular speaker, he had presented papers on the history of fantasy and science fiction literature at numerous writing programs, book conventions, and college campuses every year. He still filled auditoriums when he gave infrequent readings at Longfellow College where he taught in the creative writing program.

As Cooper breathed heavily, face suffused with color and rage, Liv recoiled. His claims seemed highly improbable. Was this guy stable? She glanced over his shoulder. Cooper stood between her and the exit. Best to let him have his say, hand him her card, and give him the standard brush-off.

"You're Mason Falwell's student?"

"Yes. Or I was. He was my advisor, that ambulatory shell of a decaying has-been!"

"Well, you trash-talk like a writer, I'll give you that much."

He glared at her, clenching his fists. "You think I'm crazy?"

"I'm sorry, but this is very hard to believe. Why would Falwell steal your story?"

"Because he hasn't written anything for years!" Cooper shoved his hands into his pockets, hunched his shoulders. "Look, I know it's hard to believe, but it's true. He was my MFA advisor. My mentor. I'd been revising my manuscript for months. Falwell said the story needed work but was promising. He gave me notes and suggestions. He encouraged me! Next thing I know, he's announcing this new book deal. I'm telling you, it's *my story*."

"Did you confront him?"

"Of course I did…"

The coat check attendant pushed into the room, a ticket in her hand. "You two about done in here? People are starting to leave." She reached behind Cooper for a coat.

"Yes. Just one more minute. Thank you so much."

"Hurry it up, then."

Liv turned back to Cooper. "So, in a nutshell, what happened?"

"When I accused him, he denied everything. I went to the head of the department, the dean, the president of the university. Falwell claimed I was delusional. I went to the college paper, and they wrote a story. Next thing you know, the editor of the paper's fired, and I'm kicked out of the program. The whole thing's swept under the rug." His jaw clenched and unclenched a couple of times. "I worked almost two years on that novel and my degree, and now I have nothing to show for any of it. No degree. No book. Nothing… except a bunch of student loans to pay back."

"So what do you want? Have you talked to a lawyer?"

Cooper let out a mirthless laugh. "What do I want? Let's see. Falwell's head on a platter, for starters. Barring that, I want to sue the university for wrongful dismissal. I want credit for my work. I want my MFA. I've met with a lawyer, but nothing's happened yet. He says my claims will be hard to prove. When I overheard that comment about your being a private investigator, I thought maybe you could help." Cooper looked her in the eyes. "I don't know what else to do."

Liv felt a rush of sympathy. Poor kid looked lost. Looked like someone had kicked him. Repeatedly. And laughed about it. She could at least meet with him, get more details before letting him, gently, go.

Wondering if she was making a mistake, she reached into her small clutch and handed him her card. "Call me tomorrow and we'll set up an appointment, okay?"

Cooper slid the card into his pocket. "Thank you," he said. "Next drink's on me. You like the sparkling, right?"

Liv lifted her glass. "Right."

As they made their way back to the ballroom, she sipped her wine and mulled over Cooper's story. On the surface, the case sounded like a dud, but you never knew. There might be some truth to it, no matter how far-fetched it seemed.

If there was one thing her seven years in the investigation business had taught her, it was that people did strange things and for incredibly bizarre reasons. It wasn't totally impossible that a famous writer like Mason Falwell might steal a student's work. Implausible, yes, but not impossible.

Besides, who could make up a story that bizarre?

Later, as she placed her empty glass on a tray and went to claim the Hamilton she'd successfully won, the answer came to her.

A writer. That's who.

Chapter Two

• • • • • • • • • • • • • •

When Henry Wordsworth Longfellow wrote the words, "Into each life some rain must fall," the Portland poet must have been inspired by April on the coast of Maine.

A steady shower pattered against Liv's red umbrella as she crossed the street against the light. There was little traffic downtown on such a raw Sunday morning. Only a few automobile lights reflected red and yellow streaks off the slick, wet roads crisscrossing Portland's Old Port.

At least it wasn't snow, she thought, but anyone with sense would be home curled up in their squishy chair, reading the *Sunday Telegram* and drinking coffee. If not for her mandatory once-a-month Sunday brunch with her parents, that's just what she'd be doing.

The historic Portland Regency Hotel rose just ahead, and she picked up her pace so as not to be too late. She'd tried on and discarded several outfits that morning, finally settling on skinny jeans, an oversized sweater, a raincoat, and a pair of high-end rain boots. A brown fedora completed the look. Her mother would frown at the jeans. Her father would compliment her on the hat. And her feet would stay dry. Win. Win. Win.

Liv reached the hotel and shook out her umbrella before stepping inside. She checked her raincoat and the umbrella, glanced in the mirror to make sure her lipstick wasn't smudged, and made her way to her parents' usual table in the center of the hotel's warm and intimate dining room.

A cheery fire blazed in the brick fireplace. The subtle clink of utensils against tableware blended with the groovy jazz playing on the sound system. The familiar aroma of bacon, good coffee, and scones smelled delicious. Okay, so maybe she didn't completely hate Sunday brunch. In some ways, it was a comforting ritual.

Comforting, with one major exception.

"Hello, Olivia," her mother said, holding out her cheek for a kiss.

"Hi, Mom. Hi, Dad." She took her seat and placed a linen napkin in her lap. "Sorry I'm late. Did you order already?"

"Of course not." Her mother sipped her mimosa. "We did tell the server to bring coffee and scones as soon as you arrived. In case you arrived."

"You know I'd call if I couldn't make it." Liv turned to her father. "How have you been, Dad?"

"I've been fine, Olivia. Just fine."

"The hospital merger still on track?"

Gilbert Lively nodded. "Yes, thank you for asking. I believe it will be very beneficial to our staff and patients once the MainePatientCare merger is finally completed. Not everyone agrees, of course, but they'll come around."

She noted the exhausted droop of his face. "Still having PR problems?"

"Oh, just the usual. A few glitches with systems and whatnot, and some of the newspaper editorials have been brutal, but we'll manage. How's the investigation business going?"

"Don't encourage her, Gilbert," Tiffany Lively interrupted. She turned to Liv. "I understand you attended the Glitterati Ball last night. The Telling Room is a wonderful organization, Olivia. I'm so pleased." Tiffany smiled at her.

Feeling irritated about Tiffany keeping tabs on her and also a little guilty, Liv shrugged. All her mother ever wanted was for her only daughter to graduate from a prestigious university, marry well, and take her place in the Livelys' social circle. Not only had

Liv failed to snag an appropriate husband, but she'd also chosen an embarrassing and potentially dangerous profession.

In Tiffany Lively's world, a career as a private detective, or as she liked to put it, "snooping around in other people's affairs," was low-class and certainly not a topic for polite conversation.

Then again, no matter what she did, her mother found something to criticize. She might as well please herself, she rationalized. At least one of them would be happy. Ish.

She decided to throw Tiffany a conversational bone. "I did attend the ball. It was fun. In fact, I picked up a Rick Hamilton in the silent auction."

No sense telling her mother she'd also picked up a potential new case.

Her mother sat back, looking pleased. "That's fantastic. Tell me all about..."

Her mother's voice trailed off as a man walked up to their table. Liv's eyes traveled from his dotted tie and navy blue cardigan to his dark and tousled hair, damp from rain. "I hope I'm not interrupting," the man said. His voice was warm, his wide smile slightly crooked.

Liv sucked in a breath. *Hello.*

"Jasper!" Tiffany beamed a thousand-watt smile. Gilbert glanced at Liv and quickly away.

Suspicious, Liv looked from one to the other and then up at the beautiful man who looked like he dressed straight from the Ralph Lauren catalog.

"Good morning, Tiffany. Gilbert." He put up his hand as Liv's father started to stand. "Please. Don't get up."

Liv's father lowered himself back onto the chair.

"Are you here alone?" Tiffany said, gesturing to the chair next to her. "Won't you join us for breakfast?"

Liv narrowed her eyes as this Jasper, whoever he was, thanked her mother and seated himself at their table. A server materialized, briskly organizing a fourth place setting. Another server poured coffee. Liv's suspicions grew.

Tiffany made the introductions. "Olivia, I'd like you to meet Dr. Jasper Temple. Jasper, my daughter, Olivia."

"It's nice to meet you," Jasper said, looking across the table at Liv. His eyes were surrounded by spiky, dark lashes. He was long-limbed and rangy, and his hands looked too big for the teaspoon he'd picked up. *Elegant fingers*, she thought, watching him stir cream into his coffee.

Score one for mom, Liv thought. Not that she was interested in a set-up. Which this definitely was.

Liv sat back and tilted her head. "So, Dr. Temple, how do you know my parents?"

Gilbert answered. "Jasper is the newest cardiothoracic surgeon at Sharon Medical Center. We met a few weeks ago at a presentation regarding the merger into MainePatientCare, and then we ran into each other again last night at a dinner party."

Jasper cleared his throat. "Your mother raved about the brunch here. This seems like family time, though. If you'd rather I sat somewhere else…?" Dr. Hottie's voice trailed off, and he shot a thumb over his shoulder, indicating he would make himself scarce. Liv glanced at her mother. Tiffany gave her the death-glare.

Liv lifted one shoulder in a who-cares kind of way. "No, no. The more, the merrier." She had to admit he had a pretty great smile. She liked his eyelashes, too, and the blue eyes they surrounded. "The Lobster Benedict here is to die for."

•   •   •   •   •

When their plates arrived and they'd tucked in, Dr. Hottie rolled his eyes upward and expelled a blissful sigh. "You were so right, Tiffany. This place is my idea of heaven. Forget Sunday services. Give me brunch at the Regency."

He was so goofy and at ease with himself, Liv couldn't help but play along. "Welcome to the Lively family branch of the Church of the Mystical Mimosa," she said, placing her palms together like a prayer. A waiter arrived with a fresh plate of pastries. She shot Jasper a devilish grin. "And behold the Most Holy Platter of Warm Blueberry Scone."

Jasper grinned back and reached for a pastry. "Bless you, Sister. Don't mind if I do." His eyes met hers as he leaned forward, and Liv's heart jumped. They held each other's gaze for a few breathtaking seconds while everything around them blurred.

She broke eye contact, unnerved by the attraction humming between them. This was going to be a problem, she thought. She couldn't actually *like* a guy her mom approved of. She glanced up at him again, and he winked at her. Damn, that was sexy.

Tiffany, holding up her mimosa, interrupted the moment. "Here's to new friends," she said, batting her eyelash extensions at Jasper. The gold bracelets on her wrist clinked ever-so-elegantly as she lifted her arm.

"To friendship and future endeavors," said Gilbert, tapping his glass against his wife's and then Liv's and Jasper's in turn.

"Yes, future endeavors," Tiffany echoed, looking far too pleased with herself.

"What endeavors are you talking about?" Liv asked.

"Mergers. The merger," her father amended too quickly. He turned to Jasper and began talking about hospital business. Tiffany, the perfect hostess, interjected every so often. They'd dined here for so many years, Liv suspected her mother thought of the Regency dining room as her own.

As the others chatted, Liv took the opportunity to observe Dr. Jasper Temple more closely. He was charming, well-spoken, and warm. He deferred to her father when they had a small difference of opinion, and he took her mother's social prattle seriously—or at least, did a masterful job pretending.

Liv marveled. Was it possible that she actually liked a guy her mom approved of? An honest-to-goodness nice guy?

She sipped her coffee and peered at Jasper over the rim. She gave herself a mental shake. Next thing, she'd start believing in unicorns. There had to be something wrong with him.

Jasper turned his attention back to Liv. "I hear you run your own investigation firm. Do I need to worry about you running a background check on me as soon as lunch is over?"

"You never know. I just might." She smiled sweetly. "Why? Afraid I'll find some skeletons in your closet?"

"Actually, yes," he laughed.

"Okay, spill it, Doctor. Bad debts? Substance abuse? No, wait. Let me guess. Speeding tickets?"

"Nothing quite that exciting, no. My skeleton's name is Horace. He's an anatomy model I, um, acquired during med school."

Liv raised her eyebrows. "Acquired?"

"Let's just say some of us had a little bit too much of a good time one fine summer evening. We, um, liberated Horace from the anatomy lab, and took him out on rounds that night."

"Didn't that scare the patients?"

"No, but it gave the barflies something to talk about."

"Ah," she laughed. "Those rounds."

Tiffany giggled. "Oh, Jasper, that is such a funny anecdote. What other pranks did you get up to in med school? Yale, wasn't it?"

Liv rolled her eyes. Her mother was so transparent.

"Johns Hopkins," Jasper said.

"Oh, that's right." She gave Liv a meaningful look.

"It's okay, Mother," Liv said. "You can stop trying so hard. I like him, okay?"

Tiffany's mouth fell open. Gilbert snorted and covered it up with a cough. Jasper's eyes sparkled with humor as he watched the family dynamic play out.

Liv crossed her arms and looked around the table. "Come on. Why don't we just all be honest about what's going on here? Jasper, my mother invited you to brunch in order to set us up. You know that, right?"

"Olivia Rose Lively!" her mother gasped. "That's not…"

Liv ignored her and focused her attention on Jasper. "It is. And as it happens, I like you." She signaled a waiter to bring more coffee. "My mother likes you, and I like you. Hell might be freezing over as we speak."

Chapter Three

• • • • • • • • • • • • • •

Jasper shot her an amused look. "I like you, too, Olivia. You are definitely not what I expected."

Tiffany sniffed, not sure whether to be offended or relieved. "And I like Gilbert. And he likes me. And we both like Olivia." She speared a look at her only daughter that would have shriveled all but the most immune. "Most of the time."

Liv looked at her father. "And you!"

"Me? What did I do?"

"You allowed her to do this."

"Well, maybe I'd like to see my only daughter settled down before I die," her father grumbled.

Jasper looked from one to the other. "Uhhh… pass the scones, please."

"See what you stumbled into here, Jasper? This family is nuts," Liv said, nudging the basket of scones closer to his plate. "But cheer up. No one has died on account of a date with me yet."

"Thank you," he said, taking a scone and cutting it open. "Is this a date?"

"I hope so," Liv said, shrugging and handing him the jam before he asked for it. "Or the prelude to a date, anyway."

"Prelude to a date," Jasper said, nodding. "I like that. Maybe you should give me your number so we can talk about that in greater detail."

Liv handed him her business card. "Knock yourself out."

• • • • •

"Okay, Ruth. I have a pretty good idea of your setup here. I'll email you my recommendations for a new security system by the end of the week."

"Much appreciated." The short, gray-haired owner of Buoy Bagels stuck out her hand. "I shouldn'ta put it off for so long, but you know how it is."

She did. Owning a small business meant doing it all yourself or hiring someone to do it for you. There was never enough time in the day. When Liv got back to her office, she planned on spending the afternoon with her accounting software and stack of receipts.

They left the office, and Ruth stepped into place behind the cash register. "Getcha a latte or something before you go?"

"You know what? A latte would be fantastic. Thank you."

As Ruth made the drink, a group of female students wearing black leggings, furry boots, and sorority sweatshirts trooped into the shop. Seeing them laughing and chatting, Liv felt a not-unpleasant ache of nostalgia for her own college days.

Had it really been nine years since she and Ashleigh were roommates, smoking cigarettes over their morning coffees at the tables outside the student union? She remembered so vividly the flavor of the tobacco and the taste of burned coffee, the bad poetry in the online student 'zines they'd followed, the anxiety about papers and mid-terms, and dating drama. Wearing their low-rise jeans and tiny tees and puffy coats, they'd thought they were so cool.

Yeah, cool, Liv thought. It had taken her three years, countless acupuncture sessions, and a billion nicotine patches to finally kick that nasty smoking habit. She watched as one of the girls sneaked a puff on an e-cig and passed it to a friend. Now all the kids were vaping. The more things changed…

"Here ya go, Olivia. Thanks again." Ruth placed a large latte on the counter. "My treat."

"Thanks, Ruth." Liv waved on her way out the door and stepped into the warm sunshine filtering through the still-bare branches of the trees. Spring had finally decided to make a tentative appearance.

She took her time as she drove toward her East Bayside office. The smell of spring made her feel reckless and young, so she rolled down the window a few inches and turned up the volume on Bach's *Partitas*, which she'd been playing over and over the last few days. The trilling piano notes fit the lighter, spring mood in the air.

She caught a glimpse of fortress-like Sharon Medical Center with its old wings and new wings and recently-completed parking garage, and her thoughts turned to Dr. Jasper Temple. Was he working today? She pictured him dressed in scrubs and wielding a scalpel, a hero working to unclog an artery, repair a faulty valve, or jump-start someone's heart.

She wouldn't know.

Because he hadn't called.

It had been two days since brunch, and that meant something. She frowned. She'd liked the tall, dark, and delicious Dr. Hottie with his warm smile, verbal wit, and good manners. She thought he'd liked her, too. In fact, they'd both come right out and said it.

She tapped her fingers on her steering wheel. Ashleigh, in full school counselor mode, would have been impressed by the honesty. Except it had now been two days, and he still hadn't called.

She scowled as she contemplated what could have gone wrong. Maybe her parents had scared him off. Maybe she had. Either way, it stung just a little.

But, she told herself, still tap-tap-tapping her fingers, keeping time with Bach, it was no big deal. She could always adopt a couple cats if she got too lonely. Or start taking solo trips to Cancun or Key West. Somewhere, anywhere, that was hot, tropical, and relaxing. She'd bring along a few classics she'd always meant to read and some Agatha Christie's for when she needed a break from the heavy stuff. And she'd pay to have regular installments of juicy, sweet tropical drinks brought to her lounge chair on the beach.

She started making plans as she drove, but when she stopped at a red light at the edge of Deering Oaks Park, her phone rang through the car's speakers. She glanced at the console. She didn't recognize the number. Jasper?

She pressed a button and held her breath. "Olivia Lively." A horn blasted at a delivery truck pulling out into traffic. Pedestrians walked briskly down sidewalks wet with melting snow.

"Hi, Ms. Lively? It's Cooper Tedeschi, from the other night?"

She exhaled, trying not to feel disappointed, but failing. She tapped her fingers again, glared at the traffic light. "Hi, Cooper."

"Hi. I was just wondering if I could set up an appointment for today."

Liv hesitated. She didn't really want to take this case. There were so many reasons: Too many ifs. Too little chance of success. Too messy. Not to mention the little problem about a retainer.

Then again, business was business. "Um, hold on a second. I'm in traffic."

She thought about a recent meeting with her accountant. Quarterly taxes were due in a few weeks, and she had some time in her schedule at the moment, especially since she wasn't dating. She could accept Cooper's case on a contingency basis, and if she helped Cooper prove his story and he won a settlement, she could collect her fee.

And if he didn't? Well, even a pro bono case might take her mind off of a certain hot surgeon and his apparent inability to dial a phone.

The light changed. Traffic started to move. She had a couple of appointments scheduled for later in the afternoon, but the next hour or so was free.

"Cooper? Could you be at my office in fifteen or twenty minutes?"

"Yes, I have the day off, so anytime today would work."

"Okay. I'll see you in a few."

"Really? Thank you so much!"

He started to gush, but she interrupted him. She gave him her address. She had to do it quickly, she thought. Before she changed her mind.

· · · · ·

Ten minutes later, Olivia parked her green sedan in the parking lot of a shabby warehouse, grabbed her computer bag from the seat beside her, and walked into organized chaos.

Lively Investigations rented a two-room office for cheap in an East Bayside warehouse just off Marginal Way. The building was owned by the Fiber Fox Cooperative, a newly-established makerspace for hands-on creatives of every stripe. FFC ran their operation out of a set of offices, including a conference room, next to Liv's, but the majority of the space was taken up with industrial sewing machines, screen printers, presses, hand looms, spinning wheels, die cutters, and offset printing presses. They even had a 3-D printer.

Today a bunch of women and a few men milled around, holding up colorful swathes of printed fabric. Over to the right, another small group stood near the screen-printing table. In a back corner of the large space, books and samples spanned long shelves. A lone seamstress, satin material bunching and pooling around her, bent over one of several industrial sewing machines.

Liv swerved left from the entryway door, her mind on her upcoming meeting with Cooper Tedeschi. Preoccupied, she entered the short hallway that led to the restrooms and offices.

"Hello, Liv."

She froze, startled by the deep voice and unexpected figure lurking in the shadows. A man with slicked-back light brown hair stood beside her office door. He gave her a sardonic smile that didn't quite reach his eyes and he kept one hand in the deep pocket of his overcoat. He worked to appear nonchalant, but he twirled a keychain in his other hand, a tick she recognized.

He was angry. Nervous. Maybe both.

"Rob." Liv ignored the rapid beating of her heart as she greeted her most recent romantic mistake. "What do you want?"

Chapter Four

- - - - - - - - - - - - - -

She walked past him and pushed her key into the lock. When the door swung open, she entered the office and flicked on the lights.

"I'm not here to chit-chat," Rob said, following her in and plunking himself down into the armchair in front of her desk, legs spread, coat flaring out around him. "Just give me all the files on myself, on Gina, and anything else related to this little love triangle situation we're in, and I'll get out of your hair."

Liv took her time placing her bag next to the credenza and lowering herself into the chair behind the desk. She leaned back, propped her feet up, and crossed her ankles.

"Don't you mean love quadrangle? Or maybe pentagon is more appropriate?" She tilted her head and gave him an insincere smile. "Just how many women were you sleeping with at once, anyway?"

"If you were half the detective you claim to be, you'd know that, wouldn't you?"

"You need to leave."

"Give me the files or I'm taking you to court."

Liv examined her fingernails. "Oh really? On what grounds?"

"Breach of contract? Sexual harassment? I don't care. My lawyer will think of something."

Liv dropped her feet to the floor. "Look, Rob, why don't you save your breath and your money? There was no breach of contract. You paid me to get information, and I gave you a full report. Dates.

Times. Detailed notes. Photos. As for sexual harassment? Your name is on the credit card receipts for all those Wednesday nights we spent together at the Cormorant Hotel. Take me to court if you want. You'll lose. We both know it. Now, please. Just go away."

Rob's mouth tightened. Liv held herself still, ready to spring into self-defense mode if necessary. She wasn't at all sure how angry Rob was, or what he was capable of doing.

But Rob pulled back, playing it cool and suave. "Sending those photos to my wife, Liv? I paid you to get the low-down on Gina, but as far as I know, she didn't hire you. You did that on your own. There has to be some ethical violation there."

"You're one to talk about ethics. Let's review the facts, huh? You paid me for a service. I delivered. Contract obligation fulfilled. End of story. But I had personal reasons for following you the night you met whoever-she-is at the Cormorant." She gave a sad shake of her head. "So disappointing, Rob. You booked the same room, on the same day of the week, and even ordered up the same room service."

Nausea clawed at her stomach. That horrible night she'd never felt more interchangeable. Invisible. In her line of work, invisibility was often a good thing. Not so much in a romantic relationship. She pretended to study her manicure. "Honestly, I thought you had more imagination."

He let out a nasty laugh. "The 'woman scorned' role doesn't fit you, Liv. It's kind of ugly, if you want to know the truth."

She ignored the insult. "You want to know why I sent those photos of you and what's-her-name to Gina? I guess I wanted to level the playing field between the two of you. I didn't tell her anything about the job I did for you. She has no idea you hired me to investigate her or that you have proof of her infidelity. That's all client confidentiality stuff. I take that seriously, but there was nothing preventing me from doing my own investigation of you, on my own time, for my own reasons. So, yes, I sent her those photos. She can do what she wants with them." She focused her eyes on a spot above his head. "Anyway, my conscience is clear."

Which was true and not true, she thought. She shouldn't have had an affair with a married man, not even one who said he was filing for divorce. A moment ticked by. She glanced at her watch. "So, I think we're done here. I have a client meeting in a few minutes."

Rob stood. His eyes fell on the credenza in the corner. "Where's the Lakshmi statue?"

She shrugged. It was at home in a cardboard box, along with other reminders of their affair. "It didn't fit the decor."

"I'd like to have it back."

"Fine." It was not that valuable, just something he'd picked up on a business trip and brought home for her. She'd liked the colors and the pouty lips on the Indian goddess, the coins spilling from her hands. Mostly she'd liked that he'd thought of her while he was away. Damn him. "I'll mail it to you."

He pointed to the credenza. "The file?"

She walked to the credenza, pulled the file, and held it out.

Rob grabbed the manila folder. "I want the electronic versions, as well."

"Fine," she said again. "Now would you please leave?"

Rob glowered, opened his mouth as if he had something more to say, turned, and slammed out of the office.

Shaking, Liv sat down at her desk. She put her feet up again and stared out the window to the cracked and weedy parking lot. She watched Rob stalk to his car, and she wondered why she'd let herself fall for another creep. She knew danger attracted her like a drug. And also like a drug, it had a way of coming back to bite her.

She didn't usually date clients, though. Robert Mickelson had been a one-off in that department. When he'd hired her, Rob told her he was preparing to file for divorce. Then, when he'd asked her out, she foolishly accepted, drawn like a moth to the flame. Ten months into the affair and he was still married. Maybe he was a serial cheater, she mused. A compulsive liar. But why, then, had he hired her to investigate his wife?

She continued to stare out the window, watching the clouds roll in from the bay. Who knew why people did things? Maybe he'd just wanted leverage in the marriage. Maybe it was a kinky game he and Gina played with each other. She really didn't care anymore. She was just glad it was over.

She sat up behind her desk, started her computer, and emailed the electronic files to Rob as requested. That's it, she thought. She could forget him and move on.

Movement in the parking lot caught her eye. Cooper Tedeschi, back hunched against the brisk breeze and curly hair making him look like a wild angel with a chip on his shoulder, slouched toward the building.

Chapter Five

• • • • • • • • • • • • • •

"Start anywhere. Don't leave anything out. Sometimes the things that seem most irrelevant are the most important leads."

Liv sat at her desk, digital recorder running, pen and legal pad in hand. Across from her, hunched into an office chair, Cooper Tedeschi jiggled one knee up and down. He swallowed and looked toward the door like he wanted to bolt. "I don't know where to start."

Liv leaned over the desk toward her cute and rumpled client. He looked more boyish today in his faded jeans, black T-shirt, and gray zippered hoodie. The dimple in his chin and the curly hair reminded her of a cherub. A glum cherub. "Look, Cooper. Don't be nervous. I'm on your side, remember? You're not on trial here."

Cooper's face flushed red. "How much is this going to cost me?"

"Nothing for a consultation, which this is. We can work the rest out later if I decide to take the case." She tapped her pen on the legal pad. "Right now, just tell me what happened, as best as you can remember it. Start from when you were accepted into the MFA program at Longfellow College."

"Okay. Thanks." He swallowed. "Well, I was accepted two years ago into the program and started taking courses that September." Cooper's voice got stronger. "Two years of my life, wasted. I should have been graduating this August, but I was kicked out of the program in February, thanks to Mason Falwell and those spineless sycophants on the honor code committee and administration."

Liv nodded. This was the wordsmith she remembered from the coat room at the Glitterati Ball. "Can you give me a list of the names of the people on the committee?"

"Sure." Cooper bent down and handed her a document from the satchel near his chair. "These are the papers. All the names are on there."

Liv smiled. Cooper was nervous, but he was prepared. That told her he was serious about the situation and thinking ahead to what she might ask. She liked that in a client. "Okay, go on. Mason Falwell was assigned to be your advisor?"

"No. I requested him." Cooper grimaced. "Worst decision I ever made."

"Tell me about the program. Did you have classes with Mason exclusively?"

"No," Cooper said, shaking his head. "The first year I took graduate courses in literature, critique, and creative writing with a number of English Department professors. Last September, though, I began working on my graduate thesis—the novel— under Falwell's tutelage."

"Tutelage? I don't understand."

"The second year of the program is basically low-residency. A cohort of second-year students meets for three weeks at the beginning of the fall and spring semesters for workshops, readings, conferences, and one-on-one tutorials. After that, we're expected to work independently on our own projects, sending chapters to our advisors and receiving their feedback."

Liv jotted down a few notes. "Okay, continue."

Cooper's leg jiggled up and down. "Falwell mentored me on the novel. The work went quickly. I'd send him packets with three or four chapters every couple of weeks, and he'd either send them back or we would meet in his office to discuss the work."

"Did you use intercampus mail or email?"

"The college's email and document-sharing program called Long/Space."

Liv took the information down and then looked up. "What was the title of your book?"

"*The Eye of the Hours*. It's a hybrid, a cross between science fiction and fantasy." Cooper's voice was proud, truthful.

Liv pressed her lips together. Seemingly truthful, she reminded herself. Cooper could be delusional, believing Mason Falwell's recent book was his own. She wondered if he'd had emotional or psychological problems in the past or a family history of schizophrenia. For now, she'd proceed as if he was mentally stable, but wrote "mental illness???" in the notebook and circled it a couple of times.

"What was Falwell's reaction to your book?" she asked.

"Encouraging at first. Maybe a little hands-off. Sometimes even distracted. But he told me he saw a lot of himself in me and my writing."

"That must have pleased you."

"Yeah. I was psyched. Growing up, I practically inhaled every book the man wrote. I read and reread them. I had whole passages—*pages*—memorized. Ever since seventh grade when I stumbled across his first book, *Rune in the Crossing*, all I ever wanted was to be a writer like Mason Falwell."

Cooper let out a bitter laugh. "I guess I succeeded. His name is going to be on my novel. I actually got what I asked for. I wrote Mason Falwell's latest book. Only no one believes me. They think I'm crazy."

"Is there any way you could be, uh, mixed up about this? Maybe it's not your book that he sold. Is it possible he'd been writing his own novel all along?"

"No!" Cooper stood up and began to pace. "Why won't anyone listen to what I'm saying? I sent my chapters to Falwell, he sent them back with suggestions and corrections, and then I rewrote the pages and saved them on Long/Space. By mid-December, the first draft was done, which meant that Falwell had a copy of the entire manuscript in his possession. I was supposed to polish it up this semester and submit the final draft as my graduate thesis. It would have been reviewed by the thesis committee over the summer so that I could receive my degree in August. I was still working on the edits when Falwell sent the manuscript to his publisher and signed a contract."

"When did you discover this?" Liv kept her voice calm as she studied her potential client. Beneath the boyish good looks and charming dimple lurked an intensity that she suspected bordered on obsession.

"January." Cooper sat down again. "The third week of January. We'd just started spring semester workshops when I saw the announcement on the English Department website. I was surprised because if Mason had been writing a new novel, I would have known it."

"How's that?"

Cooper rubbed his palm on one knee, trying to stop the jiggling. "One thing I forgot to mention earlier. Last fall, Mason hired me to type up some of his unpublished papers—essays, short stories, stuff like that. He knew I needed the money, so it was kind of a favor. Or that's what I thought. He paid me through the financial aid stipend I'd received."

"Where did you do this work? At his office at Longfellow?"

Cooper shook his head. "No. At his home. He had a table set up in the library. I'd go over, and there'd be a stack of yellow legal pads beside the desktop computer. I'd put in a few hours, record the time, put a sticky note where I'd left off."

"Was he there?"

"Not usually. Sometimes he'd wander in. His wife, Karie, was there all the time. She'd bring me tea or coffee, sometimes cookies if she was baking. We'd chat about books and Mason's work. I liked her. She was nice. I thought she was a little lonely."

Liv bit the end of her pen, made another note. "Okay."

"After the news came out, I assumed the website got it wrong about it being a new novel. I figured he'd submitted those random pieces I'd typed up as a collection. It's not unheard of for big-name authors to put out a collection of odds and ends like that." He looked at Liv, eyes troubled.

"Makes sense. Go on."

"The book was big news on campus because Falwell hadn't published in over five years. In fact, in the few interviews he gave the past few years, he insisted he'd accomplished everything he set out to do as a writer. He said he'd brought all the stories into the world he was meant to and that he was going to devote the rest of his life to mentoring the next generation of writers."

Cooper snorted. "What a joke. The old fart just couldn't do it anymore. My guess is he had a major case of writer's block."

"Why would he take your work and pass it off as his own? He'd already said he was done writing. Nobody expected any more from him. This doesn't make any sense."

"Ha! You think? None of this makes any sense. The most unbelievable part is that he thought he'd get away with it."

That wasn't the most unbelievable part, Liv thought. She tapped her pen on the notepad and looked out the window. A few artists walked across the parking lot, bundles of printed fabric folded in their arms.

She turned back to Cooper. "Okay, so Falwell announces a new book deal, you figure it's this collection of old essays and stories. When did you suspect it was actually your novel?"

"There was an article in the *Press Herald* the following Friday. It contained a brief synopsis of the plot and discussed the thematic elements. I almost dropped my laptop as I read it. I was shocked. It was so surreal. The article described the plot and characters of my book, *Eye of the Hours*. Only he's changed the name to *Hours of the Crossing*."

"Uh-huh." Liv wrote down the two titles.

Cooper leaned forward, eyes intent. "Don't you get it? It's like a bookend to his first novel, *Rune in the Crossing*. That's why everyone believes him! That and the fact that we write so similarly. I guess maybe I should have tried to develop my own style more, but I loved and read his work so much, it just became a part of me. Now his publisher and everyone at the college think I'm delusional, that I wanted to be Mason Falwell so badly that I believe I wrote his latest book."

Cooper hunched in the chair, looking haunted and miserable. Liv sat back and chewed on the end of her pen. Something didn't add up.

"Don't you have copies of your work? A hard copy printed out? Files saved on a thumb drive?"

"Sure, but see, that's why Falwell hired me to type up his old stories. I had access to Mason's notebooks. He and Karie say I was hired to transcribe Falwell's manuscript pages, and that's how I know so much about the book. They've convinced everyone—the administration, the honor committee, the press—that I'm delusional. They say I copied Mason's chapters after I typed them, changed them a little bit, and told everyone it was my work. But, Ms. Lively, I swear to you, Falwell is lying. He stole *my* plot, *my* ideas, *my* characters, *my* book. The only work of Mason's that I typed were those unpublished pieces. Please believe me."

Liv steeled herself. "I have to ask you this, Cooper. Have you ever been treated for mental illness?"

He froze. Then he looked down at the floor. "Yes. I suffered from clinical depression in high school and was hospitalized for a few months when I was sixteen."

"Are you better now? Do you take medication?"

"I take antidepressants." Cooper's leg started bouncing again. "I see my psychiatrist every six months or so, but I handle things with exercise and meditation, as well. I'm not crazy."

"Of course you're not," she said.

He looked up, face bleak. "I'd be lying if I said I haven't had some suicidal thoughts lately. Getting kicked out of the graduate program, well, I just feel hopeless."

"Understandable."

"Maybe I should just let Falwell take credit for my work. I'm not even sure I can write anymore, anyway. Since this whole thing went down, I haven't been able to come up with one creative idea. Every time I try to write something, I have a panic attack. It's not good."

A few seconds passed. The room was silent except for the muffled sounds of industrial machinery in the warehouse area. Liv tapped her pen and looked down at her notes. She wanted to help this boy, and the case appealed to her, mostly because it had nothing to do with cheating spouses, routine background checks, or insurance fraud. It was something much less ordinary.

A recognizable name in the literary world. A potentially huge plagiarism case. Best of all, a mighty distraction from her sorry excuse for a love life.

She smiled at Cooper. "Let's not give up quite yet."

His eyes lit up. "You'll take the case?"

She extended her hand and they shook. "Yes, Mr. Tedeschi. I will."

Chapter Six

· · · · · · · · · · · · · · · ·

G ritty's Pub in the Old Port was quiet at four p.m. on a Tuesday afternoon.

Liv picked at the plate of poutine in front of her, popped a gravy-covered fry into her mouth. She looked around at the exposed beams, brick walls, and the scarred plank floor. She sipped her beer, enjoying the vibe. It was a little early in the day, but you couldn't sit in a traditional, Irish brew pub without having a pint and fries. She figured she'd work it off with a run later.

Cooper's lawyer, Patrick Ledeau, carried a dark amber from the bar. He joined her at the corner table. "Thanks for meeting me," he said. He took the chair opposite hers. He was a short, stout guy with close-cropped hair, the beginnings of a double chin, and a shrewd intelligence in his round, brown eyes.

He lifted his mug. She clinked hers against it. "*Sláinte*," she said. "Now, fill me in."

Ledeau, an old buddy of Cooper's from their undergrad days, had agreed to take Cooper's case on a contingency basis. "First, we'll send notices of intent to Mason Falwell for plagiarism and to Longfellow College for wrongful dismissal, defamation of character, infliction of emotional distress, and breach of contract. It would be best to settle out of court. For this to work, we need leverage."

"Go on."

"Falwell and his publisher might be willing to power through a lawsuit, but the college will want to avoid negative publicity. If we can find something about Falwell that will give the board of directors heart palpitations, they might throw the prof under the bus and be willing to settle out of court rather than risk the college's reputation, not to mention future donations and endowments. It's a gamble, but it could pay off. For both of us, Lively."

Liv nodded. She knew he was dangling a financial carrot in front of her. She could bill at a higher rate if she didn't stipulate a retainer up front. If Cooper won a big settlement, Ledeau would collect, and he'd make sure she was paid. But as Ledeau said, it was a gamble of time and resources.

Her eyebrows scrunched together over the rim of her rich stout. "Was the college really that negligent? I can see a judge taking one look and throwing the case out."

"Cooper paid tuition to the school and met all the requirements for the degree, yet they are withholding that degree from him due to a baseless dismissal. They moved very quickly. I'd argue they failed to do their due diligence regarding Cooper's supposed offenses. We claim they kicked him out of the program because of Falwell's reputation and heavy-handed influence, not because Cooper did anything wrong."

"Attacking a professor, accusing him of plagiarism in the college paper? The honor code committee might have looked at that and made what some people would consider a rational judgment."

"That's where you come in. If we can prove Cooper was telling the truth, his actions are not only reasonable but fair, and their whole defense falls apart. I'd rather settle than go to court. For that, we just need to show them the path of least resistance."

"And if they don't agree to settle?"

"I'll need a copy of Falwell's manuscript so we can run it through plagiarism software. We'll compare the manuscript to a sample of Cooper's writing. I'll request the manuscript from the publisher when I send the letter of intent. If we're lucky, they'll comply, hoping we'll be convinced and the whole thing will go away. From you, I need Falwell's and Cooper's emails, if you can get them. Cooper's given his consent. Also, find me some witnesses, MFA students who read Cooper's drafts or heard Mason talking about Cooper's work. I want a report on Mason Falwell's marital history. Any legal problems. Professional setbacks. Financial issues. Anything that might be a potential motivation for stealing a student's work and passing it off as his own."

"That's the real question, isn't it?" Liv crossed her legs and swung one of her black, leather boots back and forth. "If he needed the money, why wouldn't Falwell just write his own book? He could probably scribble any sort of garbage and it would sell, at least for a few years until the fans figured out he'd become a hack. He's already published, what, twenty, twenty-five novels. Why would he need Cooper's manuscript?"

"That's what we need to find out."

"So you believe Cooper's telling the truth?"

"I do." He snagged one of her fries. "Do you mind?"

"Knock yourself out."

"I know Coop. He's a good guy. Always had my back. He's passionate about his writing, but he isn't crazy."

"You've known him how long?"

"We were in the same dorm sophomore year. He's been talking about writing this time-travel, paranormal, utopian mashup of a story for years, long before he started graduate school. From the sounds of it, Falwell's new book runs in the same vein."

"It could be they just had similar ideas."

"Sure. It could be a coincidence, but my gut tells me otherwise. If he'd come to me first instead of harassing Falwell and going to the newspaper, he might have avoided all this drama."

"He got himself into a bind, didn't he, challenging the status quo?" Liv said. "Cooper accuses, raises questions. Falwell reacts, demands swift action. The honor code committee jumps. Next thing you know, the newspaper editor gets canned. Cooper's booted from the program. The administration looks the other way. No wonder he's angry."

"My guess is the college is afraid of scandal. Mason Falwell is a big draw for potential graduate students. They come to Longfellow in order to take classes with him, to be in the same orbit as one of the world's best-selling authors. That's a big chunk of tuition we're talking about. Think what would happen to the writing program if it came out he was plagiarizing graduate students' work. By going public, Cooper basically screwed himself." Ledeau shook his head. "He should have consulted with me first."

"You said that. Maybe you're right." A few seconds ticked by. "There's some motive there, I guess, for the university to make a scapegoat of Cooper rather than move on his accusations."

"Exactly the argument I will make."

She finished her beer and set the mug down with a thunk. "Okay, then. I guess I'll get started. I'll email a contract to you tomorrow."

"Don't worry about your fee, Lively. If you get me some leverage, I will get a settlement. Litigation was my best class in law school."

"Why doesn't that make me feel better?"

Ledeau laughed and picked up a menu. "I could go for a burger. Like to join me for dinner?"

"No thanks." She stood, pulled on her black leather jacket, and threw a couple of bills on the table. "Too many fries. Another time, maybe."

He stood, too. They shook hands, one professional to another, sealing the deal. "Looking forward to it, Lively. Give me a call when you find something."

· · · · ·

Back at the office, she checked her phone messages. There was one from her mother bugging her about the hospital auxiliary's Spring Fling dinner fundraiser. Ashleigh had called to remind her about their yoga class the next day. One of her regular corporate clients needed background checks on recent job applicants.

Still no Jasper.

After half a minute of fuming, she pushed it aside and concentrated on work. She typed up her notes from her meeting with Ledeau, went through her mail, straightened her desk. Satisfied, she changed into the set of workout clothes she'd thrown into her bag that morning and headed out to run the kinks from her body.

The sun hung low on the horizon as she jogged down Marginal Way and hit the connector path to the still-soggy swath of Back Cove Park. She breathed deep of the rich, salty smell of the cove riding a brisk breeze, stretched out into her natural stride. There were few other joggers and walkers out this late in the day, just a few dedicated road warriors wearing fleece and gloves and long, skintight jogging pants.

Her mind cleared. The day and all its noise emptied like magic as rhythm and movement took over. She enjoyed the play of sundown and shadows on the path, watched the sodium lights blink on one by one.

As the temperature sank with the sun, her breath left her mouth in long, white puffs. She wanted to finish her three-mile run before dark, so she picked up her pace as she hit Tukey's Bridge, crossing the mouth of the cove where it dumped into Casco Bay. Sweaty, breathing hard, she slowed as she approached her office parking lot.

A black SUV parked up the street caught her attention. *Doesn't fit*, she thought, narrowing her eyes.

She glanced at the parking lights, watched for movement inside the vehicle. The driver had parked beneath a burned-out street light. The interior was shadowed with only the faintest glow from a console.

She wondered what business the driver had in this mostly deserted block of warehouses and gated parking lots. If that vehicle had been parked at Whole Foods a few blocks over, she would never have noticed it. SUVs and crossovers were almost de rigueur for a certain segment of Portland's social strata, but here it stuck out like the proverbial sore thumb.

Hands on hips, Liv walked a couple of times around the lot to cool down, did a few deep, slow stretches. The SUV idled there, exhaust trickling out into the near-darkness of early evening.

Could be calling up directions on his GPS or making a phone call, she told herself, but Rob's visit to her office had her a little spooked. Shaking her hands and feet, she told herself to stop being paranoid.

Annoyed with herself, she went into the office, grabbed her things, and drove home. Just in case, she kept an eye on the rearview mirror as she headed up Munjoy Hill. A few cars snaked up the hill behind her, but to her relief, the SUV was nowhere in sight.

. . . . .

After a long soak in the tub and a Caesar salad thrown together with leftover grilled chicken, Liv felt like a new woman. She slipped into her favorite silk pajamas and poured herself a generous glass of chardonnay before settling into her chair in front of her electric fireplace.

She opened her current read, a thriller about a middle-aged woman who'd disappeared without a trace and the police investigation to find her. By the time her glass was empty and the woman's car had been found abandoned behind a shuttered mill, Liv could barely keep her eyes open.

Yawning, she marked the page in the book, turned off the fireplace and the lights, and went to bed.

Chapter Seven

● ● ● ● ● ● ● ● ● ● ● ● ● ●

"He hasn't called?"

Ashleigh whispered the question while holding herself perfectly still in crane pose—left leg planted on the yoga mat, right leg twisted completely around the left at the knee, crouching, arms pretzeled, fingers of the right hand pressed to the left palm. She wasn't even breaking a sweat.

"No," Liv whispered back, swaying back and forth like a tree in a strong wind... or a crane in a hurricane. Coming out of position before tipping over in a tangle, she placed her right foot on the floor to steady herself. "I should've known he was too good to be true."

"It's only been a couple of days. Maybe he's been busy at the hospital... uh-oh," Ashleigh said, trying not to move her lips. "Benson is staring at us." She dipped even lower at the knees and focused straight ahead toward the front of the class where their yoga guru calmly instructed the twenty students to contort their bodies in ways Liv swore were physiologically impossible.

Liv expelled her breath and tried to wrap her right leg around the left again. Today's mantra had been, "Today I will trust in the process." Liv tried. Muscles in her thighs quivered. Sweat dripped off the end of her nose. The soothing notes of flute and chimes did nothing to induce calm because the sensation of her body parts screaming at her overpowered the new-age music. Plus her mind refused to focus on the exercise.

She wasn't very good at trusting any freakin' process.

"Let your body come out of this position," Benson's voice floated across the room. "Place the palms of your hands together in prayer pose. Reach up toward the sky. Swan dive down to touch your toes."

"Oh, thank god," Liv breathed as she collapsed over her knees.

She looked over at Ashleigh, whose blonde ponytail was centered and un-mussed. How did her friend retain such perfect calm and poise throughout the class? It probably wasn't very Zen of her, but Liv sort of hoped that Ashleigh would wobble and fall on her perfect butt. Or fart. Or something, anything to get them laughing and distract Liv from her anxiety about Dr. Jasper Temple who was quickly becoming just another disappointment in the romance department.

Benson began wandering the room, helping students adjust into the positions. "Place your hands on the floor. Step back to plank. Come forward to cobra."

On the other hand, maybe Ashleigh was right. As a school counselor, she tended to give people the benefit of the doubt and had told Liv that, nine times out of ten, people lived up to your expectations of them. "Tell a kid he is bad, and he will act out," she said. "Tell a kid he is smart, and he will finish most of his homework. We are hardwired to listen to our internal voice. We are highly susceptible creatures. Change the voice, change the behavior."

"Maybe I should call Jasper after all," Liv muttered under her breath. "Tell him he's reliable and then hang up."

"What?" Ashleigh said, glancing over and frowning.

"Nothing."

They came out of cobra, rolled onto their backs, lifted their legs into the air and then back over their heads to place their toes on the floor. Liv focused on breathing. Plow pose always made her panicky. Something about the way her head was immobilized, trapped beneath her body, chin smooshed into her chest. It was hard to breathe. She felt powerless. For most of her life, Liv had hated enclosed places like closets, elevators, even restaurant booths.

One summer day when she was eight years old, she'd hidden from the housemaid by getting into a large hope chest and closing the lid. The lid got stuck. It took a couple of hours before the maid heard her yelling for help. Ever since then, she'd suffered from a mild case of claustrophobia. She carried a secret hope that yoga would help her work through the fear, but so far she hadn't noticed much improvement.

Today I will trust the process, she thought, breathing in and out through her nose.

Finally, Benson told them to lie on their backs, palms up, eyes closed for corpse pose. He dimmed the lights. Liv tried to clear her mind of any thoughts. This was the hardest part of the class. Except when she was running, turning her mind off was like trying to stop a speeding train. She might be able to slow the engine, but the wheels never completely stopped turning.

Taking another deep breath, she willed her body to relax.

· · · · ·

After class, Ashleigh and Liv pulled on their sweatshirts, thanked Benson for another wonderful class (Ashleigh) and for another torture session (Liv), and walked together to their cars.

"That man is divine," Ashleigh sighed. She then started talking about some doctor's appointment she had in a couple of days, something about the endometriosis she'd had since her teen years. Liv had been hearing about the lining of her friend's uterus since college. She nodded and mumbled, *hmmm*, in appropriate places, but her mind drifted back to Dr. Hottie. Why hadn't he called?

Ashleigh was saying something about dyspar-something or other when Liv interrupted. "So, do you really think Jasper has just been too busy to call?"

Ashleigh stopped walking. She turned, and her yoga bag slipped from her shoulder to the crook of her arm. Liv was shocked to see her friend's face contorted with anger. "You know what?" Ashleigh snapped. "No. I don't think he's been too busy. I just said that to make you feel better. I have no idea why he hasn't called. Maybe he's just not that into you."

Liv recoiled. *Whoa.* "Okay, ouch. What's wrong with you?"

"What's wrong with me? Maybe what's wrong with me is that my supposed best friend never listens to me. You're always talking about yourself, your work, your relationships. Blah-blah-blah. Did you ever stop to think that maybe, just once in a while, I might need someone to talk to as well? Someone who will listen?"

Liv caught the glint of tears in Ashleigh's eyes before her friend turned and walked away. Guilt slammed into her gut. "Hey, Ash, wait a minute…"

"Whatever." Ashleigh waved a hand over her head, unlocked her car door, got in, and drove away without looking back.

Feeling dejected, Liv trudged to her sedan. She stopped at Whole Foods to pick up deli mac and cheese and a bottle of Merlot for supper. From the store's parking lot, she tried calling Ashleigh on her cell phone, but she didn't pick up. Liv left a message saying she was sorry, really sorry, and to please call back.

Liv reviewed her situation. Her current client was potentially delusional and couldn't afford to pay her fees. The guy she'd practically thrown herself at hadn't called. And now her best friend was mad at her.

She was doing the right things, or at least trying, but so far the results of her efforts relationship-wise and business-wise were less than extraordinary.

Reaching home, she hauled the grocery bag out of the passenger seat. The bottle of wine tipped out of the bag and smashed on the wet pavement. "Perfect," she said, bending down to pick up the largest shards of glass. "Just freakin' perfect."

As she straightened, she noticed the headlights of a vehicle coming up the hill. A black SUV. It slowed as it reached her driveway. The driver must have spotted her because they stepped on the accelerator and kept going, a plume of exhaust billowing out into the night air.

Liv hustled to the door, swiped her security fob, and slipped inside. She felt better with the door shut behind her. That was the second time in two days she'd seen a black SUV, and she'd bet her mother's favorite pearls it was the same vehicle. She ran up the stairs to the third floor, put the key in the lock, and entered her apartment.

She could take care of herself, but for the first time ever, she wished she had a dog.

A big snarly one with a bad temper.

In the kitchen, she pulled the mac and cheese container from the bag, careful to avoid the shards of the wine bottle. She threw the bag into the recycling container in her entryway, hung her jacket on its hook, and toed off her sneakers. The apartment was too quiet. As if someone was waiting for her in the dark. She cocked her head, listening, feeling creeped out.

She eased open a drawer in the kitchen and drew out the container of pepper spray she kept there. She slipped around the wall and peeked into the sunroom. It was clear. She did the same for the hallway, the closet, the bathroom, the tiny guest room, and her bedroom. Clear, clear, all clear.

The tension lessened in her shoulders and she lowered the spray to her side.

Still uneasy, she padded back to the kitchen and put the spray back in the drawer. The cheery, colorful light fixture over the sink dropped a pool of warm light onto the countertops. Everything in the apartment appeared to be in place.

She opened her computer and checked the security camera footage. The first-floor renters left the building and came back half an hour later. Nobody else came to the door until she arrived just a few minutes ago. She slapped the laptop closed.

This whole breakup with Rob was getting to her. It wasn't like her to be spooked by random vehicles on the street. She warmed the mac and cheese in the microwave and brought it to the table where, in an antique vase she'd picked up at a thrift shop, some tulips had opened, exposing their dark filaments. Black SUVs were not rare, she mused. She hadn't caught a glimpse of the license plate on either occasion. Most likely it wasn't even the same vehicle. She finished the mac and cheese, washed the dishes, set them in the drainer to dry. As she poured a little fresh water into the vase on the table, one silky, purple petal dislodged from a tulip and fell, cuplike, to the table.

Soon all the blooms would shatter. Her mind turned to Ashleigh and their fight. She couldn't let their friendship fall apart. She'd call Ash tomorrow and apologize, she promised herself. Maybe suggest a girls' weekend in Boston.

They could shop in their favorite boutiques, spend an afternoon at the Isabella Gardner Museum, walk around Harvard Square, then splurge some major calories on cannolis and espresso at Mike's Pastry.

Satisfied with her plan, Liv grinned, picked up the petal, and tossed it in the trash. There was pretty much nothing in this world that a little shopping therapy couldn't fix.

Chapter Eight

· · · · · · · · · · · · · · ·

Everyone knew that the first step to getting over a failed romance—right before eating a pint of Ben & Jerry's ice cream and buying a new pair of heels—was the creation of a breakup box.

The time-honored ritual involved gathering every reminder of the relationship and hiding it away. Months or years later, when memories were no longer painful, the box could be opened, smiled over, and emptied. Why this was therapeutic Liv didn't know. She only knew it worked.

After breaking things off with Rob, Liv had scoured her apartment and office. She'd picked up all the things that reminded her of him: cocktail napkins and bottle corks, flirty florist cards and scented candles, photographs and slinky pieces of lingerie. She'd put it all in a banker's box and stuffed the box in a corner of her closet behind her luggage where she wouldn't see it until the time was right.

This definitely wasn't the right time. Digging through the detritus of her latest failed relationship held about as much appeal to Liv as a root canal. Unfortunately, it had to be done.

Pushing the luggage aside, she grabbed the box and carried it to the yellow ottoman in the center of the room. She shimmied the box open, careful not to ruin her fresh manicure, and set the top at her feet.

A wave of revulsion washed over her as the scent of Le Labo Santal 33 hit her nostrils. She'd worn the oh-so-sexy perfume on her assignations with Rob at The Cormorant, as much a part of their erotic play as the scanty babydoll nighties he liked her to wear. She pushed aside the silky, gauzy fabrics and felt for the carved, wooden figurine she'd stashed beneath them.

Seven inches tall, the orange-robed Lakshmi figure was seated cross-legged on a lotus flower base. The Hindu goddess held smaller lotus flowers in two hands, and a green jewel in a third. From her fourth hand, gold coins spilled into a bowl in her ample lap.

Liv traced a finger over the statue's golden crown. The goddess of wealth and good fortune, Lakshmi glowed with saturated colors of green, orange, pink, and blue beneath the light of the closet's chandelier.

The Lakshmi statue wasn't old or valuable or rare, but she was pretty and cheerful and Liv had been charmed when Rob presented it to her. "Sweet," she'd said, cradling the figure in her palms.

"She has your pouty lips."

He'd taken the statue from her hands, placed it on the credenza in her office before pulling her close for a kiss. "Keep her there for good luck. Now, come here," he said. "I missed your mouth."

She remembered what happened next and scowled. She'd have to get rid of that office desk, too, once she could spare the expense.

Liv sighed, wishing she could talk to Ashleigh. Ash would help her put all this into perspective. What had her friend been saying about endometriosis and fertility? Several months earlier, she'd told Liv that she and Trevor were trying to get pregnant. Worried that their friendship would change with motherhood, Liv had pushed it from her mind. Ashleigh never mentioned it again, and Liv forgot to ask how things were going.

Apparently, the baby-making wasn't going well.

Liv picked up the Lakshmi from the ottoman and sat down with the statue cradled in her hands. Maybe Ashleigh wanted to share, but Liv, always so wrapped up in her own stupid drama, never stopped talking long enough to listen. She gazed down at the serene face of the goddess, and sent out a little prayer that she'd be able to make things right.

She could live without a boyfriend. She didn't think she could live without her best friend.

Feeling pensive and out of sorts, she wrapped the statue in a few sheets of that morning's *Press Herald*, tucked it into a shoe box, and took the box to the kitchen. She called a courier service and arranged to have the statue delivered to Rob's office at the bank downtown.

That unpleasant task completed, her mind jumped to her meeting with Cooper's lawyer, Patrick Ledeau. Enough wallowing. She had a case to solve.

She returned to her closet and dressed for the day in a pair of slim jeans, a graphic tee, and a blazer. One good thing about having her own business was being able to wear what she wanted, set her own work hours, and make her own schedule. Nobody told her which cases to take, how to do her work, or questioned her use of time. She answered to no one but herself—and her clients, of course—and she loved it.

Lively Investigations was *her* baby. She was determined that her business would grow to become a multi-agented company someday, one that was highly respected and successful in Portland, New England, and beyond.

She turned, checked the back of her jeans in the full-length mirror, and nodded. As much as she hated the yoga, she loved the results. Her butt had never looked so good. All those minutes in chair pose paid off.

She flicked the light off in the closet and wandered back to the kitchen to make a pot of coffee. While it brewed, she sat down at the kitchen table and opened her laptop to do a search of Mason Falwell's website and social media accounts.

There was little online mention of the new book, and that struck her as odd. A small block on the landing page of his website had a "coming soon" notice with the book's title, but as yet there was no cover or a release date. He didn't keep a blog, but there was a "Books" tab that opened up a page with clickable book covers, ISBN numbers, publication dates, and blurbs. To be thorough, she checked the bio page, the merch page, and the contact page on the off-chance there was something of interest. Nothing jumped out at her, though.

Liv clicked onto Facebook, Twitter, Instagram, and Goodreads, but Falwell didn't have any accounts. His Amazon bio matched the website's. All in all, his online presence felt dated, tired, and slack.

Pondering this, Liv poured herself a mug of coffee, carried it into the sunroom, and drank it as she stood at the window looking out over the city. She watched the morning commuter traffic streaming back and forth on I-95 over Tukey's Bridge. A drizzly rain fell, and fog blanketed the peninsula in a gauzy haze.

So, the professor wasn't active on social media. She sipped her coffee and pondered. It could be Falwell considered self-promotion tacky, or maybe he was just one of those writers who didn't want to deal with the internet. You'd expect with a new book coming out that he would have been doing some sort of promotion, but she really didn't know much about the publishing industry, its marketing norms, and how much promotion the authors were expected to do themselves.

Maybe big names like Falwell were shielded from all that bother, but wouldn't he or the publisher hire someone to manage his online presence? It was curious, she thought, but was it significant?

She'd ask Cooper later, but for now, this angle didn't seem worth any further investigation.

The buzzer at her door sounded. She checked the security camera, let the uniformed courier in, and handed him the Lakshmi statue. Liv leaned against the door and sighed. Last tie to Rob Mickelson, cut. Now she could finally forget about him and move on.

Taking note of the time, Liv pushed herself away from the door and went into her bathroom to finish getting ready for work. She stuck some silver hoops in her ears, dabbed a little bit of taupe eyeshadow on her lids, and applied mascara. While brushing her teeth, she wandered to the round, porthole window that faced the street. She swiped at the satiny condensation that had formed and looked out.

Slowly, she took the toothbrush from her mouth. Below her and up the hill in front of her nearest neighbor's house, a black SUV idled behind an old red Saab. Scowling, she crossed to the sink, spit, and rinsed.

Enough was enough.

She ran to the apartment door, shoved her feet into rain boots, and pulled on a jacket and a baseball cap. Once outside, she eased away from the front door, hugged the side of the house, and peeked around the corner. The SUV was partially shielded by the red Saab and positioned so the driver could keep an eye on her building.

Pulling the bill of her cap low, she slipped around to the back of her building, ran across the backyards of the two houses up the hill, and emerged onto the cross street. Moving quickly, she hung a right and emerged onto her street at a spot uphill from the SUV.

She kept her head ducked as she approached the vehicle on the driver's side. Behind the steering wheel, a dark-haired man drank from a paper coffee cup and watched her driveway. Just as she reached his window, he caught sight of her in the rearview mirror. He moved his hand too quickly, nearly spilling his drink. It was almost comical.

She tapped on the window. Face impassive, he rolled it down.

She lifted the bill of her cap so that she could glare at him, eye to eye. He stared back, unperturbed. She glanced past him, caught a glimpse of crumpled fast food wrappers and empty water bottles. Her eyes settled on his face again.

"Who are you and why are you following me?" Liv said.

"Hold on, Ms. Lively." The driver lifted a finger, reached into his pocket, and pulled out a case. He flipped it open to reveal a badge and said, "Colin Snow, FBI. We need to talk."

Chapter Nine

•••••••••••••••

"So," Liv said. "Want to tell me why you've been tailing me around Portland the last couple of days?"

They were seated at Liv's kitchen table. She hadn't particularly wanted to have a conversation with a federal agent outside on the street, so she'd invited him up for a cup of tea. Agent Snow, to his credit, didn't seem too fazed that she'd burned him. "Have to admit, I'm impressed," he said. "Ever considered a job with the Bureau?"

"Um, no, but thanks for the compliment," Liv said, sipping her lavender-lemon herbal. She'd had enough coffee. Any more and her stomach would rebel.

"Well, then, would you mind answering a few questions?" Agent Snow blew on the surface of his Earl Grey and raised his eyebrows over the rim. She wasn't fooled by his nonchalant attitude. The voice recording device was running and he had a pen and small notebook at the ready.

"Depends. What about?"

"How well do you know Robert Mickelson?"

Liv froze. Rob. That figured. She said, "I should have known this had something to do with him. What's he done?"

"We're investigating him for mortgage fraud. You know anything about that?"

Liv sucked in her breath, surprised. She'd known he was a cheater and a slime-ball, but she'd never suspected him of breaking federal laws. "Wow. I'd like to help you, but no. This is news to me."

Random facts reshuffled themselves and formed a grim picture: Rob's position in commercial lending at the bank. Gina's real estate broker job. Had they been working together on some underhanded lending scheme? Maybe that's why Rob had asked her to investigate Gina, and why he'd been so angry when she'd sent Gina photos of him. Maybe the files on Gina were a kind of insurance policy, in case she considered cooperating with the feds, not for a divorce as he'd told her. Maybe he'd threatened to hurt her lover or some other kind of blackmail. Her head spun with possibilities.

Liv considered the criminology classes she'd taken and the little she knew about money laundering. If Rob was involved in a complex mortgage fraud scheme, he probably worked with a network of low-life criminals and willing mules, people who allowed him to use their bank accounts in exchange for a cut of the profits. He'd have set up dummy companies and overseas bank accounts.

Scalp tingling, she recalled Rob's many "business" trips and silently groaned. How could she have been so naive?

Disgusted, she sipped her tea and cursed herself again for getting romantically involved with Rob. Her radar had certainly gone haywire when it came to him. She wondered what else she'd missed lately. Maybe she'd already lost her edge. Or else she needed a vacation. Somewhere far. Like South America. Alone.

Her temples started to throb and she put a hand to her head. "I'm sorry," she told Snow, who'd stopped talking and was gazing at her with shrewd eyes. "What were you saying?"

"I said, we know he entered your place of business on Wednesday and stayed for twenty minutes. What did he want?"

"You were following him." Liv nodded as events clicked into place. "And then you started following me. I first spotted your SUV near my office and then again cruising past my house." She made a face. "Where's your partner? Staked out in front of Rob's bank?"

Snow's face remained blank. "Maybe."

"Ah. Right. Sorry. I guess you can't say. Well, if you've done your homework—and I bet you have—you probably already know everything about Rob and me. Just the same, I'll tell you what I know, and you can match that up with your intel. I have nothing to hide."

Liv gave him the lowdown on the job Rob had hired her to do, answered his questions, told him what she knew of his habits, hangouts, and routine. She owed no loyalty to Rob the Rover. In fact, the thought of him going to jail gave her a thrilling jolt of satisfaction.

Snow finished his tea while she talked, jotting down a time or place in the notebook every so often. "So," he said when she was finished. "He never mentioned a special bank account? Or the name of some holding company offshore?"

Liv shook her head. "Sorry. He didn't really talk about his business. Our ten-month relationship, if you can call it that, was mostly dinner dates, a bunch of Wednesday nights at The Cormorant, a couple of weekends out of town."

She gave him the names of the towns and inns where they'd stayed. She couldn't meet the agent's eyes. She felt cheap and sleazy. She certainly wasn't projecting the professional image she desired.

Snow remained unfazed. "On these trips, were you with him all the time?"

"Pretty much. He enjoyed 'wining and dining' me, buying me little presents in the local shops. Once in a while I'd take a long bath and read, and he'd stay in the bedroom working on his computer, but I don't think those trips were business." She shook her head. "No, those weekends were about the thrill of sneaking away. Cheating got him off."

If Snow found her assessment crude, he didn't show it. He'd probably encountered much worse. His line of work was very much outside her skill set. She knew very little about the workings of the FBI.

"Have you seen him since Wednesday? Has he contacted you?" Snow's voice was nonchalant, but Liv's radar picked up an edge of something. What was it?

She narrowed her eyes. "No. Why? Have you lost him?"

Snow shrugged, handed her his card. "If you see him, give me a call."

Liv took the card without glancing at it. "Sure."

"And I'm sure you won't mind if I take a look around."

Liv let out a short laugh. "You think I'm hiding him here? What's he done? Run off with the money right under your noses?"

Suddenly, Snow didn't look so affable. He pushed back his chair and stood. "Like I said, I'm sure you won't mind if I take a look around your apartment."

Amused, Liv waved her hand. "Go right ahead."

She heard him opening the door of her walk-in. She grinned when she heard him let out a long, slow whistle and yell, "This is some closet ya got here, Ms. Lively."

She opened her mouth to respond when her cell phone rang. Glancing at the screen, she didn't recognize the number. She slid her finger across the screen to answer the call. "Lively Investigations."

"Hello, Olivia? It's Jasper Temple."

Liv leaned back against her kitchen chair and crossed her legs. Her heart rate sped up. "Well, hello, Dr. Temple. Didn't think I was going to hear from you."

"I'm sorry it's taken so long for me to call. I was—"

"Busy?" Liv interrupted. "Listen, don't feel obligated to ask me out. My parents won't hold it against you. In fact, they'll probably blame me. No worries, okay?"

"Hold on, Olivia. I'm not calling out of obligation. I enjoyed talking with you at brunch, and I'd really like to talk with you some more. I'm sorry I didn't call you sooner. Let me buy you dinner tonight and make it up to you."

Snow called out from the bedroom, "How many pairs of shoes do you have in here anyway?"

There was silence on the other end of the call. "Do you have company?" Jasper asked. "I can call back later."

"Hold on a sec," she told him. She yelled to Snow, "Unless you think he's hiding inside a Manolo, please get out of my closet!"

"This is obviously a bad time," Jasper said. "I'll just…"

"It's not a bad time." She raised her voice. "My friend was just leaving."

Jasper's voice grew amused. "A friend, huh? Kinda early in the morning for a friend."

"That's none of your business, Dr. Nosy."

"You're right. You don't owe me any explanations."

"I don't just wait around for handsome doctors to call me, you know. You snooze, you lose, mister."

He laughed. "I should have called before this…"

Agent Snow sauntered back into the kitchen. Liv widened her eyes and pointed at the phone. Snow leaned against the granite countertop and stuck his hands into his pockets. He looked at her and mouthed, "Mickelson?"

Liv shook her head. "No," she whispered.

"What?" Jasper said.

"Nothing."

"Okay." Jasper sounded hesitant. "I'm not sure what to think here, but, um, I'm sorry I didn't call. There's a bad flu going around, and we've been short-staffed all week."

He let out an embarrassed laugh. "Now I think I've apologized three times, and believe me, I never apologize. Not proud of that fact, but it's true. So, do you want to give dinner a try or not? I feel as if we've gotten off on the wrong foot here, but I'd really like to see you again, Olivia Lively."

The way he said her name sent a tremor across her stomach. "All right, yes," she said. "Dinner sounds lovely." She gave him her address. "What time should I expect you?"

"Six o'clock good for you?"

"Perfect. I'll see you then."

Liv pressed the off-button on her phone and scowled at Snow. "You almost cost me a date, Agent."

He grinned. "My bad. Well, the apartment seems clear, though I have grave concerns about the safety of that closet. You get lost in there, nobody will find you for a week."

"We all have our little vices, Agent. Mine happens to be clothes. Can I see you out?"

He laughed. "I'll take the hint." He stepped out onto the stair landing, held the door open a crack as she tried to close it. "Remember to call me if Mickelson contacts you. And don't be surprised to see the SUV parked nearby. From your statement, it sounds as if he was threatening you. If you need me, I'll be around, okay?"

"Don't worry. I can take care of myself."

She closed and locked the door, watched from her bathroom window as the slim, dark-haired FBI agent looked both ways before crossing the street. *What a Boy Scout*, she thought, grinning.

Her smile faded when, at the last moment, he turned around and waved at her, knowing she'd be there watching.

Pouting, she whirled away from the window. She hated when someone had her pegged.

Chapter Ten

• • • • • • • • • • • • • •

Leaning back in her office chair, Liv looked out the window at the low, gray sky. She'd spent the rest of her morning working on her accounting software, reconciling her bank statements with the invoices and bills from the past couple of weeks. Her stomach rumbled, reminding her that she'd only had coffee and tea for breakfast.

One of Ruth's special bagels would hit the spot, and lunch at Buoy Bagels would get her close to the Longfellow College campus. She tapped her fingers on her desk, considering her next move on the Tedeschi case. She'd pay a visit to the English department, see if she could pick up any tidbits about Falwell.

She found a parking space on a narrow, residential street not far from Buoy Bagels, unfurled her red umbrella, and dashed through the downpour to the door.

The shop was hopping. The dreary weather brought plenty of customers hoping to warm up with a bagel and coffee. Liv hung her dripping raincoat and umbrella onto a peg near the door and snagged a tiny corner table just as a couple of students left.

She strolled up to the counter where Ruth appeared to be training a new employee.

"How's it going, Ruth?" Liv asked. "I'll have the First Mate sandwich and a large black coffee."

"Got it," Ruth said. She nudged the newbie. "Go ahead and start that 'Mate. I'll get the coffee." She smiled at Liv. "Have a seat.

Tanaka here'll bring your sandwich ovah in just a sec."

"Great. Thanks, Ruth."

Settled back at the corner table and nursing a large mug of dark roast, Liv opened her laptop and scanned through newspaper articles that mentioned Falwell. There were hits from national and state daily newspapers, blogs, online magazines, and indie papers, plus many science fiction/fantasy fan sites.

She clicked on an article published in the *Press Herald* the year before when Falwell accepted an award from the local Lions Club. The story gave a basic rundown of Falwell's rise to literary fame in the late 1970s with his book *Rune in the Crossing*, his decision to stop publishing and devote his time to teaching in the mid-2010s, and his second marriage to a Longfellow College graduate student five years ago, right around the same time she'd opened Lively Investigations.

"Here you go, hun." Liv glanced up when Ruth herself delivered her sandwich.

Liv bit into the thin-sliced ham, egg, and cheese on a perfectly toasted sesame bagel. A bit of yoke dripped onto her chin. She wiped it with a paper napkin and rolled her eyes in ecstasy. "Mmmm. This is so good, Ruth. You could franchise the heck out of this place."

"I like bein' small and local," Ruth said. "We need more corp'rate franchises like we need holes in our heads. I just wanted t'thank you again for the work you did, helping me get my security updated and everything." She nodded toward the new camera installed behind the counter.

"No problems accessing the video feed?"

"Nope," said Ruth. "Anytime ya need a ref'rence, just hollah."

Ruth turned to leave, but Liv stopped her, asking, "Hey, Ruth? Question for you."

"Yeah?"

"Do you have time to sit?"

The older woman nodded and settled into the seat opposite Liv.

She said nothing, but her expression was curious.

"I was just wondering... Mason Falwell lives near here, doesn't he?" Liv had already run an address search and found an online satellite photo of the house. She placed his current residence as a blue, white-trimmed Victorian a couple blocks down the street from the shop, not far from where Liv had parked. "Does he ever come in here, by any chance?"

Ruth's eyebrows shot up into the gray, curly fringe above her brows. "Are you investigating Mason Falwell?"

Liv evaded the question. "Let's just say I'm curious, okay? If I lived within three miles of this place, let alone three blocks, I'd have a hard time staying away. Your bagels are to die for. Just sayin'."

"Well, they are good bagels," Ruth said, giving Liv an amused look, won over but not fooled. The woman hadn't been born yesterday. She knew when she was being played, and Liv admired her all the more for it.

So she was grateful when Ruth decided to answer her question.

"Mason hasn't been in here for, oh, at least a year now. He used t'be a regular, though. Stopped in for an onion with lox three, four times a week. Cuppa hot tea. He'd sit down and read the morning paper. This was after his divorce from Elena, a'course."

"Elena was his first wife?" Liv remembered this from her research. Married for twenty-seven years to Elena Hegel with whom he had two grown children, Mason had filed for divorce five years ago. Two months later he married Karie Bishop.

Ruth nodded. "Yup. He married that little blonde slip of a thing. Carly? Karen?"

"Karie."

"Right. Karie. Anyway, guess she didn't know her way around the kitchen the way Elena must've because old Mason started showing up here regularly. He wasn't chatty or anything. Just tucked into that bagel, drank his tea, and read his paper. Sometimes students would meet him here and they'd fill up the whole place with talk about this character and that story. Use'ta amuse me. You know, I always thought I could write a book about this place. Maybe put in some recipes..."

"That's a good idea. You should work on that. I'd buy it." Liv said, encouraging. Even though she never cooked, she could probably handle bagels. "So what happened to Mason? Any idea when or why he stopped coming in?"

Ruth nodded her head, gray curls jumping. "It was about a year ago, I think. There was this weird thing..."

Liv's radar started pinging. She leaned closer. "Weird thing?"

Ruth's face took on a wary expression. "I don't know if I should talk about it. I liked Mason. It's all kinda sad."

Liv nodded sympathetically. "I understand your reluctance, Ruth, but this is important. Someone else has possibly been hurt, and I just need to see the whole picture. I'm not saying Falwell did anything wrong, but anything you can tell me could help this person who really, really needs somebody on his side right now."

It was the right tack to take. Ruth was a sucker for a sob story. That's why she hired more college students than she needed.

"Well, okay," Ruth said, back to almost whispering. She leaned forward so that her head almost brushed Liv's. "It was about this time last year. I was out back in the kitchen, proofing the bagels, getting ready for the day. It was about 4:00 a.m. I hear pounding on the front door, and when I go out to see what the ruckus is about, there's Mason Falwell waving to be let in.

"'What are you doing here, Mason?' I ask. 'Onion bagel and tea,' he barks at me. He pushes past me and goes to sit over there by the window in his usual spot. That's when I notice he's wearing his pajama bottoms underneath his jacket. He was kinda unsteady on his feet. I go over to him and says, 'Professor Falwell, sweetie, we aren't open yet. Your alarm must've gone off early. Come on back in a couple hours.' He looks at me kinda blank-like, and then he swivels his head, looking around the room like he doesn't know where he is. Then he looks at me again. This time I can see he's cleared up a bit."

"Interesting. Go on."

Ruth's eyes grew sad. "I thought maybe he was sleepwalking."

"Was he? I mean, how often do people sleepwalk and ask for onion bagels?"

"He got up from the table and sorta stumbled. I didn't know what to do. I asked for his home phone number. He gave it to me, and I called his wife. She came right down, rushed in, and grabbed Mason by the arm. 'Come on, Mason,' she says. 'You need to come home now.' He just sorta hung his head and followed along. Just before they walked out th'door, she looks at me square in the eye and says, 'The writing isn't going well, and he's been drinking too much and staying up too late. I'm sorry he bothered you this morning.'"

Ruth shook her head. "I told her not to worry about it. I've seen a lot in my lifetime, and a whiskey-greased professor is nothing unusual around here. She gave me a sad little smile and whisked him away. He hasn't been in here since. I kinda miss that old, blustery guy and his pack of students. Made things interesting."

"So you think Falwell has an alcohol problem?"

Ruth shrugged. "Seems like it. Maybe he's sobered up again by now."

"Have you heard any other gossip or rumors about Falwell's drinking? Students talking? Or other college employees?"

"Oh, there was talk, I guess, around that time, but I didn't listen to it. Don't like to stick my nose in other people's business. I probably shouldn't have told you that story, but... like you said, if someone needs help..."

"This will help. Thank you so much."

Ruth tapped the table with her palm. Her face brightened into her usual smile. "Okay, then. Guess I've set my bones down long enough. Poor Tanaka over there looks like he's going to fall apart."

Four or five people waited impatiently in front of the counter.

"Mind if I sit here a while and work?"

"Go right ahead, hun. That's what we're here for."

Liv finished her bagel and sucked down another coffee. She stared out the window, watching the rain and digesting what she'd heard.

Mason Falwell with a drinking problem. Interesting. Cooper said that Falwell had been distracted and stand-offish last fall, though he had been sending Cooper encouraging feedback about his book *Eye of the Hours* at that time.

Perhaps the professor hadn't been distracted so much as hungover—or even under the influence—during office hours. Alcohol addiction can have a devastating effect on a person's marriage, career, health, and social life. Perhaps Mason's decision to stop publishing wasn't so much a matter of choice as a matter of inability to cope with his addiction.

Or maybe his publisher wasn't happy with the drunken output of an aging sot.

Liv gathered her laptop and stuck it into her backpack. At least now she had a direction to explore. If Mason Falwell was under pressure—financial or career or even social—to publish something new and found himself unable to do so because of a drinking problem, would he resort to stealing his favorite pupil's manuscript and passing it off as his own?

She thought it was possible. Pride was a motive for any number of crimes.

The rain had turned to foggy drizzle by the time she left the shop. She waved to Ruth on her way out and headed toward the campus. Stopping at her car, she ditched the umbrella and tugged a black, knit beanie over her hair, checking her reflection in the rearview and finger-combing the dark wisps of her bangs into place. She slicked on some pink lip gloss, rubbed her lips together, and messed around with her hair again.

Satisfied with her more youthful appearance, she dragged the wide strap of her computer bag across her body and headed toward Longfellow College a few blocks up the street.

As she passed the stately, gingerbread-trimmed Victorians in the college district, she contemplated the lives hidden behind the walls. Every home had its tragedies, she thought. Every family had its secrets.

If there was anything to Ruth's story about Mason and a drinking problem, Liv intended to uncover it.

Chapter Eleven

• • • • • • • • • • • • • •

She headed across campus toward Wordsworth Hall, home of the English department. The scent of loam and cedar hung in the damp, spring air. Students, backpacks slung over their stooped shoulders and heads bent to the phones in their hands, trudged along the winding pathways, oblivious to the world around them.

What a shame, Liv thought. The Longfellow campus, with its brick edifices, landscaped lawns, and towering old oaks, whispered of history and learning, art and culture. She twisted her shoulders to avoid a tall fellow walking and texting, thumbs bouncing around like miniature acrobats on the screen. She grimaced at him, but, focused as he was on his phone, he never noticed.

Reaching Wordsworth Hall, Liv nodded at the landscaping team working on some beds beside the entrance. One raked compost while the other stuck bunches of pink flowers in beside the nodding, yellow daffodils, still wet from the rain. A pair of students exited the building, and she lunged to reach the door before it swung closed.

Entering the building, a faint smell of old wood and damp wool threw her back to her undergraduate days at Bowdoin. She jogged up three long steps to a paneled lobby area. Two beige couches and a few chairs formed a gathering space at one end. Bulletin boards, papered with layers of notices and sign-up sheets, lined the walls. Tiled hallways extended on either side of the lounge space, and an open door to the left drew her attention. She walked that way, taking note of several posters taped to the walls announcing poetry readings and semesters-abroad opportunities.

She reached the open double doors and stepped into an administrative office.

"Hi! Can I help you?" A middle-aged woman in a tulip-pink cardigan looked up from her desk in the center of the room. Her reddish-brown hair curved at her jawline, and she wore a polka-dotted scarf around her neck. She gave a friendly smile as Liv approached.

"Yeah, hi. I'm thinking about applying for the MFA in Creative Writing. Professor Falwell told me to stop by this afternoon to discuss my options. Is he in his office?"

The admin shook her head. "I'm sorry. He's in class right now. Did he give you a time? I don't remember scheduling an appointment." She clicked a few keys on her computer and stared at the screen.

"That's okay. I don't actually know if he put it on his calendar. Maybe I'll just meet up with him after his class. Do you know what room he's in?" Liv glanced at the nameplate on the desk. Barbara Kimbel.

"Let's see." Barbara tapped a few more computer keys. "He's in Wheaton Hall. Room 212."

"Thanks!" Liv made as if to leave then turned back. "Um, do you happen to have any information about the MFA writing program while I'm right here? That's what I'm going to talk to him about."

"Sure thing. Hold on a minute." Barbara stood up from the desk and went to a filing cabinet. "We have some brochures and an application packet."

Liv leaned against the desk and pretended to pick at a hangnail. "Cool. So, have you worked here a long time?"

"Ha! Too long," she laughed, pulling out the papers. "I've been here twenty years. Started right after high school. Hard to believe."

"Wow, that's great. You must like it then."

"It has its good points."

"I've heard such good things about the program, and of course, I love Professor Falwell's books. What's it like to work for someone who's kinda, like, famous?"

Barbara snorted in a good-natured way. "He might be famous, but he's no different from any of the other profs as far as I'm concerned."

"What are they like?"

She handed Liv the papers, glanced around, and lowered her voice. "Oh, you know. Needy. Like kids, some of them." She giggled. "They need you to pull up their class list or look up a phone number even though it's right there in our Long/Space system. I've entered in grades, collected student projects, typed syllabuses and manuscripts. I've even been sent to the convenience store to buy deodorant and toothpaste on more than one occasion."

"Wow." Liv laughed.

Barbara slid the file drawer home with a bang and laughed, too. "Yup. A prof even asked me to pick her up for work this winter because her driveway hadn't been plowed out and she was stuck. Like I was triple-A or Uber or something." She laughed again.

"No way!"

"Well, I'm used to it." Barbara sat down behind her desk again. "They're kinda like teenagers—used to getting their way but basically harmless."

Liv didn't tell her that some of the teenagers she'd seen in the course of her investigative work were anything but harmless. "Do you ever type their manuscripts? The writing profs? I mean, it would be so cool to read something Mason Falwell wrote before it was even published."

The secretary nodded. "I used to type up his manuscripts back when I first started working."

"Used to?"

"He stopped asking me a few years ago."

"That's too bad." Liv made a sympathetic face. "How long ago?"

"Four or five years, I guess. Right about the time he got married."

"Huh." Liv moved her backpack to her other shoulder. Off-hand, she said, "I read somewhere that he writes everything longhand on yellow legal pads. Is that true?"

Barbara gave her a weird look.

Liv backtracked. "I'm sorry. You probably aren't supposed to talk about him. Never mind."

The secretary relaxed. "Oh, that's okay. It's not really a secret, anyway. He used to brag about his lack of computer skills. Said he would have been better off living in the nineteenth century like Longfellow or Poe. So, yeah. He'd give me a stack of legal pads all scrawled over with black ink—always black ink." She lowered her voice. "And just between you and me, he has terrible spelling. Don't tell anyone I told you. That *is* a secret."

Barbara giggled, and Liv joined in and then said, "So, what about his new book? I guess you didn't get a chance to type that one?"

Two spots of color flushed the secretary's cheeks. "No. He didn't ask me. Nobody around here even knew he was working on a new book. We were all surprised."

"So what about that student who said Falwell stole his manuscript? Is he crazy or what?"

"Oh, Cooper Tedeschi. I still can't believe it." Barbara frowned. "He seemed like a nice young man. He followed Mason around like a lost puppy dog. He used to stop in here to chat with me, cadge a cup of coffee from the machine over there." She nodded toward the corner of the room where an electric coffee pot sat next to an overgrown spider plant. "He said he was working on a really big project. Bragged that he was going to be the next Falwell."

"Geesh, ego much?"

"Well, maybe, but he was just a normal kid. Until Mason announced his book sale. Then he went bonkers."

"Bonkers? All I know about it is from the college newspaper and, you know, gossip around campus…"

"It was pretty awful. He'd come storming into the building

and down to Mason's office. He'd pound on the door and yell for Mason to come out. We'd have to call security."

"What did Mason say about it?"

"Not much. He seemed more confused than anything."

"Confused? That's weird, isn't it?"

Barbara's lips pressed together, and she seemed to realize her mistake. "You're right. I probably shouldn't be talking about him. Well, anyway, good luck getting into the program. If you need anything else to get started, come on in."

"I will. Thank you so much. You've been really nice, not like some secretaries on campus. I bet you know who I mean."

Barbara laughed. "We will mention no names."

Liv winked at the secretary and stuffed the graduate program information into her backpack.

A heavy-set woman with bright yellow eyeglasses entered the office and walked up to the mail cubbies beside the coffeepot. "Mail come in yet, Barb?"

"No, not yet."

Liv waved as she headed toward the door. "Have a great day, Ms. Kimbel. I'll stop by and say hi again soon."

"You do that, hun."

•   •   •   •   •

Leaving Wordsworth Hall, Liv noted that the groundskeeping crew had moved to the other side of the building.

She consulted her phone with the campus map pulled up on the screen, oriented herself, and swung to the right toward Wheaton Hall, one of several classroom buildings on campus. While the first floor contained a large lecture hall and several small offices, the second and third floors were regular-sized classrooms.

She took the stairs to the second floor which was stuffy and hot. Through a row of easterly-facing windows, she could see Back Cove shimmering beyond an expanse of a parking lot full of cars.

The hall was quiet except for the muffled sound of teachers lecturing behind the closed classroom doors. Liv leaned against the wall, waiting.

At two o'clock, doors up and down the hallway opened and students streamed out chatting to each other or hustling to their next class. When room 212 had emptied of students, Liv walked into the room.

The professor was standing at a podium placed at the front of the room, staring down at some papers, apparently deep in thought.

"Professor Falwell?"

The man looked around. Liv was struck by the wild, gray hair that flared out around the rim of a bald pate. Protruding, round eyes rolled toward her from a large, pale, deep-lined face. The professor appeared not to have shaved for a couple of days. The scruff on his cheeks and chin bristled with brown and gray stubble.

He wore jeans and a baggy green sweater with leather patches on the elbows. Sturdy brown leather shoes clad his gigantic feet, size 13 or 14 if she had to guess. She'd had no idea he was so big, probably six foot four and two-fifty at least. He reminded her of an old bull, massive and wary and suspicious of anything waving a red cape.

Not to mention female students unexpectedly appearing after his afternoon class.

"What do you want?" Falwell said, his voice gravelly and tired. "Class is over."

Liv stepped closer. "My name's Olivia Lively, Professor. I'm a big fan of your work, and I'm so looking forward to your new book coming out. I was wondering if you'd be willing to talk to me about it."

He glared at her, wary. "Am I speaking with a journalist, perhaps?"

Liv gave him a flirtatious smile. "Something like that. But I'm also considering applying to the MFA program. I was wondering if you'd let me buy you a drink and ask you some questions. How about a pint at the Arrow & Song?"

She wondered how he'd react to the mention of the campus pub. If she could get him drinking, maybe he'd spill the truth, or parts of it, to the person paying the tab. "What do you say, Professor? Can I buy you a drink?"

Chapter Twelve

· · · · · · · · · · · · · ·

Falwell gathered a book and some papers from the podium. Clearing his throat, he growled at her, "I don't think that would be a good idea."

He headed for the hallway, papers stuffed into a leather satchel he gripped tightly in his right hand. Olivia scurried to catch up. For a big man, he was surprisingly quick.

Striding along beside him and grateful for her almost-daily runs around Back Cove, she reached out and touched the author's elbow. "I don't want to bother you, but if you aren't interested in a beer, how about something at the library café? You're a total legend here on campus and, well, it would mean a lot to me if you would let me buy you a cup of coffee before your next class."

Falwell stopped in the middle of the pathway and turned his head to stare at her from beneath his bushy eyebrows. "What is your name, young lady?"

Liv flashed him a wide smile. "Olivia Lively," she told him again. "Come on. Even famous professors need to eat. I'll throw in a grilled cheese sandwich if you say yes."

The author scowled, shook his head, and started walking away. Liv bit her lip, stymied.

After five or six steps, however, the professor turned around and said, "Coming?"

Liv raised her eyebrows. "Really?"

"Hurry up. I have an appointment in an hour." He turned and

took off again, uncaring whether she followed or not.

Liv jogged to catch up as the literary giant strode toward Evangeline Library. *Way to go,* she congratulated herself. She'd hooked the whale. Now she just had to figure out how to reel him in.

· · · · ·

Once inside the large brick building that housed Longfellow College's Evangeline Library, Liv ordered a sandwich and coffee for Falwell and a peppermint tea for herself.

She spotted a free table near the library café's collection of Henry Wordsworth Longfellow memorabilia displayed in glass-fronted cases along the back wall. Students and professors crowded around the fifteen or so wooden tables. The room was awash in voices and smelled like damp wool, old books, and strong coffee overlaid by the aroma of the café's signature grilled Gruyère and ham sandwiches.

The whole place reeked of academia.

"So what publication are you with?" Mason Falwell took a bite of his sandwich and fixed her with his bulbous eyes. Crumbs from the toasted bread sifted down onto his green sweater and clung, but he didn't seem to notice or care.

"You could call me a freelancer." Liv resisted the urge to brush the crumbs away. She waved her phone. "I'll write this up and submit it on spec. Maybe get a publishing credit to my name before grad school. You don't mind if I record this, do you?"

"What do you want to know?"

"Well, first I just want to say how excited I am about your new book. Congratulations! You must be very pleased."

"Mmm-hmm." Falwell took another bite of his sandwich and his eyes wandered away from her to scan the room as if he were bored with the topic.

"I'm sure everyone is asking you this, but you pretty famously said you were done publishing books. It was such a surprise—a *wonderful* surprise—when you announced this new book deal. I mean, a new Mason Falwell on the shelves. What made you change your mind?"

Falwell shrugged and slurped at his cup of coffee. "My agent sold the book. It doesn't matter to me one way or the other."

"Really? You don't care about publishing a book you spent five years writing? You seem awfully ambivalent about the sale, especially considering the amount of money they say you are going to make." She knew the question of money was crass, but she was desperate to get him talking.

Falwell picked up his cup and set it down again. He reached for the coffee spoon to the right of the now-empty plate on which his sandwich had been served. He moved the spoon to the other side of the plate, picked it up, moved it back to its original position. Finally, he spoke in a measured, practiced voice more suitable to a lecture hall than lunch.

"I've spent my whole life writing, young lady. I don't care about the money—never cared about the money—and I certainly don't need the validation of a publishing contract. *Rune in the Crossing* is a commentary on the nihilistic impediments hobbling man's true greatness. That is what I am interested in exploring, always what I've been interested in exploring."

"Cool," Liv said, hesitating a moment before asking, "But don't you mean *Hours of the Crossing*? That's the title of your new book, right?"

"Yes, yes. That's what I said."

"Actually, you said *Rune in the Crossing*. I guess it's easy to get the titles confused."

Falwell's expression went blank for a moment and then darkened. Agitated, he lifted his coffee cup and took another loud slurp. When he put the mug down, he seemed to have composed himself.

"I know what I said, young lady. *Rune in the Crossing* was my first novel. It took me ten years to write that damn thing."

He went off on a monologue about agents and publishing companies and commercialism and the evils of computers. "If I were starting out today, I doubt any agent or editor would consider a manuscript like *Rune*. It's too big. Not commercially viable, you know. That's why I prefer to spend my time writing for my own pleasure and teaching."

"So what about this new book?"

"My agent's the one who wanted me to publish another book. I didn't care one way or the other."

"Right. Okay. That makes sense. What about the trouble you had with that student? What was his name? Cooper Trudeau?"

"Cooper Tedeschi? That little pissant!"

"He was trying to pull something, wasn't he? I mean, it's one thing if you don't want to publish your novel, but you certainly couldn't let someone else take the credit for it. Is that right?" Liv had the feeling she was goading a bull. With any luck, the bull would charge.

"Cooper Tedeschi tried to get me fired from the university, that's what he pulled! Tried to say he wrote my book." Falwell raised his voice. "After everything I'd done for him. After all the encouragement and mentoring and smoothing of his nervous, little feathers, helping him mold his spastic prose into something resembling art."

"So, you're glad he was dismissed from the program?"

"He got what he deserved. Tedeschi? Writing *Rune in the Crossing*? Ridiculous!"

Heads swiveled their way. Bodies leaned forward over tables. Voices murmured.

Liv frowned. Again, he'd gotten the name wrong.

The murmuring voices grew louder as a petite woman rushed through the café toward their table. She was around thirty, blonde, and dressed in a pair of slim khaki pants, ballet flats, and a conservative, floral-printed shirt. Worry lines had etched themselves into the corners of her mouth.

"Mason, what's going on?" she demanded before turning her suspicious brown eyes on Liv. "Who are you?"

"Just a fan," Liv said, sending her an enigmatic smile. "Who are you?"

Mason moved his hand, clattering the spoon. "Karie," he said. "I'm just having lunch with, uh…"

"Olivia." Liv stuck out her hand. "Hi there. You must be Professor Falwell's wife. Nice to meet you. I'm boring the professor with questions about his new book. It's so exciting! You must be thrilled."

Ignoring Liv, Karie reached down and tugged on Falwell's sweater. "Come on, Mason. Time to go. You have an appointment, remember?" As she herded Falwell from the room, Karie turned to glare at Olivia. A warning to stay away from her man.

Liv leaned back in her seat, stopped the recording on her phone. *Very interesting*, she thought. *Very interesting, indeed.*

Chapter Thirteen

• • • • • • • • • • • • • • •

L iv reached down to the taps on the clawfoot tub and ran water for a bath.

Head aching, she reviewed the events of the day. Her morning confrontation with FBI Agent Snow felt like days, not hours ago, and the Tedeschi case, while fun, had further drained her energy.

Streaming her favorite classical music station, Liv sprinkled a generous amount of rose-scented bath salts into the steaming water. When the tub was full, she shed her clothes and immersed herself up to her neck with a moan of pleasure.

It hadn't helped to come home to find the box she'd couriered to Rob sitting in her entryway with a slip saying the recipient could not be located.

According to the signature on the carbon, her second-floor tenant had signed for the returned box. She'd carried the box up to her apartment and stashed it under the yellow ottoman where it wouldn't get in the way. She'd take it to Goodwill next week or something.

The FBI agent must be right, she mused. Rob Mickelson was on the run.

The soothing moodiness of Dubussy's "Clair de Lune" eased some of the tension knotting her neck, and the hot, scented water worked its magic on her headache. She closed her eyes, relaxed, and pushed all thoughts of Cooper Tedeschi, Mason Falwell, stolen manuscripts, fickle lovers, and government agents from her mind.

The most pressing issue at hand had nothing to do with investigative work. Jasper Temple would be here to pick her up at six. What was she going to wear?

He'd said dinner, but that could be anything from Sicilian-style pizza at Slab to something fancy and locally-sourced at Hugo's. She really wanted to make a good impression on Dr. Hottie, not just because he'd pushed all the right buttons at brunch with her parents but also because she wanted to break her bad habit of dating losers.

Water sloshed around her ears as she slid herself further down the tub, stuck her feet onto the water spout, and felt the taps with her toes. Something about the bad boys appealed to her. Even in high school, she'd gravitated toward the pranksters and pot-heads rather than the jocks and debate team cuties.

In high school, she'd dated a tattoo artist wannabe for a semester, oohed and aahed over the designs in his sketchbook, and sneaked out of the house to meet him at Limbo on the weekends where he knew a bouncer—a friend of an older cousin—who'd look the other way when handed their fake IDs.

Then there was the summer camp counselor, a college junior, who she'd slept with just before her senior year. He bought her and her friends Boone's strawberry wine and cigarettes, pulled down her shorts in the boathouse, and introduced her to certain oral activities. A revelation, to say the least.

Of course, they'd been caught. Either her friends tattled or it was just bad luck. Either way, he'd been fired and she'd been sent home. Her mother didn't speak to her for the rest of the summer. Her father couldn't look her in the eye.

Then in college, there'd been Curtis, the townie bartender whose father ran a numbers game out of the back of his laundromat. Curtis wore silver rings on his fingers and played in a grunge band on the weekends. When he touched her hot skin, the cool metal made her shiver.

Unfortunately, he'd had a taste for coke and pornography, so she'd dumped him and moved on to someone more appropriate, a poli-sci major with big ambitions whose corporate father pulled strings to secure Junior a summer intern job in D.C. He'd bought her a tennis bracelet, boffed her one last time at his family's Kennebunkport cottage, and stopped returning her emails and texts the very next day.

Since then there'd been a single dad with anger issues and a commitment-phobic restaurateur—both long-term relationships that ended in hurtful words and bitter breakups. After that, she'd kept it casual. She dated men with awkward fetishes, men who couldn't communicate, men who hated women, men who really liked other men, and men who lied as easily as they breathed.

By the time Robert Mickelson showed up, she was too jaded to care about forever, settling instead for fun while it lasted. She'd overlooked Rob's marital status, choosing to believe him when he assured her the marriage was over. He ticked off all the boxes. Business degree. Head of commercial loans at a bank. Handsome. Fit. Cultured. Fun. Naughty enough in bed to satisfy her baser cravings.

You had to admit, she thought as she opened her eyes and picked up her loofah, he looked good on paper.

"Yeah, Lively," she said, gripping her pumice stone and rubbing at her heels. "You really know how to pick 'em."

Which brought her to Jasper and their upcoming date. The last time her mother set her up with a boy was a seventh-grade cotillion, an afternoon that had ended in vomit—his, not hers—but still. If this night went well, it would be a freakin' miracle.

She pulled the plug on the drain, wrapped herself in a fluffy towel, and padded down the hall to her closet. Frowning, she slid hangers back and forth. She held one top up and then another, checked her image in the mirror, and settled on a silky, coral top paired with slim, navy pants and one of her grandmother's vintage Hermes scarves. She'd finished her makeup and spritzed on a fine mist of Miss Dior when the doorbell rang.

"You look... wow," Jasper said when she opened the door. "Amazing."

Liv blushed. "You look nice, too," she said. "Love the jacket." He wore destroyed brown leather over a forest-green button-up shirt. With his dark blue eyes and floppy black hair, he looked more like a model than a surgeon. Yum.

"Ready to go?"

"Sure. Let me just grab my bag." She threw a lipstick and her phone into a small cross-body, ignored the nerves jumping in her stomach. "All set."

He led her to his car, a dark gray Toyota hybrid. Nicer than her sedan, but not pretentious like a Mercedes or muscley like a Dodge Charger.

He got in and smiled at her, and her heart did a little somersault. Don't get too excited, she scolded herself. Remember Rob. Just 'cuz they're pretty and charming and smell amazing doesn't mean they're worth your time and attention, let alone your heart.

He started the engine and indie rock blasted from the speakers. "Sorry about that." He reached over and turned down the volume.

"That's okay. I like Coldplay as much as the next person."

"I heard you were a classical music aficionado."

"My mother likes to talk."

He glanced at her, then turned his attention back to the road as he pulled out onto the street and headed downtown. "So, you don't like classical?"

"Oh, I do. Just don't know how I feel about you and my mother talking about my preferences. What else did you discuss? My abhorrence of broccoli? The way I used to bite my fingernails when I was a kid? My fear of small places?"

He nodded, feigning seriousness. "No broccoli. Got it. But what are your thoughts on brussels sprouts? Because I like a good brassica now and again."

She laughed.

They chatted about inconsequential things as he navigated the few blocks to Congress Street. "I hope you don't mind waiting a bit for dinner. There's someplace I wanted to take you first."

She was too nerved up to eat anyway. "Okay."

Jasper parked at the curb, and they walked side by side past Geno's, the Burnham Arms, and Local Sprouts where a few hardy Portlanders were sitting outside at café tables and sipping hot beverages. The night air was cool, but the rain had stopped. The tangy-salt scent of the ocean drifted between the buildings.

"This way," Jasper said, hanging a right down a small street between The Green Hand Bookshop and Joe's Smoke Shop.

As they rounded the corner, Liv broke into a wide grin. "I know where we're going. The International Cryptozoology Museum, right? I love this place."

"You know it?"

She took his arm. "Haven't been in a while, but yeah! It's cool."

They walked into the large room crammed full of crypto artifacts. There were plaster casts of Bigfoot prints, samples taken from Sir Edmund Hillary's explorations, photos of Giant Pandas that were once thought to be mythological creatures until they were discovered by Ruth Harkness, toy replicas of Nessie the Loch Ness Monster, and, of course, a giant statue of Sasquatch in all his hairy glory.

Liv and Jasper walked around the museum, reading bits of information, laughing, discussing the various creatures and whether or not they could be real, and discovering a similar love for the mysterious and unknown.

"I wouldn't have pegged you for a paranormal fan," Liv said, nudging Jasper aside so she could get a better look at a sample of Yeti hair.

Jasper cleared his throat. He stuck his hands in his pockets and managed to look sexy and sheepish at the same time. "I have a confession to make," he said.

"Oh, yeah?"

"Yes," he nodded. "The handsome, debonair specimen of a man

you see standing before you was once a geeky little kid growing up in the Midwest. I know it's almost impossible to fathom, but it's true. I was the youngest of eight children in the family, and I was pretty much left on my own. Had to keep myself occupied. Living right in the middle of farm country, I became fascinated with crop circles, aliens, cryptids, and eventually *The X-Files.*" He shrugged. "I figured you might as well know the truth about me right away. That is, if you haven't already dug up my entire history, P.I. Olivia Lively."

"Well, thanks for telling me." She punched him lightly on the arm. "I guess I can deal, especially since I'm a closeted paranormal geek myself. You're a doctor."

"I am."

"I'm surprised you didn't go into forensics like Dana Scully."

She paced over to look at the collection of colorful, bold artwork. "I would so love to get my hands on a couple of these pieces," she whispered. "Do you suppose the director would consider selling any of it?"

"Doubtful," Jasper said, following along behind her. "And you're right. I thought about becoming a medical examiner, but I didn't like the idea of looking at dead people all day. I wanted to fix people. You know what I think?"

"What's that?"

"Life–biology, the living human body—is as mysterious and alien as anything in this museum. We carry within our microbiome a multitude of organisms all eating, reproducing, colonizing, fighting, and dying. There's a whole world inside each of us."

"I never thought about it that way." She moved away from him, touched a small figurine dressed to represent a cryptozoologist out in the field. He was interesting, Dr. Hottie. He looked at life from a different angle than most, and she liked that.

The docent joined them in front of the artwork, and they chatted about the newest exhibits and the famous people who had wandered in over the years to the world's only museum dedicated to the study of unknown creatures. The docent told them that the museum was expanding to a bigger space at Thompson's Point where they could display their growing collection. "We're bursting at the seams here," he said, a proud look on his face.

Jasper mentioned some recent sightings of a mysterious wolf-like creature in northern Maine. When the docent launched into a lecture on Lycans versus werewolves, Jasper looked over at Liv and winked. She just about melted into a pool of lust on the spot.

Which, when she thought about it, would be kind of fitting for a cryptozoology museum.

Chapter Fourteen

• • • • • • • • • • • • •

After thanking the docent for his time and promising to visit the new digs at Thompson's Point, Liv and Jasper walked a couple of blocks to Empire Chinese Kitchen, a local place known for its dim sum. As they entered the restaurant, Jasper put a light hand on her back, held the door, and allowed her to enter ahead of him. He gave his name to the hostess while Liv looked around.

The cream walls were illuminated by bulbs encased in rustic, wire lanterns and canning jars. Simple table settings and pale wood gave the restaurant an atmosphere of warm functionality. Good smells of garlic and spices and *umami* wafted through the air, promising an enjoyable meal ahead.

"Mr. Temple? Your table is ready if you'd follow me?" She seated them at a banquette near a window where they could look out at passersby, but that didn't seem to matter. The view was wasted on them since they couldn't seem to stop staring at each other.

"This is nice," Liv said, smiling at Jasper. "I've never been here, if you can believe it."

"It's one of my favorites," he said. "Do you like dim sum? If it's okay with you, I can order for both of us."

Liv, remembering her mother's etiquette instructions over the years, nodded. She knew the rules, even if she often chose to break them. "Sure. My palate is in your hands."

He chose well. Over Empire Eggrolls, Chinatown Roast Pork, and a selection of dumplings, they chatted about their mutual love of *The X-Files*, argued about Roswell, and speculated about a Bigfoot sighting in the famous "Turner Triangle," an area of central Maine known for having an unusual number of strange reports and unexplained phenomena.

"I mean, it could be a bear," Liv said, dipping a dumpling into a little dish of sauce.

"I prefer to think it's a Yeti."

She grinned at him. "Have you ever gone on a crypto expedition?"

He grinned back. "Can't say that I have. Want to give it a go this summer? With your investigation skills and my extensive knowledge of anatomy and physiology, I think we'd make a pretty good team."

"Might be fun. I haven't been camping in a really long time, but it would be fun to get out in the woods."

"So how did you happen to get into investigative work? Were you inspired by Mulder and Scully, too?"

"I think it started earlier," she said. "My mother hates my career, but I like to tease her sometimes and tell her it is all her fault for giving me the complete set of Nancy Drew books when I was ten."

"Ah, Nancy Drew." Jasper poured some more wine into her glass. "It all makes sense to me now."

"You can't knock Nancy," Liv said. "She had nice clothes, a great car, fun friends, and was never bored. I graduated from Bowdoin with a liberal arts degree and no clue what I wanted to do with it. When I saw an advertisement for an investigator's assistant, it was like, ding! Light-bulb moment. I worked as an apprentice for two years, took a criminal justice course, and started my own agency five years ago."

"Do you think you'll stick with it? For the long haul, I mean?" The light-hearted banter in Jasper's voice became more serious.

"I'm good at it. I enjoy it. Why not?"

"I just wonder if you'll change your mind when you start a family, that's all. Isn't it a little dangerous?"

Liv shrugged. "You have to be cautious and sensible, and most of my cases aren't dangerous at all. For instance, the one I'm working on now involves a college professor. An author, actually. You've probably heard of him. Mason Falwell?"

This time, Jasper looked surprised. "You're investigating Mason Falwell? Why?"

She filled him in on as many details as she could without breaking her client's confidentiality. The story about Cooper's allegations had been in the papers anyway, so giving him the basics wasn't a problem.

"I have to admit, I'm skeptical," Jasper said. "I read Falwell's books when I was in middle and high school. He's brilliant. I can't imagine why he would take anyone else's work."

"I know, that's what makes this case so intriguing."

"Why did your client hire you? Wouldn't it be pretty easy for him to prove he wrote the manuscript? Doesn't he have copies?"

"That's just it. He has copies, but Falwell claims he hired my client to type his manuscript and in doing so my client became delusional, believing he wrote the book."

"So the two manuscripts match?"

"I don't know. I haven't seen a copy of Falwell's yet. We'll run it through plagiarism software once we get it. Even if that scan is inconclusive, there's copyright infringement to determine."

"How is that different?"

"It's more about the content of the material versus the wording. In order to win a lawsuit for copyright infringement, my client will have to prove that the two novels are substantially similar in substance, setting, plot, theme, and language. What we need is proof that my client wrote the novel first and that Falwell knowingly submitted the work as his own. It is going to be a tough case to prove."

"Did Falwell have access to your client's manuscript?"

Liv nodded. "Falwell was his advisor. My client sent chapters to Falwell who would critique the work and send it back with notes, corrections, that sort of thing."

"So why can't your client simply produce those critiques?"

"You would make a good investigator," Liv said. "That was my first thought. Unfortunately, there was a malfunction of the college's email system. All the emails and attachments were wiped out."

"That's a bit coincidental."

"Yeah, isn't it? I need to get back over to the university. Talk to some people about the system malfunction. I imagine many of the students lost work. I'm sure they are working to restore the data, but so far, my client hasn't been able to get his old files and emails."

"If Falwell really did steal your client's work, I hope you can find the proof." Jasper reached for his wallet, drew out a credit card, and placed it on the table. "I still can't believe it, though. Now I want to dig out those old novels and reread them."

They discussed books and authors on the way home, discovering they had some overlapping interests and favorites. He pulled into her driveway. She reached for the door. "Hold on," he said. She watched with amused eyes as he bounded out of the car and ran around to open her door.

"What a gentleman," she said, teasing.

"You know it." There was seriousness behind his light tone. He took her hand as they walked toward the door.

The street was quiet. Three doors down, a neighbor walked his large dog. One or two windows in every home glowed with lights. A cat ran lightly across the street and into a sloping backyard. The air smelled of salt spray and spring.

"You must have a great view of the city from up there," he said, pointing at her big westward-facing windows.

"Are you angling to come up?" Their hands swung between them, fingers lightly clasped, comfortable. It felt like a real first date, the old-fashioned kind with a goodnight kiss at the door and nothing more. Romantic. The kind she didn't expect or much want anymore.

"I can't," he said. "I have office appointments stacked back to back starting at seven-thirty tomorrow, and I'm heading out of town for the weekend. Some other time, though? How about Monday evening? I'll bring dinner ingredients and my *X-Files* DVDs."

She squeezed his fingers. "That sounds nice."

The space between them hummed. Jasper let go of her hand, reached up to graze her jawline with his fingers.

His eyes dropped to her mouth and lingered there. She held her breath, dizzy with anticipation.

He lowered his head and brushed his lips against hers. It was a nice kiss. Tantalizing. Just enough to ignite a few sparks. She leaned into him, smiled against his mouth. Jasper smiled too. They stood there like two idiots, smiling lip to lip, for a few seconds before he murmured, "I should go."

"You could stay. I'll still respect you in the morning. Promise."

"Tempting." He kissed her again, a quick light smooch, as if he couldn't resist, and then he stepped back. "Thank you for a wonderful evening, Olivia."

She looked at him through half-closed eyes, sultry and seductive so he'd have something to think about later on. "This date definitely made my top ten list... maybe top five."

He stuck a hand on his heart and pretended to double up over it. "Ouch. Only top five? I was shooting for number one."

"Don't get too cocky. I'll see you Monday. I'm looking forward to some Mulder and Scully." She walked backward to her door. Leaned against it. "Sweet dreams."

"You better believe it."

She opened the door, laughing, and ran up the stairs to the third floor. Later, cozy in her silk pajamas and with a mug of chamomile tea in her hands, she replayed the evening from start to finish. Through the big windows, the lights of the city below glowed through the fog, pinpricks of light. She sipped her tea, thought about the shape of Jasper's mouth, the way his fingers brushed against her skin, and the heat shimmering between them.

Despite what she'd told him, tonight had been her best first date. Ever.

Chapter Fifteen

●●●●●●●●●●●●●●

She was dying to tell Ashleigh about her date. It wouldn't seem real until the two of them had gone over every detail, dissected every word of conversation, analyzed what it meant that Jasper hadn't tried to get upstairs.

But Ashleigh still wouldn't take her calls.

Liv held her cell to her ear, closed her eyes, and willed Ashleigh to forgive her and pick up. The phone rang six times and went to voicemail. Liv's shoulders drooped as Ashleigh's voice instructed her to leave a message. She could almost hear an unspoken, "Unless this is Olivia, in which case, bug off."

Liv sighed. Of course, Ashleigh would never record a message like that. That was much more Liv's style.

The phone beeped. "Ashleigh, please call me back. I'm really sorry. I didn't realize how upset you were when you tried to talk to me. I mean, you've had endometriosis ever since I've known you. I didn't know you were having worse trouble with it or that you and Trevor were struggling to get the baby thing going."

She winced, tapped the phone against her forehead, brought it back to her ear. "I'm sorry. That's probably not the right thing to say either. I know you would have told me if I'd given you a chance to talk instead of me hogging the conversation all the time. Now I don't know what I'm supposed to say."

Liv pulled her knees up to her chest and hugged them tight with her free arm. "Well, I'm just going to keep calling until you decide to forgive me. If you want to talk, I promise I'll listen. I miss you. Just call me. Okay? Bye." She held the phone away, put it back to her mouth. "Call me."

She pressed the red button, let her hand with the phone fall against the couch cushions, then rested her forehead on her knees.

She and Ashleigh had never gone this long without talking, not since the time in college when Ashleigh got plastered at a party and announced to everyone present that Olivia Lively was a rich, spoiled snob who left her dirty Victoria's Secret thongs all over the floor of their dorm room.

Liv, standing behind her with a cup of beer in her hand, had heard every word. She'd snarkily commented that if fancy underwear made Ashleigh feel inferior, then she should go to student housing and request a single. Everyone around them had laughed and stopped talking to Ash.

They hadn't spoken for a week.

Liv had tossed every article of clothing she owned onto the floor and stayed up late every night reading Raymond Chandler novels and smoking cigarettes out the dorm window. For her part, Ashleigh gave her the silent treatment, showing up at their room only to sleep and basically acting as if Liv didn't exist.

What happened next was one of those friend-legends that was told over and over again, often aided by the lubricating influence of a couple of cocktails.

The following Saturday, when Ashleigh turned up around midnight, Liv pulled out a small, crumpled, but distinctive pink shopping tote with a beribboned handle. "Here," she said, shoving the Victoria's Secret bag toward Ashleigh. "I'm sorry for being a total B."

Ashleigh took the bag, stared at it a moment, and then smiled. "Hold on a minute," she said.

She navigated the war zone of clothing on the floor, reached into her very neat closet, and pulled out an identical bag. "Guess we are more alike than we thought."

Liv pulled out the red silk thong and squealed. "I love it! Open yours."

Ashleigh held the pair of lace-edge printed cotton hip huggers in both hands, gave the panties a little squeeze to her chest. "They're so pretty! Thank you, Livs."

"You know that's not the body part they're meant for, right, Ash?" Liv joked.

Ashleigh picked up a shoe from the floor and tossed it at Liv's head, and they both laughed so hard the uptight girl next door pounded on the wall. They hadn't had another serious fight since.

Until now.

Needing some distraction, Liv decided she might as well go to the office and get some work done. It was either that or laundry. She made a face. Work. Definitely.

After a shower, she felt more like herself. She didn't have any appointments, so she opted for cropped black leggings, a hoodie, and a pair of canvas high tops. She looked up and down the street for Agent Snow's SUV. He must be harassing one of Rob's other girlfriends, she thought, tossing her computer bag into the car. She's promised Snow she'd let him know if Rob contacted her, but he hadn't. Maybe he really had skipped town. "Good riddance," she muttered.

She headed toward her Bayside office. At an intersection, she spotted a shaggy-looking guy with a handmade sign asking for money for a bus ticket to Florida. A dismal sky threatened yet more rain. She grimaced. Couldn't blame the poor guy for wanting to escape Maine this time of year.

She reached into her cup holder where she kept a few extra dollars and handed them out the window. "Good luck to you," she said as the driver behind her laid on the horn.

Resisting the urge to flip the impatient driver off with a well-manicured middle finger, Liv turned into the parking lot at the warehouse. A smattering of cars told her that a few artists were already hard at work inside.

She waved at a couple of guys at the 3-D printer, juggled her travel mug and keys as she walked down the hall to her office. A cool draft snaked under the door, twining around her bare shins above her canvas sneakers. Odd.

She stuck her key in the old lock, jiggled it, and opened the door to chaos.

Books and papers lay scattered on the floor. Her sturdy philodendrons and ferns had been dislodged from their pots, and the soil made sad piles beside broken stems and ripped leaves. Heart pounding, Liv scanned the room for signs of forced entry. It wasn't difficult to spot. The casement window was smashed. Shards of glass like pieces of an evil jigsaw puzzle glittered on the industrial carpeting. Exposed to the brisk April air, the room felt as cold and damp as a tomb.

Liv picked her way through the mess, and took notice of the open desk drawers, the cracked computer monitor, the desktop tower pulled from beneath the desk, cords attached, and tipped on its side. Her eyes fell on the dented sides and broken handles of the credenza.

She spat out an expletive and walked over, careful not to move anything. She crouched down to inspect the lock. Scratch marks, most likely from a screwdriver, indicated that the lock had been tampered with. Fortunately, it appeared to have held. She straightened and took a deep breath.

Pulling her phone from her bag, she called 911, explained that she'd had a break-in, and gave the dispatcher the address. She then dialed the number she had for the owner of the building, told her about the situation, assured her that the police had been notified.

Leaving her office, she strode into the main area to talk to the crafters working there.

"Someone broke into my office," she told them. "They came in through the window. Have you noticed anything out of place? Anything missing or broken?"

The mostly group looked at each other, eyes wide. They shook their heads. "Nothing suspicious that we can tell," an older woman said. "I was the first one in this morning. The door was locked as usual."

"Okay," Liv said. "The police will be here soon. They might ask you some more questions."

On her way back to her office, Liv checked the bathrooms, the doors of the main office and conference room, and looked for any signs of further mischief. Finding none, she went into her office for her computer bag, and grabbed her laptop.

The light on the security camera she'd installed in the corner of the room was still blinking, so she knew it hadn't been disabled or broken. She opened the camera app and began scanning the video footage from the previous night. At 2:11 a.m., a dark figure appeared outside the window.

She crossed her arms, watched as the burglar smashed the window with what appeared to be a hammer, cleared the shards of glass from the frame, and crawled through the window. He dropped a backpack and then himself to the floor. He wore baggy jeans, a dark hooded sweatshirt, and a dark bandana over the lower half of his face and nose.

Hissing, she drew back when he looked up at the camera and waved.

She stopped the recording, zoomed in on his face. She didn't recognize his small, round eyes. There was a scar on his left eyebrow, though. "Idiot," she said, pressing the play button again. "You should have worn a full mask."

Her face was stony as she watched the perp trash her office, looking for... what? He checked for hiding places behind her shelf of books, crawled beneath the desk, and tilted paintings to look for hidden storage spaces. Finding nothing, he withdrew a screwdriver and some lock-picking tools from the backpack, worked at the credenza for a few minutes, and grew frustrated.

Liv pressed her lips together, watching as he smashed at the drawers with the hammer and tried to pry them open with the screwdriver. The drawer locks held.

"How do you like that, you loser?" Liv muttered.

On the video, the beam of headlights swept into the window. Looking up, the perp hustled to the spot beneath the window and tossed the backpack through. In the glare of the headlights, he jumped to grab the sill and hoisted himself through the window frame. She froze the screen, checked the time indicator.

He'd been in her office for just under ten minutes.

She sat back in her chair. She stared at the computer screen, locked on the image of the broken window and the dark blur of a car leaving the scene.

He'd gone away empty-handed, she thought. The question was, what had he been looking for?

Chapter Sixteen

• • • • • • • • • • • • • •

After talking to the police who arrived a half-hour later, Liv took a bunch of photos and then cleaned the mess in her office. She scooped soil back into the plant pots, placing them back on the shelves along with her books. She sorted papers, stacking them in her desk organizer trays, and swept the window glass into the dustbin.

She placed a phone call to a window replacement company and her renter's insurance assistance line. The window company promised to send someone within the hour. The insurance company asked her to email them photos and to send a copy of the police report when she got it along with an itemized list of damages and replacement estimates.

She scanned the room with a critical eye. She'd need to buy a new desktop monitor as soon as possible, and the warehouse owner needed a come-to-Jesus sermon about getting security bars on the windows and a camera to monitor the parking lot. Liv had mentioned both options several times, but she hadn't wanted to preach too much. She liked the cheap rent and convenient parking.

The window tech arrived, took measurements, and left. An hour later, a carpenter came in and boarded up the window, leaving the room gloomy and dungeon-like. Liv's head began to pound from the stress, noise, and lack of caffeine.

In desperate need of coffee, she took off on foot toward Coffee

By Design for a large dark roast, taking a moment to chat with her favorite barista and enjoying the cool, artsy vibe and chatter.

Feeling somewhat revived, Liv exited the coffeehouse. Oh, she was still plenty perturbed about the break-in, but she pushed the negativity into a corner of her mind so she could focus on the positive. Most people in life, she reminded herself, were good. In her line of work, she happened to deal with the more negative impulses of humanity.

Once back in the office which had warmed up enough to be comfortable, she sipped her coffee and thought about the break-in. The police promised to check their profiles for a guy with an eyebrow scar, but because nothing had been stolen, she knew it wouldn't be high on their priority list.

Most likely the target had been petty cash, small electronics like phones and tablets, or even silver photo frames and expensive pens, anything the burglars could quickly pawn. Luckily, she took her gun home every night, and she didn't keep petty cash or expensive gadgets in the office.

Her eyes fell on the credenza. If these guys were part of an organized crime ring, they may have been looking for financial records, social security numbers, anything they could use for identity theft. The police had told her there'd been a rash of similar break-ins over the past few months with a corresponding uptick in credit card fraud and even compromised bank accounts. Most likely, she'd been the victim of this group of low-lifes.

An uneasy feeling roiled in her stomach. The break-in wasn't personal, but she felt violated just the same. If only she could call someone and vent…

She picked up her phone to call Ashleigh before she remembered they still weren't talking. She thought about calling her mother or father, but decided against it. They'd only tell her once again that running a private investigation business was both dangerous and foolish.

She'd simply have to deal with it alone.

• • • • •

That afternoon, Liv approached the Tedeschi case as if she were an archaeologist or historian, analyzing the data for clues or possible avenues for further inquiry that would help his case.

After retrieving Cooper's file from the dented but functional credenza, she opened the folder onto her desk, picked through the sheaf of papers and documents Cooper had left with her, arranged them into piles, and examined them one by one. She perused his undergrad application, acceptance letter, transcripts, and class schedules. With better-than-average grades, he'd graduated cum laude from the state university, emerging with a degree in English literature.

So, she concluded, Cooper was no slouch. Not brilliant or anything, but a good student with no academic probation periods or any glaring inconsistencies.

She put those papers aside and then scanned his MFA application and letters of recommendation. Nothing unusual there. She read the letter of acceptance to the creative writing program. He must have been psyched to get that, she thought, adding it to the pile of inconsequential documents.

She picked up the next piece of paper. It turned out to be a financial aid form that listed Cooper's loan amount as well as the awarded work-study stipend. *Aha!* Now she was getting somewhere.

Liv shuffled the papers looking for actual income statements and found several paper-clipped together. The statements included Cooper's title of graduate assistant in the English Department as well as the dates of the pay period, hours worked, and the amount of compensation.

She frowned. Cooper admitted he'd often worked in Falwell's home library. The statements in her hand proved that Cooper had been given significant hours of access to the professor's personal computer and papers, evidence that backed up Falwell's story, not Cooper's.

Her client had not only motive, but means. Something the administration would have taken into consideration when deciding his fate.

She scanned the letter of dismissal from the college, and then she looked through her notes on the meetings she'd had with Cooper, his lawyer, Ruth at the bagel shop, and Mason himself. She jotted a few more notes into her notebook and then continued to dig through the pile of unread documents.

She loved this aspect of her work, searching for the truth beneath the surface, exposing secrets and motivations that led to wild impulses and problematic human behavior. Being a private investigator wasn't all stakeouts and long-range cameras. Much of it was just this: trawling through paperwork for data, connecting the dots, coming up with a plausible theory, investigating to see if the facts fit, finding hard evidence, and creating a narrative where everything fit.

In this case, either Cooper or Falwell was telling the truth. One of them wrote the novel. The other one didn't. It was a classic he-said, he-said situation.

Liv tapped her fingernails on the arm of her chair. The Longfellow administrators had opted to accept Falwell's version of the events because that version benefited the institution. It was easier to kick out a troubled student, claiming he was incompetent and delusional, than confront their illustrious faculty member.

However, Liv mused, Cooper's academic record showed him to be a competent student, one that was more than capable of succeeding in the two-year writing program. The pages of writing he'd submitted with his application seemed solid, not that she was anyone to judge. At least they'd been good enough to get him accepted into a very competitive program.

She picked up his graduate transcript and related documentation. He'd earned excellent grades in literary criticism and the other interdisciplinary courses taught by a number of faculty members, and the file included hard-copy printouts of feedback from faculty regarding his writing assignments completed before he began working with Falwell exclusively last fall.

Most of the feedback had been positive, she noted, with the type of suggestions and criticism you would expect from teachers in a creative writing program. Her eyes traveled up to the tops of the critiques and settled on the Long/Space logo prominently displayed on top.

She felt a tingle at the back of her head. What exactly was Long/Space anyway?

She reached for her desktop keyboard before remembering the monitor was cracked. "Crap," she muttered and grabbed her laptop from her bag. A quick search on the college's website revealed that the Long/Space course delivery system had been developed in-house by a Longfellow College graduate and was used by professors for both distance and web-based courses as well as in conjunction with their traditional college classes on campus.

Lectures were uploaded by teachers and viewed by students at their convenience. Assignments were saved in communal folders with permissions for access given to specific individuals—the professor, the students, and sometimes whole study groups depending on the way the course was designed. Grades were posted on the student accounts. Long/Space included the college's email system, as well.

Liv searched through the notes she had taken when she met with Cooper last week. Based on what she'd just learned, he should have been able to provide copies of chapters from his novels along with Falwell's critiques, corrections, and suggestions as evidence of his authorship. However, a freak glitch in the Long/Space system wiped out not only all of Falwell's online class materials, but also Cooper's email history and folders. Everything associated with Cooper's final writing project disappeared into the ether.

A bizarre coincidence or intentional sabotage?

The loss of data certainly worked to Falwell's advantage—assuming the professor had, indeed, stolen Cooper's novel. All the feedback that Falwell had typed onto Cooper's manuscript pages in the shared folder was gone, poof, into thin air. All the emails they'd sent back and forth between them had likewise disappeared. All Cooper had left to show the Honor Code Committee was a printout of the manuscript with his own handwritten notes in the margins, no date stamp on the pages to indicate when the document had been written or by whom.

The idea that a system like Long/Space could totally crash and that files could be lost with zero hope of recovery stretched the imagination. Liv knew It was very hard to completely delete electronic files. For that much information to be irrevocably lost, something extremely major had to have happened to the college's server during that upgrade.

Had Cooper's Long/Space account been specifically targeted? And if so, by whom?

Liv closed the laptop with a slap. The whole Long/Space snafu seemed fishy to her. Like rotting lobster shells in a dumpster fishy. She added the abbreviation "IT Department" to her list of possible leads.

Out of habit, she glanced toward the window to check the weather and cursed when she saw the plywood. It was past five p.m., anyway. She should go to the gym, work the kinks and frustration out on the punching bag, and practice her self-defense moves. It had been a while since her last martial arts class, and the break-in definitely had her spooked.

She yawned as a wave of exhaustion rolled over her. On the other hand, maybe she'd just go home, order up a pizza, and watch a Netflix movie.

She replaced the bulging Tedeschi file into the credenza and shoved her small spiral notebook with its lengthening list of potential interviewees into her bag. After locking the office door behind her, she stepped into the shadowy hallway. The crafters had closed shop for the night, and the workspace lay shrouded in gloomy darkness. Only one emergency light glowed near the door.

A shiver of apprehension crawled up Liv's spine. She hurried through the building to the front door and jogged to her car, computer bag slapping at her hip. Glancing around, she threw the bag into the car and slid into the driver's seat. "Nobody's watching you," she whispered to herself as she started the engine. "It's just your overactive imagination."

With a last, quick glance around the lot and a flash of her taillights, she took off for home.

Chapter Seventeen

•••••••••••••

On Monday morning, Liv headed to the campus. She wore a pair of slim, dark-wash jeans, a Longfellow College T-shirt, and a tiny yellow cardigan sweater. Temperatures were set to climb into the mid-60s by noon. Spring, finally.

Liv dropped her car near the bagel shop and hiked over to the creative writing department. The secretary, Barbara, was on the phone talking about registering someone for a summer class, but she gave Liv a smile and a friendly wave.

Unzipping her backpack, Liv pulled out a thin stack of papers stapled at the corner. She plunked herself onto a chair with the college seal embossed on it.

From the hallway, there were sounds of doors opening and closing. A few voices greeted each other. Someone whistled as he walked down the hallway past the office. In the secretary's office, the morning sun streamed through the wide slats of the window shade, and the smell of coffee rose from the machine next to the spider plant. Barbara asked the caller a few questions, clattered away on the computer keyboard, and peered at the screen.

Liv pretended to read the papers in her hand. She was hoping to build some more rapport with the secretary, see if she could learn more about Karie Falwell. There had been something panicky and desperate about the way she'd barged up to them in the library café last week. But what would she be trying to hide? And did it have anything to do with Cooper?

"Hello, hello," the secretary said when she'd hung up the phone. "I was wondering if we'd see you again." Barbara beamed at Liv. "What can I do for you today? I'm sorry I've forgotten your name."

"Olivia," Liv said, standing and walking to the front of the desk.

"Yes, that's right," the secretary said, nodding her head. She'd tucked one side of her reddish-brown hair behind one ear and held it back with two gold bobby pins. She wore a vintage-style dress and a gauzy white scarf tied around her neck.

"I was wondering if Professor Falwell was in this morning?"

"I'm sorry, he hasn't come in yet today. Is there something I can help you with?" The secretary's eyes fell to the papers in Liv's hand.

"I have this piece I wanted to drop off for him to read. He said he'd take a look at it for my MFA application. I'm kinda nervous about it. You can probably tell." Liv faked an awkward laugh.

"He did? That's unusual." Barbara frowned. "You were able to meet with him after all?"

Liv nodded. "Yes! Thank you so much for pointing me in the right direction. I just went up to him after his class and begged him to talk to me. Finally, he agreed to coffee in the library, and he was quite helpful. At least until…" Liv bit her lip, feigning reluctance.

"Until?"

Liv shrugged. "Well, until his wife came along and dragged him away. She was all suspicious, like I was trying to seduce him or something."

The secretary shook her head. "Oh. That one."

Liv lowered her voice. "Yeah, is she always like that, or was it just me, do you think?"

"Huh! It's not just you. Don't worry about it. That's just Karie." She made a face and lowered her voice. "Between you and me, she's had him on a tight leash ever since she married the poor guy."

"What's she so worried about?"

"Oh, who knows," the secretary said, waving her hand. "Probably afraid some younger, prettier college student is going to tempt him away from her the same way she stole him away from poor Elena."

"His first wife? That must have been a big scandal."

The secretary glanced toward the door. "You don't know the half of it. Most of the college faculty were calling for his resignation because Karie was a student here."

"She was Falwell's student?"

"No, no. She was a graduate student in Comparative Lit. She had applied for the MFA program but wasn't accepted. It's very competitive, as you know."

"Yeah, I'm worried about that."

"Don't worry, hun. I'm sure you'll be accepted. Anyway, about five years ago, it seemed like all of a sudden wherever Mason was, there was Karie Bishop hovering nearby, agreeing with everything he said, making eyes at him, putting a hand on his arm, that kind of stuff. It was very obvious she was after him. Everyone in the writing department knew what was going on and didn't mind talking about it, either."

"That must have been embarrassing for Professor Falwell."

Barbara shrugged. "Nothing embarrasses him. He's... what's the word?"

"Impervious?"

"That's it. Anyway, all that attention paid off for Karie."

"Paid off? Monetarily, you mean?"

Barbara looked abashed. "No. That sounds worse than I meant it to."

Liv heard voices in the hallway, and Barbara made a zipping motion in front of her mouth.

Brushing past Liv, a couple of faculty members bee-lined for the coffee pot in the corner and chatted about someone's low summer class enrollment.

"It'll be canceled. You'll see. And our classes will fill to overflowing," the man said.

The woman sighed. "More papers to grade." She picked up her coffee cup. "Did you finally fax my symposium registration over to USWM, Barb?"

The admin's body stiffened. "Yes, I did. Friday afternoon. I'll call and check with them today and make sure everything is finalized."

"Fabulous. Thank you." The woman's eyes landed on Liv, sized her up, and walked to the mail cubbies.

Barbara said to Liv, "I'll get your story to Professor Falwell." She held out her hand for the stack of papers Liv held.

"Um, if you don't mind, I'd rather give it to him personally."

"He's in and out a lot. You could always slip it under his door."

"Oh, okay. Thank you so much. You've been a big help."

"No problem, hon'. Hey, wait a minute." Barbara clicked a few buttons on her computer and the printer behind her whirred. She twirled in her chair, grabbed the paper, and handed it to Liv. "The MFA students have readings at the Arrow & Song on Tuesday nights. You might want to check it out."

Liv took the paper, "I will for sure! Thanks again. You've been super helpful."

On her way down the hall, Liv folded the paper into a square. Emerging into the bright sunshine, she tucked the square into her bag and decided to attend the reading the following evening. She'd talk to the other MFA students about Cooper and Falwell and the Long/Space crash. One of them, without even knowing it, might hold the key to proving Cooper's story.

Pleased with her work, Liv pulled out her phone and checked her schedule for the rest of the day. She had a couple of phone calls to return, an appointment with a potential client in Fallbrook at eleven, and a one o'clock meeting with the volunteer coordinator at The Telling Room to discuss ways she could get involved.

Her thoughts jumped to Jasper and their upcoming *X-Files* marathon date that evening. He'd phoned her on Sunday night to confirm, offering to bring ingredients for a chicken dish if she'd take care of the salad fixings. That had set off a few warning bells. She'd expected takeout pizza and a bottle of Chianti. Was cooking together on a second date just a little too intimate?

Walking toward her car, Liv listened to her voice messages and wished for the umpteenth time she could talk to Ashleigh for advice. She'd give Ash one more day to get over the fight, and then she'd be forced to take more drastic action.

She returned a call from Port City Sash & Blind who'd left a message to let her know when her replacement windows would be in. That reminded her to contact the Portland PD to see if they had any leads on the break-in. They didn't. She threw her phone in her bag and gave up on work and phone calls for the day.

Humming along with Bach's zippy "Coffee Cantata" as she drove home, she considered what to wear for her date that night. Like food, wine, and music, clothing set the mood for a date. So, what was tonight to be? Classy with a cashmere cardigan and her grandmother's emerald earrings? Or maybe something sexier, like silk. A little camisole under a sheer blouse. Heels.

She thought about the way Jasper's mouth felt against hers, the way he'd winked at her in the museum, the reluctant step away from her as he said goodbye.

Silk and heels, she decided. Definitely.

Chapter Eighteen

• • • • • • • • • • • • • •

Jasper arrived with two canvas shopping bags.

"Lead me to your kitchen," he said. A bouquet of grocery store flowers peeked out the top of one of the bags. She showed him the kitchen. "It's small but functional," she said, pointing here and there. "Counter, knife drawer, measuring cup drawer."

"I like it." He placed the bags on the floor, and she gave him an appreciative glance as he began to unpack the groceries. He looked adorable and casual in jeans and an untucked, light blue button-up. His dark hair, still damp from a shower, brushed the back of his collar.

She touched his back and leaned over to watch as he lifted items from the bags. "Watcha got there?"

He grabbed the flowers and thrust them out to her. "Daisies, for starters. Got a vase?"

"Yes, doctor." She took the flowers, discarded the cellophane wrapper, rummaged around beneath the sink, and produced a blue vase. "Vase, check." He grinned over at her, flirty and bashful, while she snipped the stems, ran water into the vase, and worked the sturdy orange daisies into a pleasing arrangement.

By the time she finished with the flowers, he'd emptied the bags. The dinner ingredients lay on the counter.

"Spinach?" She wrinkled her nose.

He handed her a bottle of white wine. "Open that," he said. "It was my understanding that it was broccoli you objected to."

"Oh, I definitely object to broccoli. But you know what happens with spinach." She moved a fingernail back and forth between her two front teeth.

He laughed. "I'll make a deal with you. You let me put spinach in this dish, and I promise I'll tell you if any gets stuck between your teeth."

She pretended to give it some thought. "Okay. Deal. What are we making?"

"You are making salad." He held up a package of chicken. "I'm making my famous *poulet au boursin*. Do you have a cutting board?"

"Yup." She put the board on the counter as he grabbed the handle of a copper skillet and twirled the skillet in his hand. "You brought your own pan? Who are you, Gordon Ramsay?"

"It's my only good pan, so don't get excited. And this is my only dinner recipe."

She batted her eyelashes. "So what you're telling me is that you make this for all your girlfriends."

He winked at her. "Maybe."

Her body did that melty thing again. Oh, boy.

She watched him fillet the chicken breasts. He spread them with deft fingers on a plate, and he glanced over at her. "I'm getting performance anxiety here. Don't you have a salad to make?'

"All done and safe in the fridge. I'm much more interested in what you're doing over there with the knife, Doc. It's not every day I get to watch a famous surgeon at work."

"Hardly famous. And this knife isn't exactly a scalpel. Mixing bowl?"

He melted some butter in the pan and threw in handfuls of the baby spinach. "Catch any bad guys today?" he asked her as he stirred the greens until they were wilted.

"No, but I did get some more insight into this Falwell case. The administrative in the English department is real chatty. She had lots to say about Mason and his second wife, Karie. It was quite the scandal at the college, apparently."

"Do tell."

"Well," she leaned her hip against the counter, "according to the gossip mill, Falwell divorced his first wife so he could marry hot little Karie Bishop, a graduate student in the English department, with whom he'd been carrying on for a while. There was an uproar, but Falwell's a big name, and because Karie wasn't his student, the powers-that-be looked the other way."

Jasper scraped the wilted spinach into the mixing bowl, stirred in a tub of herbed boursin cheese, and mixed it all together. "He used his clout to avoid repercussions for his actions. Did people feel sorry for Karie, see her as a victim?"

"Just the opposite. The admin said Karie had been the one to pursue Falwell, not the other way around. She all but called Karie a gold-digger."

"Hmmm. So how does this play into Cooper's accusation?" Jasper spooned the spinach and cheese mixture onto the chicken breasts, smooshed the bottom and top pieces together over the mixture, and placed the chicken breasts in the pan to brown.

"I was thinking about that this afternoon. I've come up with a theory, but I could be way off. I don't know."

Jasper poked at the chicken, adjusting the gas flame under the pan. "Who knew academia was such a soap opera?"

She nudged past him, opened a cupboard, and snagged a couple of white wine glasses. She poured the wine, handed one to him. "Cheers."

He touched his glass to hers. "Cheers."

They both sipped, watching each other over the rims. Liv felt a little flutter in her belly. The night was young, and Dr. Hottie looked really, *really* good to her right now.

"So," he said, putting his glass on the counter. "Tell me about this theory of yours."

Liv tapped her wine glass with her fingernails. "Here's how I see it going. Falwell leaves his wife and kids for a pretty, young graduate student named Karie Bishop. She pursued him, and that appealed to his ego. Everything is wonderful at first. He's switched out the old, worn-out wife for a smart, nubile grad student who caters to his needs, hangs onto his every word, makes him feel young and virile again. He thought all that excitement and passion were behind him, but now he has this second life with a beautiful, fresh, young woman at his side. What man wouldn't love that?"

"I probably shouldn't answer that question."

"Better not. Anyway, it's easy to see the appeal for him, but I'm asking myself, what's in it for her? I've seen the guy. He's not Warren Beatty or Robert Redford, if you know what I mean. She's a comparative lit major. She geeks out on Henry David Thoreau, Virginia Woolf, Colette, or whoever."

"Virginia. Colette. I'm with you." Jasper sipped his wine.

"So maybe she thinks being married to a famous writer's going to be all conversations about literature over breakfast and intellectual dinner parties at night. Maybe she's hoping for trips to London and New York City to meet with publishers and editors, that she'll accompany him to literary conferences and award ceremonies. She thinks he's her ticket to a big life."

Jasper took the bottle of wine, poured a little bit into the pan with a splash and sizzle. The kitchen filled with the aroma of wine sauce and spices. "Maybe she saw herself as his muse," he said.

Liv stared at him for a second. "Huh, that's good! I hadn't thought of that."

"What? You never wanted to be a man's muse?"

"Not my calling."

"Shocker."

She picked up the dish towel and flicked him with it while he laughed and dodged out of the way. "So, anyway, a few years into the marriage, Karie realizes she'd pinned her hopes on a dud. The great Mason Falwell turns out to be a grumpy, irascible, alcoholic, old has-been. Maybe he's tight with his money. Maybe the trips to Europe and New York never materialize. Whatever. The thrill is gone.

"That's when I asked myself—what would Mason do if Karie, fed up, threatened to leave him? I mean, he destroyed his first marriage, broke up his family, put his career on the line for her. Not only would he be alone if she left, but also he'd look like a fool in front of his colleagues and the whole literary community. Everyone would know. Everyone would talk. They'd gossip. Laugh. Or worse, feel sorry for him."

"You think Mason needed to do something to hold on to his marriage and his status, so he stole Cooper's book."

"Maybe."

Liv crossed to the refrigerator and took out the salad and a bottle of vinaigrette dressing. "He's in a bind. He needs to produce another book so Karie won't leave him, but when he sits down to write, nothing. He's blocked. Karie pushes him, nags him, tells him this isn't working out, that she's not happy, and threatens to leave him—just as he'd feared."

"Enter Cooper."

"Right. At Mason's darkest hour, along comes this young writer by the name of Cooper Tedeschi whose work reminds Mason of his own early writing. Cooper's novel is right there, tantalizingly close, so similar to Mason's work that he could have written it himself forty years earlier. The temptation is too great to resist."

Jasper raised his glass again. "It fits. I like the way your mind works."

She shrugged. "It's a theory, anyway."

· · · · ·

After dinner, she booted up the old laptop she saved for just such occasions and placed the first disc of Jasper's *X-Files* DVD collection into the pop-out tray on the side. They settled onto the couch and watched two episodes.

Halfway through the first episode, Jasper put his arm around Liv, and she snuggled in close to him, arm around his waist. His arm tightened, and he looked down at her. "I like this," he said, brushing the top of her head with his lips.

"Me, too." She felt secure, she realized, and as soon as she recognized this, the doubts crept in.

Nobody was this nice, this perfect. Here was this gorgeous doctor in his mid-thirties, single, never married, no kids. A guy with good taste in clothes, restaurants, and cult TV. Something must be wrong with him. Had to be. Not that it mattered all that much to her. After all, she was used to enjoying relationships when things were good and moving on when they weren't. *Just be careful*, she warned herself. *Don't get too attached.*

When the second episode finished, Jasper looked at his watch. "It's getting late, and I have an early surgery tomorrow. I should get home." He slid his arm away from her and reached over to pop the DVD from the computer.

She watched as he walked over to the big windows to look down at the city. She appreciated the way his jeans sat on his hips and the way his shoulders filled out the shirt. He had the build of a basketball player, tall and long-limbed. She wondered if he'd played in high school or college.

"There's so much I don't know about you," she said, tucking her legs beneath her. "You let me go on and on at dinner, and I never got to ask one thing about you."

"There's plenty of time for that." He glanced over his shoulder at her. "At least I hope so. I really enjoyed cooking with you tonight."

She laughed. "You mean cooking *for* me. I enjoyed it, too."

He went to the kitchen to pack up his knife and pan in the canvas bags. She pulled a plastic container from a cupboard, put half the leftovers inside for him to take home. She was startled when he came up behind her.

He put his hands on her hips, bent down to nuzzle the back of her neck. "Mmmm, you smell good."

Liv leaned into him. "I clean up well on occasion."

"Is this an occasion?"

Delicious little thrills ran down the back of Liv's legs. She turned her head so that his lips brushed her cheek. "It could be," she said, her voice low and seductive. "If you changed your mind and stayed. You could set an early alarm."

"I like you too much to go too fast."

"For the record, I don't believe there's such a thing as too fast. I like you, too. Guess I'll just have to be patient a little bit longer."

She searched his eyes, read desire and a little bit of regret there so she knew he wanted her, too, and that made everything okay.

"I'll be fantasizing, too," he said. "Here's something to go by." He held her firmly by the hips and bent his head to kiss her. For a few delicious seconds, there was nothing but sizzle and heat and she grabbed onto his arms, holding herself steady, wanting to pull him down on the floor right there in the kitchen and have her way with him.

Liv half-laughed, half-groaned with frustration, and pushed him away. "Get out of here before I change my mind, tie you up, and take advantage of you."

He hesitated a second, as if enjoying the thought of such a thing, but then he gave her one last quick kiss. "More material for the fantasy. I'll call you tomorrow."

She swatted him on the butt as he walked out the door. "You better."

When he was gone, Liv took a book with her into the bathtub, read until the water got cold, and she finally cooled down enough to sleep.

Chapter Nineteen

• • • • • • • • • • • • • •

The Arrow & Song was crowded on Tuesday night.

Walking into the dim, pine-paneled interior of the pub on Forest Avenue, Liv was hit by the smell of beer, burgers, and onion rings. In a corner to the right of the door, a ratty-looking stuffed moose surveyed the tables from behind a pair of gigantic, red plastic sunglasses. Someone had sewn an oversized Longfellow College sweatshirt on him. His name, Liv knew, was Bruce. Bruce the Moose. The unofficial mascot of the college.

From the doorway, Liv surveilled the scene.

Crowded around the one-room pub were sturdy chairs and tables made of dark wood, shiny with varnish, and built to withstand decades of abuse by college students. Most of the tables were filled by college students, but a few older folks were scattered throughout the room.

Servers wearing jeans and Arrow & Song T-shirts carried trays of beer and meals over their heads. A small stage with a microphone stood in one corner across from the bar. A group of seven or eight older-looking students occupied two tables directly in front of the stage.

Liv guessed these were the MFA candidates. Only one way to find out.

At the bar, she ordered a dark, foamy beer, and then she wound in and out around the tables, making her way toward the stage. Pretending to look for a seat, she walked up to where the grad students were leaning their heads close together, talking and gesturing. One young woman with a bright, gauzy scarf wrapped around her hair waved a few papers, and said, "I stayed up all night reworking these! I can't even tell if they're any good anymore!"

A chorus of compliments and encouragement rose from the table.

"Excuse me," Liv said, bending down to talk to a chunky woman who was wearing a long black skirt, a baggy T-shirt, and square, dark-rimmed glasses. "Do you know when the reading is supposed to start?"

The woman turned startled eyes toward her. The smile she gave Liv transformed her plain, round face from nondescript to pretty in a second. "In a few minutes. At seven. If you want to read, you need to sign up on that clipboard."

"No, that's okay. Do you mind if I take that chair?" Liv nodded toward the one empty chair at the table.

"Sure. Help yourself."

"Are you students at Longfellow?" Liv sipped her beer and looked over the rim of her glass at the group.

"We're graduate students," the young woman said. "In the creative writing program. I'm Marion. This is Ethan."

"Olivia," Liv said. They shook hands. "Actually, I was hoping to talk to some students from the creative writing program about Mason Falwell and Cooper Tedeschi. That's why I came here tonight."

Marion's eyes widened. "Are you a reporter? What do you want to know?"

"I'm trying to help Cooper out. Did you know him very well?"

The young man with the goatee leaned over. "Did we know Tedeschi? Yeah, we did." He made a face. "What a douche!"

Marion shot Ethan a frown and said to Liv, "Yes, we know Cooper. He was part of our cohort. We all started two years ago. He should have graduated with us at the end of this summer, but, well, there was all that trouble."

Ethan pulled his chair closer. "He made trouble for himself. Thought he was so special. Falwell's little pet." He took a gulp of his beer. "You ask me, he deserved to be kicked out just for being such a douche."

"What, exactly, do you mean?" Liv asked. "You didn't like him personally, or he wasn't the writer he claimed to be? I was under the impression he was talented."

"Sure, the guy had chops," Ethan admitted, his bearded chin lifting slightly. "At least when he lowered himself enough to share his oh-so-precious work with us."

"He didn't work well with the rest of the group?"

Marion shrugged. "He wasn't that bad."

Ethan snorted.

"Okay, yes, he was pretty bad." Marion turned back to Liv. "Cooper was a little, um, stuck-up, I guess. Arrogant. Like he was better than the rest of us because he was working so closely with Falwell. He didn't seem to care about our opinions or suggestions. He was always saying that the workshop assignments were of no interest to him because his project was something bigger, something special."

Ethan snorted again. "Yeah, right. Special as in copying his mentor's manuscript!"

Marion ignored Ethan. "Or maybe he was hoping Falwell would connect him to agents, publishers, that sort of thing. I think he saw himself as Falwell's literary heir or something."

Liv nodded at Marion, then turned back to Ethan. "You're pretty sure Cooper copied Falwell and not the other way around? Did he share his parts of his novel with anyone in the group?"

"Nah," Ethan shook his head. "Tedeschi was always, 'It's still in draft. It's not ready. I'm rewriting. It needs polishing.' That sort of thing. Bunch of excuses if you ask me. All of our work's in progress. That's why it's called a writing *workshop*. That's why we have *mentors*. If we already knew what we were doing, we wouldn't need to be here, would we? That's what I couldn't stand about Tedeschi. He was always acting like he was better than the rest of us."

"Maybe he was better than the rest of us," Marion said.

"Speak for yourself," Ethan said. "I think he had a screw loose. I don't think there ever was a manuscript. The stuff he shared our first year was just okay, nothing spectacular. Not Mason Falwell quality."

"I thought his writing was solid," argued Marion. She turned to Liv. "Ethan's style is more literary, but Cooper could really set a scene. He wrote fantasy and science fiction, and his descriptions were outstanding."

"I guess. If you like that sort of thing," Ethan said. "Alien species with transparent skin and black veins. Blue ears. That sort of crap."

Marion gestured toward Ethan, supplicating. "But see, there you go. You remember what he wrote. And that was almost two years ago!"

"Doesn't mean he had talent."

Marion shrugged and looked at Liv. "I don't know. I think he had something."

Liv sat back. "So to change direction. What happened with the Long/Space accounts this winter? Cooper said Falwell read and commented on his manuscript, but then the system crashed and he lost shared files and emails. Did you lose your work, too?"

Ethan shook his head. "That's just more of his b.s. Everyone on campus lost a few emails. Maybe one or two days' worth. For a couple days after the crash, we couldn't access our shared files or participate in the class message boards. It was annoying, but they got it running again, like I said, within a couple of days. It was nothing like what Tedeschi claims. Nobody else 'lost' all their files." He emphasized the word lost with air quotes.

Obviously, this had been discussed at length among the graduate students.

Liv looked to Marion who made a rueful face. "Yes, Ethan's right about that. Cooper went around ranting that his entire account had been wiped clean, but nobody believed him. Why would it happen to just him? It seemed kind of convenient that he wasn't able to produce that manuscript or notes or emails with Falwell's feedback. I felt bad for him, though. I think he really believed he wrote that book. And to get kicked out of the program after all that time. That's rough."

Ethan and Marion fell silent, pondering such a disaster. Ethan picked at a scratch on the wooden table. His expression was conflicted. "There was one thing, though."

"What's that?"

Ethan glanced at Marion and back to Liv. "There's this guy in the program. Jeremy Crete. He works for the IT department part-time. Right around the time Cooper came forward claiming Falwell stole his work, a bunch of us were here, shooting the shit. We were talking about Cooper. Crete, being a little toasted, said that Cooper might be telling the truth. We all shouted him down because…"

"Because Cooper's a douche." Liv finished the sentence for him.

"Right," Ethan said.

"Did anyone ask this Jeremy why he said that?"

"Yeah, and this is the weird thing. Crete said something ambiguous along the lines that Cooper could write and Falwell hadn't done squat the past five years. Then he shut up real fast. Like he'd said too much. The conversation didn't go any further than that, but maybe since he works in IT, Crete knows something we don't. That's who I'd talk to if I were looking for answers."

Chapter Twenty

• • • • • • • • • • • • • •

Since she was already there and on her second beer, Liv decided to stay at the Arrow & Song and listen to the readings. By the time the bar closed down at eleven, she felt like part of the gang. Ethan and Marion threw drunken arms around her shoulders, told her to come back next week and hang out with them again.

She complimented them on their readings, said she'd enjoyed their work very much, and that she'd make it a point to come back again.

Because she'd switched to diet cola after her second beer, driving wouldn't be a problem for her, but Ethan and Marion called for an Uber. Liv waved as they crawled into the back seat of the vehicle. They seemed like decent people—passionate about their writing, maybe a little competitive but mostly friendly and encouraging, clapping and whistling after each others' readings, lifting their glasses and mugs when they returned to the table.

If Cooper had given them the chance, they would have had his back, Liv mused. Instead, he'd held himself aloof and refused to let them read his work in progress.

Now look at the mess he was in.

Driving home, she took Forest Avenue up to Cumberland, enjoying the light traffic and clear skies. She turned her radio to WCYY, the city's alternative rock station. She sang along with an old Goo Goo Dolls single and thought about her date with Jasper. She enjoyed their conversation, liked the way he'd kept up, and especially liked the way he kissed her.

She should have asked him about himself, though. There was so much she wanted to know. What had it been like to grow up with seven older siblings, she wondered? Liv had enjoyed her status as an only child. Her parents made sure she had plenty of playdates and activities. She never had to share her toys, her clothes, or her parents' attention—unless you counted their busy social life, which, especially when she was older, she hadn't minded. The less attention paid, the better.

Jasper's childhood must have been so different. She pictured him as a gangly, raw-boned, Midwestern kid sitting up in a treehouse and reading about mysterious, mythical creatures, dreaming up adventures, avoiding chores in order to read just one more chapter in solitude hidden away from the business and crowdedness of a houseful of siblings.

Tapping her fingers on the steering wheel, she considered what she knew. He could cook. He liked eggs benedict. He made a living saving people's lives. He had a sense of humor and a kindness she found appealing, if disconcerting. A start, she thought, but not enough. She wanted to know more.

That was a good thing, she decided, as she pulled into her driveway and got out of the car. They'd scheduled a third date for Friday—lucky Friday she hoped—but maybe she'd give him a call tomorrow night just to talk. Without her hormones distracting her, she could shut up and listen instead of trying to get him into bed.

Tired and ready for some shut-eye, Liv trudged toward the house. She frowned, noticing the entrance light was dark. Either one of the renters accidentally turned it off, or the bulb had burned out. If so, she'd have to fix it. It wasn't safe, blundering around in the dark for keys, even in this relatively safe part of town.

The words "safe part of town" had just crossed her mind when she was blindsided. A blur of motion to her right preceded a sudden swing toward her face. From instinct and training, she shifted just in time to deflect the worst of it, but the blow grazed her cheek, knocked her off balance. Stars danced in front of her eyes as she pivoted to face her attacker.

The dark-clad figure reached for her bag, a red leather tote that held her wallet, phone, pepper spray, and her Glock G43. He grabbed the handle and pulled. Liv stuck her left arm out straight, pushing his shoulder, and swung her other hand into his face.

She felt her fist connect with his nose in a satisfying crunch. He stumbled backward, letting go of her bag. She reached into the bag for her pepper spray, but before she could grasp it, he growled and came at her again. She kicked out, straight into his solar plexus, and let out an ear-splitting scream. The attacker grunted and doubled over. Lights in both first- and second-floor apartments came on. The assailant turned his head for a second, long enough for her to grab the pepper spray.

They squared off. She held her spray out while he eyed her warily between the slit of a woolen ski mask. She couldn't see his eyebrows, but his build matched the one she'd seen on her camera footage.

A car started up the street, and the ski mask guy took off running. He jumped into the vehicle, some kind of sports car, black or dark gray paint, and was gone by the time her first-floor tenant peeked out the door and yelled that she'd called the police.

By the time Portland P.D. arrived, Liv's adrenaline surge had ebbed, leaving her shaky but lucid. She gave the two officers an account of what had happened and mentioned the break-in at her office earlier in the week.

"That's quite a coincidence," one of the cops said.

"A little too coincidental," Liv countered. "I could buy a random burglary, but to be attacked in my own driveway a few days later? Feels like someone's out for revenge or sending me a message."

The officer held his notepad and pen. "Any idea who?"

Liv shrugged. "It could be any number of people. Someone I've served papers on, possibly. I've helped several women get free from abusive spouses and boyfriends, and those kinds of guys don't take kindly to people interfering. A few of my investigations have led to arrests—criminal threatening, assault charges, attempted rape, forgery. After serving their time, they might be out for revenge. I'm working on a case right now, as well. Maybe someone's warning me to back off or trying to distract me. I don't know."

She didn't say anything about Rob, but his name popped into her mind. She hadn't heard anything from him since the FBI showed up. The way Snow talked, he'd gone underground. He'd been pretty mad about those photos she sent to Gina, but Liv thought Rob wasn't likely to mess with her if he wanted to keep a low profile. Plus, he knew she was capable of defending herself.

Keeping these thoughts to herself, she told the cops, "It would be easy enough to get my address, pick a night I'm out, and wait for me to come home. Give me a little payback." She tightened her jaw. She almost wished she'd gotten another poke at her attacker, but it had happened too fast. "I noticed the front door light's out. I bet he broke it before I arrived."

"We'll check the perimeter, the windows, make sure you didn't catch him on his way out. If you find anything missing or disturbed, let us know."

She nodded. "Thanks, officers."

The younger cop gave her a look of concern. "Are you going to be okay alone here tonight? Is there anyone you can call to stay with you?"

Liv twisted her mouth into a bitter smile. "I'll be fine. Thank you for coming. Let me know if you find anything. Right now, I just want to take a shower and go to bed."

· · · · ·

Lying in bed, Liv replayed the attack over and over in her mind. The attempted purse-snatching hadn't been random. Those kinds of crimes tended to be perpetrated by opportunistic slimeballs on the street waiting for a likely-looking victim walking by.

This had been premeditated, all too similar to the break-in at her office. Guy in a mask and dark clothes doing the dirty work. Another person driving the car. Both times, they'd attempted to take something from her. Papers from the credenza. Her purse. She had something they wanted.

All this had started when she'd taken the Tedeschi case. She sat up in bed.

She'd been asking a lot of questions about Mason and Karie Falwell around campus and at the bagel shop. Barbara, the English department admin knew her name and liked to gossip. Faculty members and students were in and out of her office all day long. She'd been talking to the MFA students tonight. Mason also knew her name.

She remembered the look Karie had thrown over her shoulder on her way out of the library café. Was it possible that Cooper had given her some paperwork that incriminated Mason only she hadn't recognized it yet? She'd examined those documents thoroughly, and nothing had jumped out at her, but it was possible.

She slumped back down onto her pillow and pulled her comforter over her shoulders. She was tired but too keyed up to sleep. Her eyes refused to close.

She considered possibilities for moving forward. She tossed and turned. What could she have missed? Tomorrow she'd go over the documents again with the proverbial fine-toothed comb, see if there was anything she'd missed that could prove her client was telling the truth.

Finally, exhausted, she fell asleep.

Chapter Twenty-One

• • • • • • • • • • • • • •

Standing next to Ashleigh's car in the parking lot of the elementary school, Liv held out the pink striped bag with a pink ribbon handle. Dark pink tissue paper peeked over the edge of the lingerie store bag.

"What happened to your face!" Ashleigh stared at the scrape and bruise on Liv's left cheek.

Liv gave her a brief explanation, keeping her tone light.

"Oh my gosh. That's so scary. Please tell me you'll be careful. Is it something to do with the new case? If it is, I'll blame myself for dragging you against your will to the ball."

"No way is this your fault. Anyway, I'm here to apologize to you. I know we talk about me and my problems and drama all the time. I forget, sometimes, to ask how you're doing. I'm sorry, Ash. I brought a peace offering." She held out the bag again.

Ashleigh's face softened into amusement. "Okay, give it to me. I can't believe you're pulling the old college panty apology on me." She snatched the bag out of Liv's grasp, dug through the tissue, and dangled the gray and pink striped, laced-edged thong on her index finger. She quirked an eyebrow. "Well, maybe half an apology, anyway."

Half a second passed. Finally, Ashleigh smiled. "Okay, you nut. Come here." She held out her arms. "Give me a hug."

"Thank you, thank you. Anytime you want to talk, I promise, I am ready to listen, okay?" Liv said, giving Ashleigh one final squeeze before stepping back. She gave her friend an assessing look. Ashleigh's blonde hair was thick and shiny and highlighted. A light tan gave her long, thin face a glow. "You look good."

Ashleigh pushed the thong back into the bag. "I took an extra couple of days off and spent a long weekend at a spa in Vermont. Did yoga. Got a massage. Meditated. Tanning bed. Had my hair done," She shrugged. "Amazing what a talented masseuse and stylist can do for a girl."

"I guess!" Liv laughed. She leaned against Ashleigh's little blue Prius. "So how's the other thing going? You know. The endometriosis?"

Ashleigh's face closed up again. "Not so good. Look, no offense, but I'm not really ready to talk about it with you yet. It still feels a little raw, and I'm having to work through some things that I don't think you'd understand."

"Okay, sure," Liv nodded even as her chest tightened.

Up until now, the two of them had never *not* talked about anything. What if her friendship with Ashleigh had changed forever? Ever since their freshman year in college, Ashleigh had been there for her, sharing every high and low.

"Well, I'm here for you when you're ready, okay?"

"I appreciate that," Ashleigh said. "So what's up with you? Still working on the Falwell case?"

"Yeah. I'm making some progress, but I haven't put all the pieces of the puzzle together yet, and I could use a break. Do you want to have a girls' night tonight? Face masks and pedicures and a romantic comedy? We could have a sleepover, two old roomies, just like the old days."

"I'd love to but Trevor wants to take me out on a date," said Ashleigh, her mouth tightening. "He thinks it will help."

She didn't seem inclined to elaborate, and Liv thought it was strange the way she'd talked about having a date with her husband. Like they needed to get to know each other or something. Not like they'd been married for almost seven years.

Liv decided this was another something her friend didn't want to talk about so she dropped the subject. "Okay, well, I'll see you at yoga tomorrow night, right?"

"Sure."

The two women embraced again and promised each other a long chat soon. Liv hoped so. Her conflicting feelings about Jasper had her rattled. She really needed a friend right now.

Liv watched the Prius leave the school lot. She pulled sunglasses from the top of her head, stuck them on, and frowned. She turned toward her dark green sedan and thought about the look on her friend's face when she mentioned the endometriosis. She was pretty sure Ash needed a friend even more than she did.

Question was, would she let Liv be that friend again?

•   •   •   •   •

"Before you say anything, it looks worse than it is."

Liv stepped aside to let Jasper into her apartment. It was Friday evening, and she hadn't told him about the attack Tuesday night.

They'd spoken several times on the phone since then. She'd learned the names of all his siblings, knew his parents were evangelical Christian farmers who took the Bible's instruction to "go forth and multiply" at face value, and that he had, indeed, played center on his high school's basketball team.

She'd learned that his father still farmed, with the help of Jasper's oldest brother and youngest sister, and that his two other brothers lived in the same Iowa town. One was a dentist, the other a car dealer. A sister lived in California, another in Nebraska, and a third in New York City where she was pursuing an acting career.

Some of the siblings were close; some were not. There were factions and fighting, alliances and grudges. Some of the siblings still went to the Baptist church. Others were agnostics or atheists. One sister practiced Wicca.

Jasper was the only one speaking to her at the moment. Now he bent down to inspect the scrape and the fading green and yellow bruise on Liv's face, his eyes searching, his fingers gently probing. "Ouch," he said, straightening. "What happened?" "I'll tell you if you promise not to freak out," she said. "But first, here's the takeout menu. It feels like a pizza night, don't you think." He laughed. "Guess that means you don't want to cook." "Bingo."

They settled on a pepperoni with extra cheese, and while he placed the order, she mixed up a shaker of martinis. She carried the drinks and a small tray of olives, pickles, and pretzels to the living room where the westward sky glowed pink and lavender. The sun had already set on a beautiful spring day. Liv set the tray on the wicker coffee table.

She and Jasper settled into her grandmother's vintage floral chairs which she'd turn to face the view. Coldplay streamed from the speakers because she knew he liked their music. Going for a sexy but casual look, she'd paired black cropped pants with a striped silk blouse and strappy heels, and now she leaned over to pick up a martini glass, giving him a quick glimpse of skin beneath the neckline, and handed him a drink.

Jasper accepted the martini, eyes intent as she sat back in her chair, crossed her legs, and swung her foot seductively. He cleared his throat, and struggled mightily not to look at her cleavage. "Tell me what happened."

"Some perp jumped me outside my door here on Tuesday night. He grabbed my bag, and I fought him off. When my tenants yelled out that they'd called the police, he ran. No big deal."

Jasper processed this for a moment. "You fought him off? You could have been seriously hurt! What if he'd been armed?" He put his drink on the table. "Why didn't you just let him take the damn purse?"

She gave a little shrug and grinned. "It's a nice bag?"

He ran a hand over his mouth. "Is this neighborhood safe?"

"Totally. Munjoy Hill used to be rough back in the day, but we're all gentrified up here now." Liv made a face. "I'm afraid this was personal."

"Why would you think that?"

"Well, there was a break-in at my office, too"

His eyebrows shot up. "You didn't tell me that either. We talked on the phone for hours this week, and you didn't think to mention it?"

"It was my problem to deal with, and I dealt with it. They didn't take anything, just made a mess, tried to get into my credenza. It was a random burglary—at least I thought so at first. But now I'm not sure. One attack could be chalked up to bad luck. Two feels deliberate."

She leaned over and selected an olive. "Like I told the police, there are any number of low-lifes who might be giving me a payback. Maybe I served this guy papers or helped his abused spouse get a restraining order or tracked him down for missed child support and now his wages are garnished. Who knows. There are some people out there who aren't too happy with me. I can expect this sort of thing to happen from time to time, I guess."

Jasper said nothing, just sat there staring down at his hands.

"Tell me what you're thinking," she prompted.

"Here's what I'm thinking. It's not my place to tell you how to live your life. I get that. But have you considered how other people, your parents, for instance, would feel if you were hurt or killed? Are you sure this profession of yours is worth the risk? You're smart. You could do any number of things. Less dangerous things."

"Like sitting on the board of charitable organizations and planning hospital auxiliary fundraisers?" She struggled to keep her emotions in check. She liked Jasper, wanted to keep seeing him, but not if he couldn't accept her for who she was. Not if he wanted someone more like her mother, a woman happy to support her husband's career rather than build one of her own. "I like what I do, Jasper."

"I was thinking more along the lines of lawyer. Don't read more into this than there is. I'm just saying you have other options." He looked over at her. "I'm not sure how I feel about my girlfriend putting herself in danger. The thought of some guy... I can't even say it. What if he'd really hurt you?"

"Then I'd deal with it." She put down her martini. "You have to understand. I know the risks, and I've taken self-defense classes. I practice at that. I keep myself in shape. I have a permit to carry. I could have pulled a gun on the guy the other night. I reached for the pepper spray instead. I can take care of myself. I fought the guy off, and believe me, he's in worse shape than I am."

"Oh, that makes me feel better." His tone was sarcastic.

"It should."

"And you're too cocky. I know you're tough, but sometimes even tough people get hurt."

She fumed inside about the cocky comment but kept her temper in check. "Listen, Jasper. It's important to me, the work I do. You know how you love helping people, making their hearts work again? I feel the same way about my job. Instead of bodies, I help people make their lives work again. I'm good at it. Every profession has its dangers. I mean, you could be sued for medical malpractice, lose your license because some scheming patient and slick lawyer decided to take advantage of a bad outcome."

"Losing my license isn't the same thing as losing my life or being sexually assaulted."

"Maybe not, but my desire to help people, by doing work I'm good at, is greater than my fear of being hurt. I'll be smart. I'll do my best to be prepared and aware. I refuse to live my life afraid. That's just not me."

He looked at her then, his eyes full of mixed emotions: frustration, admiration, concern. "I can see you've given this some thought. I hear you and I'm trying to understand. Like I said, it's not my place to say."

"True, but what was that about me being your girlfriend?" She stood up, sat down in his lap, and smiled. "Am I your girlfriend, Doc?"

He kissed her. "I hope so."

She ran a hand over his face, curled her fingers into his hair, and gave a little tug. "Do that again."

They were breathing heavily and he'd unbuttoned her shirt when the doorbell rang. "The pizza," she muttered against his lips.

He groaned and put his forehead against hers.

She gave him a quick kiss on the cheek. "It's okay," she said. "We have all night."

Buttoning a couple of buttons, she ran down the stairs to get the pizza. By the time she returned, he'd pulled plates from her cupboard, found the napkins in the drawer, and was opening a bottle of Merlot.

"*X-Files*?" he asked.

"Definitely."

Chapter Twenty-Two

• • • • • • • • • • • • • • •

A couple of hours later, the pizza demolished, she asked him if he wanted espresso.

"Okay."

As she fussed with the tiny cups and the machine whirred and hissed, Jasper stood next to her, running his fingers up her back. She could feel his eyes grazing over her body, and her stomach fluttered a little as she manipulated the machine.

She handed him a cup, a little saucer and spoon. He took it from her and drained it before she'd even taken a sip. His eyes were intent on her, a look no grown woman could misunderstand. He put the empty cup on the counter.

She laughed, "What's your hurry, Doc?"

"Come here," he said.

She put her espresso down and went to him. Her arms drifted over his shoulders, her fingers ruffled his dark, thick hair. He bent his head, kissed her, rocked her a little back and forth. "I've been thinking about this for two hours."

"Me, too," she said. "Days, actually."

"Good." He ran a hand along her hip, up her side, fingers grazing her breast. She murmured something unintelligible against his lips and pushed herself into him. He responded, pushing back, pressing her against the kitchen counter, hip to hip.

When he cupped her breast and ran his thumb back and forth, all the cells in her body hummed. They kissed like this for a few minutes, hands traveling here and there, exploring. She liked the way their bodies fit, the way his hands spanned her hips, pulled her in tight.

She wasn't prepared for Jasper to pull away, but he did, leaving her panting and so turned on that she could barely think. He took a couple of steps back. Cool air rushed across her heated skin. She gazed at him, eyes slightly unfocused. "What's wrong?"

He reached out, took her hand. He brought her hand to his lips, and she thought he'd do something sexy like suck on her fingers, maybe even lightly bite. But no. He pressed a kiss into her palm.

"Nothing's wrong," he said, twining his fingers into hers and turning to stand beside her, back against the edge of the counter. "I told you. I want to take this slow."

That's it, she thought? Her espresso hadn't even grown cold!

"Why wait? We're both grown-ups here. It's our third date. We have this incredible chemistry. Why put off what we know is going to happen sooner or later?"

"We should have talked about this before." He ran his thumb over hers. "I'm thirty-five years old, Olivia. I've been in two serious relationships that didn't work out for reasons too complicated to go into right now. I've had my share of no-strings-attached sex partners, the occasional one-night stand. I know myself. That's not the kind of guy I am. I'm not a player. I'm a relationship kind of guy."

Liv stood there, letting him hold her hand, and hating every second of it. She wanted to pull away. She wanted him to stop talking. She wanted him to kiss her again. He was ruining the whole night.

She pouted, and he ran a finger over her bottom lip and smiled. "I really like you, Olivia. I respect you. I respect your parents. I can see us having a real relationship. I don't want to rush into sex too soon. I want it to be special."

She rolled her eyes.

"Hey, I'm trying to be honest here." He dropped her hand. "Are you sure that's it?"

"What else would it be?"

"The assault rattled you. You don't like that I'm a P.I. You're wondering if I'm a little too low-class to be a respectable surgeon's girlfriend."

"You're partly right. I don't love your work. It is dangerous. You do put yourself in bad situations and deal with sketchy people." He reached out then, held her chin, and turned her face so she'd look at him. "But there's nothing low-class about you, Olivia. I'm intrigued by you. You're smart, beautiful, and too brave for your own good. You like the Sci-Fi Channel and can discuss Roswell intelligently. It's just that I want to be sure."

She twisted her head to shake off his fingers. "It's okay, Jasper. Really. This is not my first rodeo. If you don't want me, you just have to say so."

"You think I'm rejecting you because I don't want you?"

"I've been pretty clear about wanting to sleep with you. I like sex. I'm attracted to you. Sleeping together wouldn't have to mean everything, or even anything. It could just be two people enjoying each other's bodies, having a little fun. If respecting me means putting me on a pedestal, I don't want it. I'm not some high-society, hot-house flower you need to handle with care. I like things a little rough around the edges. I like to get a little spicy."

"Oh yeah?"

"If you want bland vanilla whatever, you won't find it here. I'm any flavor but vanilla."

"I'm aware, believe me. And I do want you, Olivia."

"Then let's not ruin the night. Let me convince you that delayed gratification isn't all it's cracked up to be."

"You don't know how tempted I am."

She searched his face. "But you're still going home. Fine."

"You're upset. I'd hoped you'd understand, but guess we both need time to think." He grabbed his jacket near the door and she followed him, reached past him to open the door. "I'll call you tomorrow," he said.

"G'nite." She closed the door after him, leaned against it, and let out a frustrated growl. Jasper came across all sophisticated and sexy, a gorgeous doctor with good manners, a killer smile, an off-beat interest in the paranormal, and kisses that left her breathless.

But it was all a ruse.

Underneath Dr. Hottie's sophisticated persona lurked a hopeless romantic, a guy who wanted a conventional life. A little wifey who stayed home. A couple of kids. A labrador retriever. Vacations to Disneyland. She wanted an amazing career, a cleaning service, a fantastic art collection, and trips to exotic locales around the world.

Maybe it was good they'd had this conversation early on. They were only three dates in. Better to end it before they wasted any more time.

She poured herself a large glass of the Merlot and curled up in her chair.

Some men appreciated assertive women who liked sex for the fun and simple pleasure of it. Rob Mickelson, for example. She tapped her fingers against the glass. Weasel or not, at least he'd been honest and enthusiastic about sex. Those Wednesday nights they'd spent at the Cormorant had been fun. They'd laughed, talked, played lots of inventive games beneath the covers.

He'd never promised her marriage. She'd neither wanted nor expected that. But he'd delivered in so many other ways.

As the fireplace flickered, Liv thought back to the last night she and Rob had spent together, the two of them stretched out on the Cormorant's king-sized bed, both wearing the hotel's plush robes, nibbling on sweet potato fries ordered up from room service, and washing the fries down with good champagne.

Rob had been talking about some yacht he was contemplating buying and how the two of them would sail to the Caribbean. He painted a picture of bright sun, clear skies, aquamarine water, and tangy margaritas on the deck as they made their way to where? Puerto Vallarta?

Liv frowned and stared at her wine. No. Puerto Plata. There were resorts there, he said, and an airport, and it wasn't too far from the Caymans. Liv let herself sink into the dream for a moment. He'd made it sound so glamorous and exciting.

She sat up, sloshing her wine. "Puerto Plata," she said aloud.

Rob had mentioned the Dominican Republic on more than one occasion—usually after they'd killed a couple bottles of champagne. Whiling away a few lazy, post-coital hours, they'd fantasized about sailing through tropical seas, pulling into port once in a while to stock up on supplies, hit a restaurant and a nightclub, and check into a resort hotel for a night or two before heading out again.

Now Liv's mind jumped to Agent Snow. Did he know about the boat? Rob had said something about buying it under an alias so Gina wouldn't find out and try to take it in the divorce settlement. Feeling a little woozy from the wine, Liv stood up and found her bag. She searched in all the nooks and crannies for the card Snow had given her. Where was it? There.

She wondered if the FBI agent was outside her building again. She went to the bathroom and peeked out the window, but didn't see the black SUV on the road. Looking at the card, she punched in his number.

He answered on the second ring. "Snow here."

"Hi. This is Olivia Lively. Do you have some time? I just remembered something that Rob told me. It's about a yacht. And a Caribbean destination spot. Interested?"

"Yeah, I'm interested. What can you tell me?"

"Not over the phone. What are you doing right now? Can you come over?"

"It's a Friday night, Ms. Lively. I won't be busting in on a hot date?"

"I'm alone." *Not lonely*, she thought. *Alone.* There's a difference. And okay, yeah, she was lying to herself, but she'd think about what that meant later.

On the other end of the call, Agent Snow said, "I'm on my way."

Chapter Twenty-Three

• • • • • • • • • • • • •

L iv swung the door open. "Come on in, Agent Snow. Have a seat," she said, gesturing toward the kitchen table. "The water's hot if you want some tea."

"Thank you," he said, giving her a tired smile. She was amused to notice his rumpled shirt and crooked tie but then felt a twinge of guilt. His eyes were puffy and shadowed, his boyish face slightly haggard. "Got any chamomile, by any chance?" Snow pulled out a chair and sat down.

"Sure," Liv said, moving to the cupboard, aware that he was watching her every move. "Having trouble sleeping?"

"Nah. No more than usual. Overnight surveillance always messes with my sleep patterns. You probably know all about that."

Liv brought two pottery mugs to the table and set them down. The sweet, sunny scent of chamomile rose with the steam. "It's a hazard of the trade."

Snow ran a hand over a stubbled jaw. "I was trying to catch some shut-eye when you called. I'd been staring at the hotel ceiling for two hours, trying to will myself to sleep. It was a relief to stop trying." He gave her an appreciative glance, taking in her low-cut shirt and heels. "You're all dressed up. Hot date out on the town?"

"A lukewarm date here at home, actually. Disastrous. Don't ask." Liv plopped into the chair across the table from Mr. FBI. She let out a tremendous sigh. "Do you find that your job interferes with your relationships as much as it does your sleep?

Immediately, she regretted asking the question. She felt heat rise to her cheeks. "You don't have to answer that. I shouldn't have asked. Never mind."

Snow's eyes fell to the welt on her face. "What happened, Lively? Did you scare off the poor guy tonight offering to teach him a few exotic defense moves? That's quite a bruise you got there."

She told him about the attack. "The assailant got it much worse, believe me. I doubt he'll be back."

"Good." Snow winked. "But back to this date. Let's see. What could have gone wrong? I know. You ran a background check on the guy, right? And he wasn't happy about it. Got all offended."

Liv shook her head. "Wrong again, Agent. I like to keep a little mystery in my relationships. Keeps things spicy. Running a check seems so, I don't know, not romantic."

"Is that what you tell your clients?"

"Of course not."

"So, you think you have some sort of super-duper girl-detective radar that tells you when someone is lying to you? Is misrepresenting himself? How did that work out with Robert Mickelson?"

Liv forced a smile. "Touché. Anyway, what about you? Do you run a check on all your potential girlfriends?"

"How do you know I'm not married?"

"I just assumed. Sorry."

An awkward silence fell between them, and the hands of Liv's black-kitty wall clock ticked in the quiet room.

"I'm not, by the way. Married." Snow set his mug down on the table. "To answer your question, yes. My work interferes with my relationships. The job takes me away from Boston three or four days a week, sometimes longer. The hours are erratic. I decided a while back to forget having any serious romantic relationships, at least until I've moved up to a supervisory job and regular office hours. Keeps things simple."

Liv caught his eye. "I like simple."

They stared at each other across the table. The FBI agent was handsome, all sharp cheekbones and shrewd hazel eyes. His dark brown hair was wavy in front, cut close over the ears and in back. She liked the way he was looking at her, as if he knew just what she was thinking. Like he liked what she was thinking. It would be easy to take their mild flirtation and mutual attraction to the next level, especially since neither of them was looking for a serious relationship. It could be fun, she thought, at least for a little while.

But what about Jasper?

To Liv's chagrin, some of her mother's uptight, conservative values penetrated her conscience. She couldn't start the night off with one man and end it with another. She frowned. As much as she claimed to live life by her own rules, some lessons she'd been taught rose from the murky depth of her subconscious and surfaced at the most inopportune moments.

Like this one.

As much as she'd like to see if Agent Snow had any interesting ideas about how to use his handcuffs, it wasn't going to happen. Not tonight. She wasn't going to sleep with someone just because she'd been rejected by someone else. She had more self-respect than that.

Feeling a little bit like a kid whose triple chocolate, gummy-bear sprinkled ice cream just fell off the cone and splatted on the hot, dirty pavement, Liv broke eye contact.

"Well," she said, her voice brisk. "I asked you to come over for a reason, and it wasn't to talk about our personal lives. How are you doing on Rob's case?"

"You know I can't tell you that," Snow said, reading the message loud and clear. He snapped into professional mode. "So what's this about a boat?"

"He used to talk about buying a yacht and sailing away to the Caribbean." She didn't tell Agent Snow, however, that the conversations had been post-coital. He didn't need to know all the gory details.

She continued. "I didn't pay that much attention because I

thought it was just talk, you know, a romantic fantasy. I mean, he had a high-powered position at the bank, a home, a life here. He made a good salary, but I didn't figure it was enough for him to retire this early." She shrugged. "Of course, I didn't know about the ill-gotten gains."

"So what about this alias?" Snow pulled out from his shirt pocket a small notebook and pen. "Any idea what name or names he might be using?"

"Not really. He didn't get specific about that, but he did mention one particular boat broker, some guy he knew from high school up in Belfast. Al or Hal Skoog, I think the guy's name was. If I were you, I'd give Skoog a visit, and I'd check his recent sales information. If Rob has disappeared, it's possible he went through with his plans, bought the boat, and headed toward the Caymans or the Dominican Republic." She smiled at him. "But you don't need me to tell you how to do your job."

"Nope. I don't." Snow tucked his pen and notebook in his shirt pocket. His eyes looked even more tired than when he'd arrived. "If there's nothing else, then, I guess I'll head back to the hotel and resume not falling asleep."

"Poor Agent Snow. Maybe the chamomile will help. I could have put a shot of whiskey in it. Would you like one now?"

"Probably not a good idea. I'd get punchy, end up staying here, and keep you up all night."

Because she couldn't resist, Liv grinned and said, "Doesn't sound so bad to me."

He laughed. "You and I both know you don't mean that." Snow stood up and walked toward the door. "Thanks for the info tonight, Lively. I realize this can't be fun for you. I'm sorry you got mixed up with Mickelson. You seem like a nice person. You deserve better than him."

For some reason, the agent's kind words were like lidocaine spray, taking some of the sting out of her evening. "Thank you, Agent Snow. Good luck. I hope you catch him soon."

Snow turned around in the landing and held the apartment door open just as she was about to close it. "One more thing, Lively."

"Yeah?"

His eyes traveled from her tousled hair to her high heels and back up again. His eyes darkened, and he gave her a little, sexy smile. "You look damn hot in that outfit. For the record, I think the guy tonight was an idiot. See you around."

Chapter Twenty-Four

● ● ● ● ● ● ● ● ● ● ● ● ● ●

Monday morning, Liv got up just as the sun broke free of the horizon. Dressing quickly, she headed out for a long run.

Along the Eastern Prom, the air was brisk despite the sun, and Liv was glad she'd dressed warmly. She wore the hood of her navy-blue sweatshirt pulled up over her hair, and sunglasses protected her eyes from the glare. Comfortable in her black yoga pants and running shoes, she felt anonymous and solitary, alone with just her thoughts, the ache in her muscles, and a satisfying burn in her lungs.

While her body moved, she pushed all thoughts of Jasper and Rob from her mind and concentrated on the Tedeschi case instead. She was done with relationships. She'd concentrate on her career instead.

Pounding along the pavement and enjoying the view of the ferries plowing through Casco Bay, Liv turned the Mason Falwell problem over and over in her mind, like a coin with two very distinct sides. On one side of the coin was a literary giant, a respected author with a forty-year publishing record, a teacher and mentor to countless students at prestigious Longfellow College.

On the other side, however, was a very different image. According to the people she'd talked to, Falwell was a faltering has-been, possibly an alcoholic, who had trouble remembering appointments and most likely hadn't written anything new in years.

Rounding the hairpin turn near the elementary school, Liv pushed her body, determined to beat her fastest time. And then, she thought, there was the question of evidence.

As she pushed herself through the miles, she reviewed everything she'd heard and read, and she realized she was no closer to proving Cooper's innocence than when she started. The slimmest sliver of hope was that second-hand comment attributed to Jeremy Crete, one of the grad students she hadn't yet interviewed. She still needed to talk to the IT department about the Long/Space crash, as well. And had Ledeau been able to get his hands on Mason's manuscript from the publisher? She'd check in with him soon.

Her body clicked into a rhythm of motion and breathing, forcing her mind to be quiet as she entered the zone. By the time she hit mile five, she felt she could go on forever, but that was just the endorphins. Sprinting the last few yards, she turned the corner toward her house, and then she slowed to a walk, hands on hips. Moisture ran down her spine beneath the sweatshirt in a satisfying way.

When she reached the driveway, she put her hands on the bumper of her car and pushed to stretch her calves. A vehicle rolled slowly down the street. She twisted her head. Of course. Black SUV. Agent Snow.

He rolled his window down and stuck his head out to greet her. "Good run?"

"You ought to know. You were tailing me the whole time."

Snow smiled. "Just keeping an eye out for you, Lively. Still haven't caught up with that boyfriend of yours. You ought to be careful."

"Ugh, Mickelson's not my boyfriend. Keep on driving, Agent. I promise I'll let you know if he shows up on my doorstep."

"Make sure you do."

Liv grinned as Snow sped up and took a left at the next street. She kinda liked knowing he was around. Not because she was afraid—Rob was probably well on his way to the Dominican

Republic by now, and besides, she could take care of herself—but it was nice, in a way, talking to Snow.

He understood better than Ashleigh, certainly better than her parents or Jasper, about her job and its perks and pitfalls. Who else but a fellow detective would know what it was like to be on surveillance at three in the morning and be hit with the sudden need to sleep? Or pee? Or worse? Who else would get the satisfaction of finding the proverbial needle in the haystack going through public records for the one piece of information that would make or break a trial?

Scanning her key fob and trotting up the stairs to her apartment, Liv realized she felt good, strong, ready to take on the world. She didn't need a man in her life to be happy and complete. She was healthy, unencumbered, and the owner of her own business.

She had good friends, parents who drove her crazy but loved her, a fabulous apartment, and a closet full of clothes and accessories that most women would die for.

Her work kept her sharp and introduced her to interesting people with complicated problems that she was capable of solving. In fact, she had a feeling that if she pushed just a little bit harder on this Tedeschi case, she'd find the proof that Cooper needed to get his place back at the college and graduate.

She'd know more today after she visited Longfellow College's IT department to find out what really happened to Cooper's Long/Space account.

· · · · ·

The runner's high lasted until she checked her phone and listened to a rambling message from her mother bugging her about the Spring Fling dinner on Thursday night and offering to make Liv an appointment for a facial and mani-pedi at Bonne Vie, her mother's favorite spa. Tiffany also wanted to know if that nice Dr. Temple had ever called, and should she add his name to the seating chart for the dinner?

"Ugh!" Liv deleted the message, tossed the phone onto her bed, and went down the hall to shower.

She stood beneath the hot spray and scowled.

Maybe if Tiffany stopped pushing so hard, Liv would make more of an effort to see her. In fact, a spa treatment at Bonne Vie sounded heavenly.

She closed her eyes and imagined sitting in a vibrating pedicure chair, feet resting in deliciously scented water. Then she imagined listening to Tiffany's opinion on the color of the polish Liv had chosen and why it was totally wrong. Then Tiffany would tell the nail tech to give Liv a French pedicure, so much more refined. After all, everyone knew French women were the chicest in the world, so Olivia could hardly go wrong taking a page from their book. And speaking of that, had Olivia ever bothered to read that copy of *French Women Don't Get Fat* that she'd lent her? So clever and practical.

Liv loofahed her leg and imagined how it would play out. She'd admit to Tiffany that she *had* read the book and realized how much she enjoyed drinking Veuve Clicquot while rendezvousing with her married lover at the Cormorant Hotel. And then she'd say that was before he cheated on her, of course, and got caught up in an FBI investigation for alleged mortgage fraud and money laundering.

Imagining her mother's horrified face cheered her up. She'd call Tiffany later, maybe agree to that spa treatment after all.

•   •   •   •   •

"Hey, Lively. Hoping we can meet sometime this week to discuss Cooper's case." Attorney Patrick Ledeau rang her just as she was heading out to Longfellow College.

"Funny you should call. I'm about to head over to the IT department to get the low-down on this Long/Space crash." She crossed the parking lot, avoiding a puddle of oily water, jumping over it in her leather, peep-toe booties. "It's almost lunchtime. Do you want to meet me at the Arrow & Song first? We can compare notes and possible strategies. You might have some other angles."

"Perfect. I'll bring Coop along. That way he can hear from you first-hand what you've learned and the line of investigation you're following now."

She beat them to the pub and secured a semi-private table in a corner of the room. They walked in, Ledeau short and tubby but full of energy and Cooper still a depressed cherub with his light curls and dimpled chin. He looked thinner, and the lines on his face gave him the appearance of someone either gravely sick or under a lot of stress.

When the server came to take their order, Cooper ordered a cup of soup. She noticed how he'd studied the menu, probably worried about the prices. She put a hand on his arm. "You need a big, juicy burger, medium rare, and a plate of french fries. It's on me." She met Ledeau's eyes. "You, too."

Cooper looked at her as if she were a goddess, blinked back quick tears. She glanced away, not wanting to embarrass the poor kid. "When you win your settlement, you can return the favor."

He swallowed hard and nodded.

Ledeau interrupted the awkward moment. "Thanks, Lively. What have you managed to dig up?"

She gave them the run-down, and by the time they'd finished the burgers and fries, Ledeau and Cooper were caught up. "My next step is to have a talk with the IT department, get an explanation about this system crash. If they could restore your files and emails, Cooper, this whole thing would be over."

Cooper looked over at the door and went white as a sheet. He ducked, eyes wide, like a small animal hunted by a pack of wolves.

Liv glanced over her shoulder at the group of people gathered at the entrance. She recognized Ethan, the graduate student she'd met at Tuesday's open mic night. Behind him was Marion and an older, mustachioed man wearing a baggy jacket with leather elbow patches. A professor, maybe. Several others she didn't recognize crowded in behind them looking for a table. "Are they all MFA students?" she asked Cooper.

He nodded, still keeping his head down. "Second-year cohort. Most of them, anyway. That's Professor Calder with them."

Ledeau stood up. "We should get you out of here."

Marion glanced over and her mouth dropped open. Her eyes traveled from Cooper to Liv. Liv put a finger to her mouth. Marion nodded, said something to the group, and pointed to a table on the other side of the room. The crowd shuffled in that direction.

"I'll email you later," Liv told Ledeau.

"Good. Let's go, Coop."

They left, and Liv paid the bill and made her way to the MFA students' table. Ethan said hello. Marion stood, gave her a little hug, and sat down again. The professor squinted up at her with a look both shrewd and calculating.

She smiled at the Ernest Hemingway mustache, an obvious homage. She wondered if he copied Hemingway's style of prose, as well. Mimicking his mentor was why Cooper was in so much trouble, but maybe when the major writer in question was dead it didn't matter so much.

"Orin Calder." The professor stood and stuck out his hand. His grip was firm, almost painful. "Short story and personal narrative."

"Olivia Lively." She lowered her voice. "I'm a private investigator interested in the Falwell-Tedeschi incident. Do you have a few minutes to talk?"

"Sure. Let's go up to the bar." He put his hand on Ethan's shoulder and leaned over the table. "Please excuse me, ladies and gentlemen. I'll rejoin you shortly."

Calder led them to the far end of the bar. A Red Sox game played on the large-screen TV. Calder pulled out a stool, motioned for her to take it. He sat down next to her while a bartender tossed coasters with the image of Bruce the Moose in front of them.

"Getcha?" the girl said.

"Give us a minute, love." Calder winked at her.

The bartender rolled her eyes and moved away. Calder contemplated the fifteen or so microbrew handles lined up below the pub's selection of spirits and asked her if he could buy her a drink.

"No thanks," she said. "But feel free."

He held up a finger and the bartender moseyed over to take his order. The girl set the glass on the coaster in front of him, and the thick layer of foam flowed over the rim. Calder looked disgusted, but he grabbed a napkin from the holder nearby and wiped the glass without making a fuss.

He turned to her. "Marion and Ethan told me they spoke to you last week. If there's anything you want to ask me, fire away, but it has to be off the record. I don't want my name on any official reports or legal documents. The administration's keeping a firm hand on public relations. We've been told not to speak with the media. I'm guessing that would go double for private investigators."

She wondered why he was so eager to offer information. Professional grudge against Falwell? Or genuine concern about a student?

"I appreciate your talking to me. What can you tell me about Mason Falwell? General impression."

"I hate to tell tales on the old gent, but over the past couple of semesters he's really started to slip."

"What do you mean, slip?"

"Forgets what he's saying in the middle of a sentence. Misses department meetings. Seems confused when he does get the day and time right. Repeats himself. Sometimes you'll see him wandering around campus, bumping into people, muttering. Stumbling sometimes. He's always been a drinker, but now I'd say he's, well, a drunk."

"Have you actually seen him drinking? Like at faculty functions?"

"Sure. Yes. Always a full glass. Dark stuff, on the rocks. Whiskey I'd say if I had to guess. Never wine. His pretty, little wife takes care of him, always bringing him a fresh drink."

"That's Karie, right? You think she's enabling him?"

"*Pffft*, enabling. That's one way to put it. I didn't know him before his second marriage. Karie had snagged him by the time I got to Longfellow, but I heard the stories—nothing like academia for gossip and intrigue."

"Snagged him?"

Calder took a gulp of beer. "What I heard was, *she* chased *him*. Got him to divorce his first wife. They ran off together one weekend and came back married. She's not well-liked by most of the faculty, but everyone puts up with her because they don't want to offend Mason."

"In the time you've been here, has Falwell mentioned writing a new novel, or that he was working on anything at all?"

"No. All of us were surprised by the news. If you knew academics, you'd understand that most of us can't resist talking about our current projects, so when we heard Mason had a new novel coming out, we were all quite shocked."

"What about Cooper Tedeschi? Did he ever share parts of his novel with you? Maybe he showed you a chapter or two during the workshop or emailed you a sample as part of a class assignment. Anything you can remember?"

Calder lifted his glass. "Sorry, but no. He took a short story course from me his first year. Decent writer. But these were stand-alone pieces written for specific prompts."

"How about his style? Do you think you'd recognize it if you saw it?"

Calder considered, tilting his head. "Long, complicated prose full of metaphors, a little bit H.P. Lovecraft, if I had to compare."

"Or like Mason Falwell?"

Calder raised his eyebrows, gave a slight nod. "Or Mason Falwell, I suppose."

"Do you think it's possible that Tedeschi's telling the truth?"

Calder folded his hands on the bar, shoulders hunching beneath his jacket. "I find it hard to believe. Falwell might be a sad, old drunk, but that doesn't mean he lost his ability to write. He might have been keeping it quiet, especially if he wasn't sure he had it in him anymore. But once a writer, always a writer. Even the ones who stop publishing are usually writing for their own enjoyment."

Calder looked over at Liv. "The library is full of books written by sad, old drunks, Ms. Lively. The writer's mind is mysterious. None of us knows where the spark comes from. I see it in some students, even if their technical skills are lacking to nonexistent, and not in others. Tedeschi showed some promise. *Some*," he stressed, making sure she got the point.

She nodded, and he continued. "He had a bit of that spark, but he wasn't any Mason Falwell. Tedeschi had access to Mason's computer. From what I understand, he struggles with mental illness. Maybe the pressure got to him. Maybe he really believes he wrote that book. But I'm confident Falwell's editors could tell an imposter from the real thing. I'm sorry if that isn't what you hoped to hear."

"I'm still trying to get a clear picture of what happened. I appreciate your honest insights, Professor Calder. I hope I can call you again if I need to?"

"Sure thing. I'm in the Longfellow directory. Contact me any time."

Chapter Twenty-Five

• • • • • • • • • • • • • • •

After her conversation with Orin Calder, Liv made her way to Danforth Hall on the far northern edge of campus. The building housed the college's distance education department and career center on the two main floors. Instructional design and information technology resided in the cave-like basement level. She found the correct door and knocked. Without waiting for an answer, she entered a large but low-ceilinged space divided into workstations. She recognized Jeremy Crete from his Facebook page profile and made her way to his space at the end of a row.

Crete looked up from his workstation—three large monitors positioned as a kind of screen within the larger screen of the cubicle—and said, "What do you want? I'm busy."

Shifting on her peep-toe ankle boots and popping a hip, Liv looked him in the eye and waited. He was tall and lanky, folded up like a beige poolside lounge-chair on the off-season, hunched over a keyboard in a chair much too small for him. His light brown hair was short and ragged, most likely cut by himself in a bathroom mirror, and he wore wire-rimmed glasses reminiscent of the 1970s.

Behind the glasses, his blue eyes were nearly lashless, but sharp. He held her gaze for a full three seconds, and then he lifted his hands and let them fall against his thighs.

He inhaled deeply and sighed. "Okay. What? Either tell me what you want or go away."

"Do you have a few minutes to talk to me?" Liv said. Two other IT workers clicked away on their keyboards, but she could see they were rigid with curiosity. "Somewhere more private? It's a sensitive topic, but I promise I won't keep you long."

Jeremy looked her up and down, taking in her black jeans and bright, red leather bag. She'd slicked her hair with gel, poked large silver hoops in her ears, and colored her lips shiny red. She knew she looked sexy, edgy, and kick-ass, hopefully a little intimidating. No one to mess around with, certainly.

The basement workspace was dim and windowless. The only light fell from a few low-intensity spots from the ceiling and the glowing computer screens. Liv had done a bit of research. Back in the 1990s rows of computers had been set up for student use down here, but now dorm rooms were equipped with wi-fi, and students used their own laptops.

The Danforth Hall space had been converted into central command for the tech geeks in the ever-growing IT department. They installed, monitored, and troubleshot the technology for the entire campus. There were ten or so large workstations in the room.

"I'm not scheduled for a break for another twenty minutes." Crete twisted around in his seat, dismissing her, leaning toward the monitors again.

"Fine. We'll talk here then."

She almost laughed when the other two workers gave in and turned to watch what would happen next. "I'm Olivia Lively. I'm looking into the Cooper Tedeschi and Mason Falwell controversy, and I was told both their Long/Space accounts crashed right around the time Tedeschi accused Falwell of stealing his work. I'd like to ask you a few questions about that."

Jeremy continued to stare at the monitors. He clicked a few keys and pressed the enter button. All three screens went black. "What does this have to do with me? You should talk to my supervisor, Dustin Pfiester. He should be back from a meeting soon."

"I heard you might have some information that would back up Tedeschi's story. Something you said at the Arrow & Song one night. Want me to continue?"

The other employees were openly staring now. Crete went still. He seemed to consider his options, pushed back his seat, and stood.

Liv craned her neck back. The top of her head reached his nearly non-existent biceps. He was so skinny, his belt was pulled to the last notch and the tail end flopped in front of his crotch.

Crete reached out a long arm. "After you," he said pointing to the door. The sleeve of his faded, yellow T-shirt gaped. "There's a break area out back. We can talk there."

They stood outside the dented metal door on a concrete patio surrounded by a weed-filled lawn and scraggly bushes. A splintered, wooden picnic table listed to one side near a chain-link fence that separated the break area from a parking lot. There were two large oak trees that would provide nice, deep shade in the summer, but now the whole area seemed decrepit and unused and bleak.

Crete stuck a cigarette in his mouth. He lit it with a *thwick* of the fancy metallic lighter he pulled from the back pocket of his saggy jeans, and inhaled deeply.

"So, fire away," he said, blowing out a stream of smoke. "I don't know what you've heard, but we've been trying to recover those account files for weeks. As far as we can tell, they've been permanently compromised."

"I was talking to a couple of your classmates the other night over at the Arrow & Song, and they said you made a comment once that Cooper might be telling the truth. Why did you say that?"

A pink flush rose up Jeremy Crete's long, thin neck and spotted his face. "I don't remember saying that."

"Do you have any reason to believe that Cooper might be telling the truth about Falwell stealing his work?"

"Not really."

"How about this, then. Did you see Cooper's manuscript, or parts of it, before Falwell announced his sale? Maybe you and

Cooper critiqued each others' projects, and you saw some of Fallwell's responses to Cooper's work? Comments that would prove Falwell was critiquing Cooper's manuscript as an original piece of fiction?"

She knew she was asking leading questions, but she was used to reading faces. What she saw on Crete's face told her nothing and everything. The flushed skin, the skittering eyes, the lowered head—all spelled g.u.i.l.t. But what was Crete feeling guilty about, exactly?

"Come on, Jeremy. You're in the program. You know how much work goes into it. Cooper Tedeschi was just a few months away from graduation. If he's telling the truth and Falwell really did steal his manuscript, how unfair is that? How would you feel if it happened to you?"

"It sucks, okay!" Jeremy's mouth tightened. He shook out another cigarette but didn't light it. He tapped it on the pack, held it between his thumb and forefinger. "I'm sorry for what happened to Tedeschi. If he's telling the truth... and that's a big if... then he has every right to be angry, to go to the press like he did, to make a stink with the administration."

"But you aren't sure? If someone did mess with the files—say destroyed emails sent between Cooper and Mason or deleted the critiqued chapters sent between the two of them—that might lend some credence to his accusations. Is there anyone in the IT department who might have wanted to target Cooper?"

"No." Jeremy shook his head. "There's nothing solid."

"But maybe something not so solid?" Liv pushed.

"I..."

An older model black Jaguar made a wide arch into the parking lot and pulled up near the back fence. Crete's head lifted, startled, and he abruptly turned and pulled the door to the building open. "Break time's over. That's Pfiester who just pulled in. If you have any more questions, you need to talk to him."

"But..."

Crete stared at her from behind the wire rims of his glasses. "Talk to Dustin Pfiester. That's all I can tell you."

With that, he was gone. Liv bit her lip and turned back to watch the Jag. A stocky man got out of the driver's seat and walked toward the main entrance of Danforth Hall.

Pfiester was dressed in loose-fitting khaki chinos and a white button-down shirt, and he had the swagger and going-to-fat face of a former high-school football star starting to age. She pegged him to be in his early thirties. His blond hair was already receding at the temples, but he had the kind of showy confidence that some women found attractive.

Once he was inside, Liv started to turn toward the door. Movement from the Jag caught her attention. The passenger door opened, and a slight, blonde woman wearing dark sunglasses scooted around the back of the car, slid into the driver's seat, and pulled the Jag out of the driveway.

Liv watched the Jag speed toward the center of campus. The woman's face, even hidden behind the glasses was familiar. Liv had last seen her at the library café with Mason Falwell, and now here she was driving around with the head of the IT department.

Liv's heart sped up. This could be the connection she'd been looking for between Mason and the lost computer files.

The woman in the Jag was Karie Falwell.

Chapter Twenty-Six

•••••••••••••••

L iv was getting more annoyed by the minute.
"The files were not recoverable. They've been removed."
Dustin Pfiester folded his hands together on top of his desk and
gave her a tight, but somehow satisfied smile. His small, beady eyes
reminded her of a ferret. Not only that, but if his blond eyebrows
were any shaggier, they would completely obscure his vision. A
musky odor rose from his armpits. He looked–and smelled–
practically feral.

"Removed?" Liv gave him a skeptical stare. "Permanently?"

"Yes. Removed. Wiped. Erased. We attempted to recover the
information stored on the accounts, but we were unsuccessful in
decrypting the files in-house. We spent a few weeks on it, wasting
hundreds of man-hours, but in the end, we had to move on.
Frankly, we don't have the resources to squander on a situation
that was limited to just a few accounts, even if one of them is the
great and powerful Mason Falwell."

Pfiester's voice was both patronizing and sarcastic. "There's
really not much else I can tell you."

"You haven't told me anything." Liv swung her foot back and
forth, considering her next line of questioning. What Pfiester said
merely echoed what Jeremy Crete had already explained. They were
all spouting the party line around here. "Aren't you worried about
this encryption malware attacking other computers on campus?"

"That's unlikely. Mason Falwell has a new account, and Tedeschi is no longer a student. We haven't had any more complaints about malware that fits this description. It is no longer a priority situation. Frankly, we have more work than we can handle just doing the day-to-day maintenance of the systems on campus."

"I see."

Liv's eyes roamed the room. They were in Pfiester's office just off the main room of the IT department. Large glass partitions allowed the department head to keep an eye, however hairy, on his staff. Jeremy Crete and the two extra staffers—one male and one female—hunched over their keyboards and stared at their computer screens in their cubicles.

Liv sat in one of the Longfellow College insignia chairs placed in front of Pfiester's desk. Hanging on the wall next to her were a few plaques that looked like athletic awards. A photo of Pfiester in a Longfellow rugby team jersey had pride of place above the awards.

Pfiester was an alumnus of the school, she realized. Just like Karie Falwell.

Liv tucked that information away and glanced past Pfiester. On the workstation behind his desk, three large computer monitors were in screensaver mode. One showed a digital readout of the time, another Longfellow's Bruce the Moose mascot, and the third a *Lord of the Rings* image with the words "One ring to rule them all" scrolling along the top.

"You must have some theories about how the accounts became encrypted in the first place," she said, pulling her eyes from the screensavers and fixing them instead on ferret-face looming in front of her. "These things don't just come out of nowhere."

"Sometimes they do. Falwell and Tedeschi likely opened an attachment that contained the virus," he said. His voice was reluctant, guarded. Because he thought she was dissing him professionally? Or because he was hiding something?

"Who sent the attachment, then?"

"We don't know, and frankly I doubt we'll ever find out. What is important is that we've made the necessary adjustments to our anti-virus shields, so we don't expect it to be a problem in the future. It's too bad about the lost info, though."

He didn't sound sorry, but she let that go.

"Could the loss have been prevented?"

"Certainly! We encourage our staff and students to back up their files consistently to safe storage, either elsewhere on the cloud or external drives. Obviously, Tedeschi and Falwell did not do so." He glanced behind him to check the clock counting out the seconds on his screensaver. "If you don't have any more questions, you can see yourself out."

To annoy him, Liv uncrossed and crossed her legs, taking her time. She tapped the arm of her chair.

"Oh, but I do have more questions. Cooper Tedeschi claims that Mason Falwell stole the manuscript he'd been writing and sharing via their shared Long/Space files. Emails between the two men might have shown who was the originator of the text. Doesn't it seem suspicious to you that the malware attacked at just that time, on just those accounts? Is it at all possible that someone could have sabotaged those two accounts on purpose? Sent the malware as an attachment to them on purpose just as the system crashed? Or even hacked in and installed it?"

"Is it possible? Yes. In fact, I have to wonder if Tedeschi didn't plant this bug himself."

Liv leaned forward, back muscles tensing beneath her shirt. "What makes you say that?"

Pfiester leaned back in his chair, putting his hands behind his head. He looked smug, as if he had everything figured out. "No reason. Just a theory. I never met Tedeschi, but it *is* suspicious the way it played out. Like you said, the timing's interesting. Falwell sells a book. Tedeschi's manuscript and emails 'mysteriously' disappear right around the same time, and then all of a sudden he accuses Falwell of stealing his manuscript. Seems to me he either planned it or took advantage of the situation."

"I see. By your same reasoning, though, couldn't it also follow that Falwell stole Tedeschi's work, sent it to a publisher, and then introduced malware that would erase any proof that his student actually wrote the manuscript?"

"I suppose, but who's the more likely culprit? A best-selling author who peaked well before the computer era or a no-name creative writing student who grew up in the information age?" Dustin abruptly tipped forward in his chair. "In any case, it really isn't my concern. What matters to me is that we weren't able to decrypt the files, and I don't like how that looks for my department. We will be doing some extensive training, upgrading, and testing of our protection systems over the summer. We will also be implementing more regular communication with our staff and students about how to protect their computers and accounts from malware and viruses. So, if that's all…"

"One more thing, Mr. Pfiester. You said you don't know Cooper. How about Mason Falwell?"

"Only since this encryption problem. He wanted to make sure he got set up with a new account right away so he could continue teaching this semester."

"But you aren't friends socially?"

"No."

"How about Karie Falwell?"

Dustin's eyes skittered. Not much, but a little. His face remained impassive, though. "Again, yes, I've met her since Falwell's computer crash, but we aren't friends. Why do you ask?"

"No reason." Liv smiled and rose from the chair in front of Dustin's desk. Let him sweat that one out after she was gone. Dustin Pfiester was lying. Lying for sure about Karie Falwell. Possibly lying about the encryption virus, as well.

Liv reached out her hand. His beefy palm pressed against hers, and she repressed a shudder. "Okay, well, thank you for your time, Mr. Pfiester. I appreciate your talking to me."

"I wish I could have been more help." He couldn't have sounded more insincere.

"No worries," she said, withdrawing her hand, sliding it down the leg of her jeans to wipe off the clammy feeling of Pfiester's paw. She grabbed the handle of her red bag. "You've been more than helpful. I'll see myself out."

She was pleased to see his cool and overconfident expression fade. The IT staff, who had been chatting back and forth for the last several minutes, fell silent as she stalked through the room toward the hallway door. "Thank you again, Jeremy," Liv called, waving at the lanky poet. He merely scowled and turned back to his computer.

Heading up the stairwell toward the first floor, Liv tried not to feel too disappointed with her morning's work. She'd been bluffing back there with Pfiester. He really hadn't told her anything. Yes, he'd lied about knowing Karie Falwell. That was something she'd look into further, of course, but other than that, the conversations had been fruitless. Neither Jeremy Crete nor Dustin Pfiester had given her anything that would clear Cooper's name and help him apply for reinstatement into the creative writing program.

Feeling slightly nauseated, she frowned. She'd have to contact Cooper and Ledeau and tell them to forget recovering the computer files that would have proved Cooper's authorship. Those files were toast, that much was clear. They'd have to find another way.

"Excuse me?" A female voice spoke behind Liv, echoing in the deserted stairwell. "Hello?"

Liv turned. A student in distressed low-rise jeans, a plaid shirt, and a pair of worn flip-flops, huffed up the stairs. Liv waited for the girl to catch up.

"Hi," the girl said. "I heard you talking to Jeremy, um, earlier." She hesitated and averted her eyes, but then seemed to steel herself to continue. "I'm not sure if this is important, but, um, I think Jeremy does know something about that whole Mason Falwell thingy."

Goosebumps ran up both of Liv's arms. "Why do you think so?"

The girl's eyes were furtive and frightened. "I can't talk now.

Not here. If I lose my work-study job my parents will kill me. Can you meet me outside the campus bookstore at two? That's my lunch break, and, um, I need to pick up a few supplies. Dustin and Jeremy will be here all afternoon. I won't worry about them seeing us over there."

"Okay, sure." The girl turned to go, but Liv called out to her. "Hey, what's your name?"

"Morgan. I gotta get back down to IT, but I'll see you in thirty minutes, okay?"

Liv watched as the curvy undergrad clattered back down the stairs in her flip-flops. With thirty minutes to kill, she had just enough time to grab a latte at the library café and take a few notes on the morning's work, she thought. She headed up the path toward the center of campus and the Evangeline Library.

With any luck, Morgan would have some positive information to balance out the dismal results of her interviews with Crete and Pfiester. Liv hoped so, because she was down to just one other lead: finding the connection between Karie Falwell and Dustin Pfiester.

Chapter Twenty-Seven

• • • • • • • • • • • • • • •

Tall windows along the outer wall of the library café cast squares of spring sunshine onto the floor. Tiny motes of dust swirled and floated in the air above the heads of the students and staff lined up at the counter.

A happy din of voices, piped-in music, and the scrape of chairs against the floor mixed with the rich aroma of freshly-ground coffee beans. Liv's spirits lifted. Compared to the dim and dismal IT department workspace, the café was homey and bright, and after her frustrating discussions with Jeremy Crete and Dustin Pfiester, she needed something to cheer her up.

A large caramel latte should do the trick.

She ordered her drink and waited beside the counter while the machine hissed and foamed. Scanning the room for a table, she was startled to see Mason and Karie Falwell at a corner table, heads close together.

"Caramel latte!" the barista called. Liv grabbed the paper cup, said thank you, and crossed to a vacant table on the east side of the room. She took off her jacket, hung it over the back of her chair, and positioned herself so she could keep an eye on the Falwells.

What was Karie up to? Liv sipped the sweet, rich drink and watched the two in the back corner.

Less than an hour ago, Karie'd been in a car with Dustin Pfiester. Now she was in the library getting cozy with her aging hubby whose frown and furrowed brow gave his large face a fierce, but tired, leonine expression. Was it jealousy, Liv wondered? Did Falwell suspect his much-younger wife was having an affair?

Wanting to avoid recognition by either Mason or Karie, Liv slid a pair of dark glasses over her eyes. Rooting around in the bag, her fingers felt for the thin, knit beanie she always kept there. She ducked her head and stuck the beanie over her hair, hoping nobody noticed her quick-change artistry.

Looking at the pair over the rim of her cup, Liv pondered. Was Karie acting as her husband's go-between with the IT department, paying them to destroy the incriminating emails and files? Dustin could have called Karie after Liv left his office to warn her that Liv was asking too many questions about the lost computer files. Karie might have hunted down Mason to warn him of the danger. That would explain their angry expressions.

Cheered by this thought, Liv continued to sip and watch. If the Falwells were worried, she was on the right track. She wished she'd been able to snap a photo of Dustin getting out of Karie's car. That would have established a connection between the IT department and the Falwells, something that Ledeau might be able to use to build a case against the publisher and the college.

Pulling a notebook and pen from her bag, Liv jotted some notes, all the while watching Mason and Karie with quick, surreptitious glances. Mason continued to glare while Karie talked. The younger woman also appeared tense. Her hand movements were quick and jerky, and her shoulders were lifted so high, her neck disappeared.

There were any number of innocent explanations as to what Karie had been doing with Dustin Pfiester—she could be pushing the IT department to restore Mason's files, for one—but Liv's gut told her there was more here.

She scribbled a note reminding herself to investigate both Karie and Dustin's years of attendance at Longfellow. Karie's behavior in the Danforth Hall parking lot had been suspicious. Dustin and Karie in the Jag. Karie's furtive switch to the driver's seat. The way she zipped out of the parking lot wearing those dark sunglasses as if she didn't want to be recognized. Who owned the Jag, she wanted to know. And why the secrecy?

Liv chewed on the end of her pen. She'd seen that kind of behavior while investigating cheating spouses. Could Karie be having an affair with Dustin Pfiester?

Suddenly, a commotion at the Falwell table caused that side of the room to stare. An overturned soup bowl and spoon on the floor and a spreading puddle of tomato-red liquid indicated that Mason had knocked his lunch off the table.

Karie mopped at the mess with paper napkins, her face impassive. Mason sat there, scowling, while his wife tried to keep the soup from running off the edge of the small table. Kind students nearby passed Karie more paper napkins which she took with a brief smile and a nod.

Taking advantage of the commotion, Liv swung her bag over her elbow, grabbed her jacket and her coffee cup, and headed for the door. The campus bookstore was in the building next door, on the ground floor of the student center.

She couldn't wait to find out what Morgan had to say.

•   •   •   •   •

The Longfellow College Student Center was a sprawling, modern building of concrete, brick, and glass. Built into the side of a hill, the center had two stories—one above ground and one below. The main floor was surrounded by concrete patios with benches and tables, concrete pathways winding through shrub and flower beds, and an outdoor amphitheater where in the warmer months students liked to congregate. This main floor held a large cafeteria, smaller banquet rooms, the faculty dining hall, and various campus activities offices.

Once inside the building, Liv headed down a wide set of concrete steps to the lower level where there was a large food court with numerous fast-food options as well as the college bookstore.

Morgan sat on a wooden bench just outside the food court. When she spotted Liv, she rose and glanced furtively around her before giving a little wave.

Liv waved back and walked toward her.

"Hi," the girl said, her eyes round and nervous. Her hand shook a little as she pushed a strand of blue-tipped hair behind one ear. "Let's go into the store. I know where we can talk."

She led Liv past racks of sweatshirts, T-shirts, coffee mugs. They walked by art supplies, pens, and magazines and then through rows of books. Morgan finally stopped in a deserted back area where the shelves were higher and stacked with unopened boxes of books, warehouse-style. Only then did she turn around to face Liv. "Okay. I think we're safe here."

"I agree," Liv said, giving the girl a reassuring smile. "And I won't keep you long. I know you're on lunch break. What did you want to tell me about Jeremy Crete?"

Morgan bit her lip, through which a thin, silver loop was threaded. "I hope I'm doing the right thing. I got this work-study job at the beginning of the school year. I played around with coding and stuff in high school, did a little hacking, nothing serious, but, um, I knew enough to get hired in IT. Jeremy trained me on the Long/Space system. Basically, my work is like help-desk stuff. People have trouble getting into the system or lose their passwords or whatever. They call us, and I walk them through the steps to get things running again." Morgan twisted her hands.

Liv gave her a reassuring smile. "Sounds like a good job."

"I thought it would be. It's cool, helping people and stuff, but if everyone knew what was going on, they'd flip." Morgan's eyes widened. "Jeremy, Dustin, all of them? They have access to everyone's files. They sit around reading documents, emails, everything. I'm pretty sure they've even sent a code to some accounts that turns on the computer's webcam so they can spy on people. You know? In their offices? Even dorm rooms?"

Liv nodded, keeping her face impassive. "Go on."

"They're a bunch of cyber creepers. The whole IT department." Morgan shuddered. "I hate working there, but I need the money pretty bad. I figure I'll request another job for next year, but for now, I just have to go along with it." She looked at Liv with pleading eyes, as if she were asking for some sort of validation.

"It sounds as if you're in a tight spot, Morgan."

"Yeah," she whispered. "I guess."

"So, who exactly are they targeting? Students and faculty?"

"Both. Even administration. These guys, um, they don't try to hide what they're doing. It's a joke to them. They even have this game where they see who can find the most embarrassing email. They read the messages out loud and then everyone votes. It's so sick and creepy!"

Liv made a sympathetic face but kept quiet hoping the girl would go on.

Morgan twisted her fingers together. "I mean, their whole excuse is that people are supposed to know that nothing is truly private on the college email system. No one is supposed to use Long/Space except for college stuff, but of course, no one follows that rule. Staff, professors, students, everyone. Except, the administrators not so much. From what Dustin and Jeremy and those guys say, the admins are a little more paranoid and careful. But everyone else writes the most, um, personal emails, you know? Stuff about dates, divorces, family. Even medical conditions. Not to mention the photo files. It's all a big joke to those guys."

"Have you ever done it, read other peoples' emails?"

"No! I think it's sick. I wish I could turn them in."

"So why don't you?"

"I really need the job. Plus..." Morgan looked away.

"Let me guess. They've threatened you in some way."

"They get dirt on everyone who works in IT. Secrets. Photos. Stuff like that. They make it clear that if you blab, all your embarrassing, personal stuff will get published on social media."

"This is Dustin?"

"Yeah. They're all in on it."

"Does Dustin have something in particular on you?"

Morgan looked down again. "Yeah. I was pretty stupid when I was a freshman, before I started working in IT. As soon as he hired me, Dustin made sure I knew he had some photos and things. He was all jokey about it and everything, you know? But still."

She raised her head and locked eyes with Liv, pleading. "Please, please don't tell anyone I talked to you. I just want to get through this semester and move on. And one more thing. I don't know if it means anything, but once I forgot my keycard and came back to the department to get it. Dustin and Jeremy were sitting together at Jeremy's computer and talking about something called Red Eye. I didn't pay much attention at the time, but since then I've seen it mentioned on a few IT message boards. It's a new encryption malware program that is popping up here and there. It got me thinking that maybe that's the code that messed up Falwell and Cooper's files, and Dustin doesn't want to admit he can't fix it."

"Do you know anything else about this Red Eye malware?"

"No. Just chatter on the boards. It isn't that widespread, so regular people haven't heard about it."

"But you think that's what attacked Tedeschi and Falwell's files? Where would they have picked it up?"

Morgan shrugged. "I mean, someone could have sent an email with an attachment."

Liv nodded, but her mind was going a hundred miles an hour. Maybe her friend Agent Snow would know something about some new encryption malware threat called Red Eye. The FBI investigated cyber crimes. Maybe he could point her toward decryption software.

She got excited for a second, and then she remembered: Pfiester had told her the files had all been erased. Even with the decryption code, it would be too late to recover the files. Still, it would be worth mentioning to Snow.

"Okay, I'll look into that Red Eye thing," she told Morgan. "But you said Jeremy knows something about Cooper Tedeschi and Mason Falwell?"

"Oh, yeah," Morgan said. "Jeremy snoops into all the creative writing student accounts. He's always commenting on this person or that, reading stuff out loud that he thinks is funny. Anyway, this is what I wanted to tell you. Once Jeremy was all, like, 'Tedeschi thinks he's so great, but Falwell just ripped him a new one, haha.' He read this awful comment Falwell made on Cooper's novel, and I remember thinking that was a really mean thing for a professor to say to a student. When Cooper accused Professor Falwell of stealing his novel, I thought there was no way. Falwell didn't even like what Cooper was writing. But, of course, we weren't supposed to know that."

"Did Jeremy ever talk about Tedeschi's accusations?"

Morgan shook her head, blue hair swinging. "Actually no, and that's kinda weird. I was surprised because he'd obviously been reading Cooper's story and had seen Professor Falwell commenting on it."

Liv listened with growing excitement. If what Morgan was saying was true, Jeremy Crete not only had read Cooper's manuscript but also Falwell's critique.

When news of Falwell's new book came out, it was possible Jeremy recognized the story from what he'd read in Cooper's account files. If she could convince Jeremy to admit what he'd done and get him to make an official statement about what he knew, Cooper would at least have documentation that he wrote the original of the two manuscripts in question, not Falwell. The dates themselves weren't important. The fact that Falwell had commented on Cooper's story would be proof.

It was a little thin, and only based on one person's snooping, but it was better than nothing.

"So then what happened? When Tedeschi was dismissed from the university? Did Jeremy say anything about that?"

"Well, right around then the computer system crashed. We

were all working, like sixteen-hour shifts. But once that was all cleaned up, the administration started coming around asking for Tedeschi's and Falwell's files. Out of all the creative writing accounts that were affected, those were the only two that had the encryption issue, but no one outside of IT knew that. If anyone asked about Tedeschi or Falwell, we were told to direct them to Dustin for answers. He said it was for legal reasons."

Morgan paused. "It's almost like someone used the big system crash as a screen to install malicious code into Tedeschi's and Falwell's files."

Chapter Twenty-Eight

• • • • • • • • • • • • • •

Acting on this new information, Liv made her way back toward Danforth Hall.

She wanted to talk to Jeremy Crete again. Morgan's information opened up a new possibility. If she could get Crete to admit he'd read Cooper's manuscript and Falwell's critiques prior to the system crash and to verify that the manuscript Mason submitted to the publisher matched what he'd read in Cooper's files, she'd be much closer to proving Cooper's claims.

According to Pfiester and Crete, the actual files were unrecoverable; a signed statement from Crete attesting that Cooper was the original author would solve the case.

It was close to 2:30 p.m. by the time she entered the cool basement of Danforth Hall. The door to the IT department was closed. She opened it, walked in, glanced around. Morgan was still at lunch. Two other staffers sat at their desks, both of them on their phones. Dustin was in his office. She could see him through the glass partition.

But where was Jeremy Crete? His computer monitor was shut down and his office chair pushed beneath the work surface.

She waited for one of the work-study students to finish her call. The girl, surly and rude, glared at her and said, "If you're looking for Jeremy, he's gone home. He won't be back today."

Liv felt rather than saw Dustin's gaze fall on her. Irritated, she thanked the girl and left the department at a loss as to what to do next.

Considering her options, she decided to go back to her office and get caught up on her emails and other work-related tasks. She'd also run a background check on Crete, find out where the skinny weasel lived.

She'd root him out tomorrow one way or the other.

·　·　·　·　·

"Admit it, Liv, you've always been just a little bit spoiled."

Ashleigh waved her glass of wine around, her freshly-manicured fingernails sparkling with glued-on rhinestones. They were finally having their girl's night.

Liv tilted her head and brushed her pinky toe with green polish. A piece of cotton batting wound in and around each toe. Blue mud masks covered her and Ashleigh's faces, and their second bottle of white wine was down to the last inch. "What do you think of this color, because I don't know," she said.

"Don't change the topic. I'm giving you some good advice here. Throwing a temper tantrum might have worked when you were six," she sloshed her wine around some more, "but you can see how it works on a thirty-five-year-old cardiologist. Not well."

Liv considered this. They were curled up on either end of the couch in Liv's apartment, Ashleigh in yet another pair of to-die-for yoga pants and Liv wearing striped silk pajama bottoms and a teeny pink cardigan. Electric flames danced in the fireplace.

"Okay, maybe you're right," Liv said, "but he was giving me all these signals. Sexy talk. Flirty eye-contact. Scorching hot kisses. Other things." She wasn't going to speak aloud about how he'd run his hand over her or how she'd felt the heat searing all the way to her... never mind. She frowned at her toenails. "It was our third date. Maybe he just wasn't as turned on as I was."

"Mmm, could be. But I doubt it." Ashleigh grabbed a blue-cheese stuffed olive and popped it in her mouth, chewing thoughtfully. "Maybe it was just like he said. He wanted to take it slow because he felt a connection with you and didn't want to rush things. Maybe he wanted to, well, court you."

"Court me? What guy does that these days?"

"A guy who's thinking about marriage. One who's been raised with conservative values. You said his parents were religious? Maybe deep down he still believes that sex and marriage are, well, sacred."

They sat in silence for a moment, contemplating the possibility, and Liv poured the dregs of the wine into her glass. "I know you and Trevor didn't take it slow at all, and he's one of the nicest guys we ever met. Practically perfect."

"I wouldn't say perfect," Ashleigh said, voice dry.

"You know what I mean."

"I know. Most days, I can't imagine life without him, even if he drives me crazy with his golf and his fantasy baseball, and his men's basketball league. Ugh. He's such a jock. But he's cute. And he's good for me, keeps me from getting too deep into my head." Ashleigh held out her hand and waved her fingernails. "I think I like these. The kids at school will be impressed. But it's getting late, and I've had too much wine. Do you mind if I stay over?"

"Of course not."

"Good. Then we have time to gab a bit longer." She touched her face. "This feels like it's cracking. We should wash this stuff off."

They took turns in the bathroom, splashing warm water and mucking up Liv's hand towels. "Here, try this moisturizer. It's delicious." Liv handed the tiny glass tub to Ashleigh.

"Mmmm, smells so good! This feels like college, in a way, doesn't it? I miss those days sometimes. When we thought we had it all figured out."

When they were settled back on the couch, Ashleigh sighed. "Did I tell you Trevor planned a vacation for us without consulting me? Hawaii. I was really excited until he told me he booked rooms at seven golf resorts throughout the islands so we could play every day on a different course. The sad thing is, he thinks this is romantic."

"Well, I suppose it could be." Liv gave her a skeptical look.

Ashleigh snorted. "I said he could golf, and I'd hang by the pool with a good book, get hot stone massages on the beach, and spend his money at the hotel shops and then we could meet up for the sunsets and luaus."

"Sounds idyllic. Can I come?"

"No. But about the sex thing? Sometimes I wish Trevor and I hadn't rushed right into it when we first started dating. I mean, it was college, so we jumped into bed the second we laid eyes on each other, practically. In hindsight, it might have been nice to wait."

Ashleigh looked down at her wine, swirled it, and pretended to study the way it clung to the side of the glass.

Liv laughed. "You are so lying to me right now."

Ashleigh considered it and shrugged. "Okay, okay, you're right. I wouldn't have wanted to wait, especially if I knew how difficult it would be to get pregnant. Let's just say that trying to have a baby isn't all that hot. I miss the days of just having sex for the fun of it, or having fun with my husband without this crushing disappointment pressing in on us all the time."

"I'm sorry, Ash. What does your doctor think? About a baby, I mean?"

"We're discussing surgery as an option. I've been on the pill since age seventeen, trying to reduce the amount of endometrial cells floating around in my body. Once we started trying to conceive last year, the pain got worse, but we were hoping I'd get pregnant right away and avoid surgery. Now the doctor says he can remove the tissue from around my pelvis and fallopian tubes, and that might increase my chances. I'm thirty years old. I shouldn't have waited so long. I knew it, but Trevor... we... wanted to wait." Ashleigh pressed her lips together.

Liv handed her a cocktail napkin printed with a cheeky little cartoon. "You can cry if you want. I won't freak out. I promise." She always felt helpless and uncomfortable when people cried, but she wanted to be a better friend. She would do what she could to be supportive.

Maybe that was part of life and friendship, she thought. Doing things you don't think you can because you have to. Maybe it was time to grow up.

Just a little, though. Nothing drastic.

Ashleigh dabbed at her tears. "You know, I always wanted to have kids. I used to talk about it all the time in college, remember? It's just this pull inside me, like this big, overwhelming craving that nothing will satisfy but a child of my own. I mean, I love working with the students at school, but it isn't the same as having your own, is it?"

Liv shrugged. "I wouldn't know. I don't think I even want to have children."

"You'll change your mind once you fall in love."

"I wouldn't count on it. Is there anything I can do to help? I could call Jasper and see if he knows any good fertility specialists."

Ashleigh rolled her eyes and laughed. "You're so pathetic, Olivia. I'm happy with my doctor. He's the best in Boston. You just want an excuse to call Jasper."

"Okay, but could I use you as an excuse? If absolutely necessary?"

Ashleigh laughed again. "Fine. Do what you have to do. You really like Dr. Hottie, huh?"

Liv nodded. She did. She really did. It was driving her crazy.

"Well, tell him, Liv. Be honest."

"What if he says he's not interested anymore?"

"Then he's not interested. You'll have to accept it and forget about him."

"You mean I can't scream and throw things and get drunk and wreck my apartment?"

"Nope."

Liv stuck out her tongue. "You're no fun."

"It's hard for you. I get it. You love your parents, but you don't want their life. You never have. Then you meet a nice guy, only he's a doctor in the same hospital as your dad. In fact, your mother introduced you to him. You're afraid of his expectations. You don't want to disappoint him. You don't want to disappoint your parents. How am I doing so far?"

"Frighteningly accurate, as usual."

"Sweetie, you just have to talk to him. Keep some physical distance between you so chemistry won't muddle things up, and you talk about this. Tell him how you feel. Ask him how he feels. You might be surprised. He made himself vulnerable, and you rejected him. Maybe he's just waiting for you to make the next move."

"And if not?"

"Then you call me. And we have another girl's night and demolish some Ben & Jerry's ice cream and watch *He's Just Not That Into You* for the umpteenth time."

"Ugh. Let's hope it doesn't come to that. Did I tell you I'm training for a half-marathon? I can't be eating that much fat and sugar. Come on." Liv stood, held out her hand, and pulled Ashleigh off the couch. "Let's get you to bed. You look about ready to pass out."

"Just tired. Not used to drinking. Trying to get preggers is exhausting."

Liv thought about that for a moment, and because it was so far from anything she'd ever imagine herself feeling, she just said, "I'm glad you aren't mad at me anymore."

"I wasn't that mad at you."

"Yes, you were, and I deserved it."

"You did." Ashleigh laughed and gave her a hug. "I'm going to call Trevor and let him know I'm staying over. And *you* call Jasper. Keepers don't come along every day, you know."

Liv nodded. "Okay, I'll call him. Tomorrow."

Chapter Twenty-Nine

• • • • • • • • • • • • • •

The next morning, Liv wandered out to the kitchen and found Ashleigh finishing a cup of coffee.

"Hey, I was just about to take off." Ashleigh pulled an elastic through her blonde hair, twisted and rolled it into a bun, tucked the ends under. In two seconds she went from bedraggled to artfully casual, but her eyes sagged at the corners and she let out a deep sigh. "I'm exhausted. Wish I didn't have to work today."

"Call in sick. You can hang out here as long as you want. We can make pancakes." Liv yawned and opened a cupboard, rooted around for her favorite mug.

"Sorry. Can't. My principal has been a royal pain in the butt the past few weeks. I've had to take some time off for doctor appointments. She thinks I'm not pulling my weight with the kids." Ashleigh lifted her chin. "I've been working for her for seven years and rarely take a personal day. You'd think she'd cut me some slack."

"Why not quit?" Liv poured herself some coffee and sat down at the table. "Stress can't be helping you with, uh, Mission Conception. Besides, you always wanted to be an at-home mom. Why not consider this time as simply pre-mommyhood? Give yourself a break?"

"Mission Conception. Clever." Ashleigh grimaced. "No, work keeps my mind occupied. It's good for me to focus on the kiddos. I'd really miss them if I quit. They're so smart and funny and energetic. It'll be different once... if... I have children of my own."

"Not if. When." Liv put her hand over Ashleigh's and gave a squeeze. "You hear me? It's gonna happen."

Ashleigh sighed. "I hope so."

A few minutes later, Ashleigh hugged Liv at the door. "Thanks for last night. It was fun. Make sure you call Dr. Hottie."

Liv rolled her eyes. "Don't you have a job to go to?"

After a quick breakfast of toast and coffee, Liv dressed for the day ahead. She chose to go casual again with a pair of dark wash jeans, a pink T-shirt, and a knee-length pink raincoat. Might as well be comfortable, she figured, and the pink was friendly and approachable.

She planned to track down Jeremy Crete and convince him that telling the truth about Cooper and Falwell was the right thing to do. She hoped to appeal to his sense of fairness and ask him to put himself in Cooper's place. All that work. All those long hours working on a manuscript. The expense of graduate tuition. The loss of two years pursuing a dream, only to have it snatched away by the person you'd idolized and trusted.

To her mind, the situation smacked of power and privilege, a professor willing to ruin a young man's life in order to preserve his sense of importance and esteem. She had to convince Jeremy Crete that speaking up was the right thing to do.

And if he refused? Liv frowned, thinking about the way Crete and his boss Pfiester blackmailed Morgan into keeping quiet.

Well, they might learn that Olivia Lively wasn't above a little blackmail herself. If Jeremy refused to cooperate, she'd threaten to spill the beans to the administration and the media about his and the IT department's cyber spying. Either way, his behavior was going to come to light. If he wrote a statement, the scandal might be kept under wraps. If he didn't, the whole academic community would know what the IT jerks had been up to.

Hoping to catch Jeremy at work, she cruised down to Longfellow College and hung left into the campus's north entrance. The parking lot behind Danforth was almost full, but Liv managed to slip into a space near the chain fence. Without a sticker or visitor pass, she ran the risk of getting ticketed, but that couldn't be helped. Hopefully, she'd convince Crete to join her outside for a cigarette break where they could speak in private and she could keep an eye out for the campus police and their quick ticket fingers.

Whistling a series of notes from Vivaldi's "Four Seasons," Liv entered the building and jogged down the stairs to the IT department. Swinging the door open, she was met by a room full of blank stares. Dustin turned to glare at her. "What can I do for you today, Ms. Lively? As you can see we are in the middle of a staff meeting."

"Sorry to interrupt," Liv said, no hint of apology in her voice. "I'm looking for Jeremy."

"He's not here." Dustin turned, dismissing her. Liv held her ground, cleared her throat. The members of the IT department tried not to smile. One staffer snickered. Glancing around the room, she met the worried eyes of her pal Morgan, and quickly looked away without a hint of acknowledgment. Dustin's shoulders tightened. "Is there something else?"

"No. Just wondering. If this is a staff meeting, and Jeremy is on the staff, why isn't he here?"

"He called in, okay? Now, I'd like to get back to this meeting. There's the door. Don't let it hit you on the way out."

The staff twittered. Liv whirled and strode out of the room. She jogged up the stairs to the exit, crossed the parking lot, and slid into her car. She started the engine and rammed the car into reverse with more force than necessary. No matter what happened with the Tedeschi-Falwell case, she'd inform the administration about Pfiester's unnecessary snooping. Taking down that smug, bloated bully would be so freaking satisfying.

Tapping her fingers on the steering wheel, she decided what to do next about Crete. Consulting the address she'd keyed into her GPS, she pointed her car toward Brighton Avenue. She found a classical playlist and turned up the volume. The somber aria from Vivaldi's pasticcio, "Bajazet," sung by the magnificent Cecilia Bartoli, suited the gray, overcast sky. She rolled the window down a couple of inches to catch the scent of spring in the air.

Morning traffic was light, but she hit every one of the umpteen red lights on Brighton. Her GPS told her to turn right onto a residential road of small, run-down ranches and two-story homes. The driveways of the houses looked dismal with their cracked and broken hot-top. Bicycles and other children's toys lay scattered on many of the lawns.

Checking the numbers above doorways, Liv rolled slowly down the street. She stopped outside a light-brown ranch with a missing white shutter. Number 67. This was it.

From the privacy of her car, she took note of the residence. No toys. Two cars in the driveway, older models and starting to rust, one of which she recognized from the parking lot the other day, most likely Crete's. A few of the windows were curtained with bedsheets, and the rest were bare. Several beer bottles listed where they'd been thrown into a patch of grass beside the front steps.

Definitely a student rental, she thought, stepping out of the car and making her way toward the front door. She pressed the doorbell but heard no chime, so she knocked on the door. Waited. Knocked again. Glancing at the picture window to her left, she caught movement. A moment later, the door opened.

The smell hit her first, a combination of stale beer, cigarettes, weed, and garlic. The young guy standing in the doorway was shirtless, wearing a low-riding pair of saggy jeans, no socks. A grayish-blue tattoo of a lizard covered his chest from nipple to somewhere below the waistline. She didn't want to think where that tail ended.

Looking up toward less unsavory territory, Liv noticed his hair was standing up on his head as if he'd just crawled out of bed. Or a cave.

"Yah?" He looked her up and down, his eyes bloodshot.

"Hi, I'm looking for Jeremy."

Lizard-boy tilted his head back. "He's not here."

"Then how come his car's in the driveway?"

"Don't know. But he's not here."

"Just tell him to get out here. It's for his own good."

He gave her a leering smile and shut the door in her face.

Liv pounded on the door. She stood there for a few seconds, fuming, and went back to her car. Watching the house through her windshield, she waited for movement. Sure enough, a corner of the green sheet covering a half-open upstairs window pulled back, and she caught the flash of a face before the curtain dropped again.

Liv got out of her car and yelled up at the window. "I don't blame you for hiding, Jeremy. You got yourself in a pickle, and you know it. But you can't stay holed up in that dump forever, and hiding won't make this go away."

She waited a minute with no response, gave up, and got back in her car. A few raindrops spattered on the windshield. She tapped her fingernails. So far she'd been focusing on the IT department, but there was more than one way to approach this puzzle.

It was time to find out if and how Karie Falwell was connected to the Long/Space crash.

Chapter Thirty

• • • • • • • • • • • • •

Ensconced in her office with some Mozart playing in the background, Liv chased Karie Falwell through the social media weeds looking for a link between her and Dustin Pfiester. She searched Karie's friend and follower lists, jotted down a few names of Longfellow College connections for possible further investigation. Pfiester's name, however, did not pop up.

Disappointed, Liv clicked onto Karie's LinkedIn page and scanned her work history and job titles. Karie listed her current position as freelance editor. That made sense, Liv thought, considering her graduate degree in English. Beneath the title was a short list of publications, institutions, and companies for which she'd worked. She'd listed Longfellow College as one of her clients.

She sat forward in her seat, scrolled down the list, hoping to see a mention of Longfellow's IT department. Over the past several years, Karie had worked for several departments at the college including the alumni office, career center, and community outreach programs, mostly web copy and annual reports. No IT work. No proof of any connection with Dustin Pfiester other than what she'd seen in the parking lot.

Liv slumped back. She rolled the button on her mouse and gave the rest of Karie's resume a cursory perusal. Previous employment included tutoring for a non-profit education program and a three-month stint as a long-term substitute teacher at a local high school. Nothing, Liv thought, related to the case.

About to click off the site, Liv's eyes snagged on the very last entry. She sucked in a breath and leaned closer to the screen. She looked at the dates and did the math.

If she'd calculated the dates right, Karie Bishop had worked for the IT department during her graduate school years. Had Pfiester been working there at the same time, Liv wondered? They were about the same age.

She typed in a search for Pfiester's profile and scanned his work history.

Liv smiled. There it was.

According to the overlapping dates on their resumes, Karie Falwell and Dustin Pfiester had worked together at the Longfellow College IT department for two years. Granted, that was over seven years ago, she thought, propping her feet up on her desk, but they were still in touch. She'd seen them together in the black Jag outside Danforth Hall.

The furtive look on Karie's face, the dark glasses, the way she'd held off getting into the driver's seat until the coast was clear signaled guilt or concealment—possibly both. Either way, Karie hadn't wanted to be seen.

Liv printed out a screenshot of both profiles and stuck them into the Tedeschi case folder. Satisfied with a good morning's work, she called in an order for take-out Chinese. While she waited for her lunch to be delivered, she clicked around a few of her favorite online retailers to see what new items they had in stock. Looking at the halter-topped maxi dresses, espadrilles, and lightweight linen shifts gave her mood a boost.

One cute little dress caught her eye. It was not her color, but the pastel blue was perfect for a certain older woman who didn't know Etsy from thredUP when it came to online shopping.

Liv took it as a sign. She'd put off calling her mother too long.

She pressed Tiffany's number and waited for her mother to pick up.

"Olivia," her mother said, her voice smooth and unruffled.

"This is a surprise."

"Hi, Mom," Liv said. "I wanted to confirm that I will be at the Spring Fling on Thursday. Just me. Put me somewhere you need to fill a space. It's fine."

"Oh." Tiffany paused. "Well, if you're sure there's no one you could coerce into escorting you, I guess that will have to work."

"I'm sorry I don't have a date, mom. Believe me, I wish I did."

"Is that right? I heard you went out with Jasper Temple, but I guess it didn't work out?"

"What do you have, spies or something? You're like that character in *Game of Thrones* with your little birds."

Liv could hear her mother's gold bracelets clinking as Tiffany reached for something, probably her after-lunch cup of Earl Gray. "Is it so horrible that I'd like to see my only daughter in a relationship? I want you to fall in love, Olivia. I want to plan your wedding and shop with you for a beautiful gown and see you walking down the aisle. And I'd like to have grandchildren someday."

"No, it's not horrible. It's natural. I appreciate your trying to help, but you have to understand I need to find my own dates and choose partners who are right for me."

"And I suppose Jasper wasn't good enough for you. Well, I guess I'll just squeeze you in somewhere at the Fling."

Liv squeezed her phone. Why did this always have to be so hard between her and Tiffany? Why couldn't they communicate?

Her whole life, she'd wanted her mother to listen and understand, to really know her, and to accept her for who she was, but Tiffany was incapable of seeing things from any position but her own. Instead of worrying about how Liv's status as single affected her precious seating charts, Tiffany should tell her not to worry, assure Liv that she'd find someone perfect for her someday.

Isn't that what mothers were supposed to do?

"Do you want to know what's ironic, Mom? I liked Jasper. He may have been right for me, but I messed it all up."

Silence.

"Are you happy now? You were right. He was great. Respectful and funny and smart, and miracle of miracles, he really seemed to like me. I pushed him away, and now I'm alone again, and I wish I'd been smarter about this. But I wasn't. So I'm going to the auxiliary dinner alone, and you'll just have to find an odd seat at an odd table for your odd daughter, okay?"

"Oliv—"

Liv hung up. She couldn't let her mother hear her cry.

· · · · ·

The new wing of Sharon Medical Center boasted a soaring, glass-in atrium with potted plants scattered here and there among the shiny chrome and fabric furniture. A display case showed photos of the history of the hospital. Beyond the information desk, a colorful gift shop offered the usual candy, magazines and books, stuffed animals, and balloons. Because she knew her way around the building, Liv strode down a hallway and past the gift shop without having to consult a directory.

The hospital's main cafeteria sprawled at the back of the new wing and overlooked a charming garden complete with water feature, stone benches, hedged pathways, and even a meditation spiral outlined in smooth, river stones. Liv looked around the café, spotted Jasper at a small table near the windows, wove her way through the room before she lost her nerve.

He had his face deep into a book with a picture of Sasquatch on the cover. She gripped the handle of her green faux crocodile tote and hoped she wasn't making a huge mistake. "Hi. Jasper. How are you?"

He looked up at her, fumbled the book, and knocked it to the floor in his haste. A couple of hospital staff at the next table glanced over. "Uh, hi," he said.

Liv bent down, picked up the book, and handed it back to him.

"Here you go."

"Thanks. What are you doing here?"

It was mid-afternoon. Following her conversation with Tiffany and remembering her promise to Ashleigh, Liv decided to forgo the telephone call to Dr. Hottie and chose instead to confront her demons in person. Besides, she knew she looked sexy-cute in her jeans and pink tee and raincoat, and she hoped seeing her in person would remind Jasper of what he was missing.

"I'm here looking for you." She pointed at the chair across from him. "Do you mind if I have a seat?"

He stared at her as she pulled the chair from the table, and sat down. "Yes, go right ahead," he said after the fact. "I'm surprised to see you."

"Good book?"

He shrugged. "Passable. It's quite a coincidence, you showing up here during my lunch hour."

She made a dismissive gesture with her hand. "I'm a private investigator. Finding people is what I do. Besides, you aren't that difficult to track down. A quick call to the nurse's station in cardiology did the trick. They said I'd find you here."

"I'll have to have a little talk with those nurses. I can't have them blabbing my whereabouts to every crazed woman looking for me."

"You forget, my name has some clout around here. My father runs the joint, remember?"

He smiled, but his eyes looked serious. "What did you want to talk about?"

She pulled the edges of her raincoat around her like a blanket, protective, and leaned forward. "I've been thinking about how we ended things, and I'm pretty sure I was wrong to push you away the way I did." She searched his face for his reaction. Still that unfathomable little smile, revealing nothing.

"Go on," he prompted.

"Well, when we started dating, I wasn't thinking long-term. Not that I was ruling out long-term. I just hadn't got that far. Does that make sense? I'm a see-where-it-goes sort of girl when it comes to relationships. A jump-in-feet-first, kind of girl. You wanted to take things slow, and to me that felt like rejection. I didn't react well. I was awful. I'm sorry."

She looked down at the table, twisted her fingers together. "I recently got out of a toxic relationship. That's one of those things you wanted to talk about before we, uh, got physically involved, and I get it now. We should know these things about each other. Someone hurt me, but my being in that relationship potentially hurt someone else. I'm not proud of it. I haven't always made the best decisions about men. I certainly messed up with you. You didn't deserve to be treated like that. I'm sorry about my behavior and the things I said. I hope you can forgive me. If you can, maybe we could try this dating thing again. On your terms."

Why wasn't he saying anything?

She unclasped her hands, traced her finger along the edge of his book. "So, I was thinking, if you want, maybe we could go out for coffee sometime?"

"Stop that. You'll give yourself a paper cut." Jasper reached for her hand, ran his thumb over her knuckles. "Liv, you know I really like you, but I don't think coffee is a good idea."

"Why? Do you have something against coffee?" She tried to pull her hand away. He held on.

"Coffee's fine, but I have something better in mind."

"You do?"

"Yup." His thumb made little circles on the back of her hand. "I've been thinking about the other night, as well. I was going to call you after work, to talk, but you beat me to it. Maybe you'll always be a little faster than me. The truth is, I thought about our argument and decided you were right. We don't need to make a commitment. This thing between us doesn't have to be serious. We're attracted to each other. We have fun together. Let's just go with it and see what happens."

"Really?" She gave him a skeptical look. "That's quite a turnaround."

He twined his long fingers into hers, leaning forward to speak in a low, intense voice. "This thing between us? It's hot. It's fun and exciting, and yeah, maybe I do think it could be something more serious, but it doesn't have to be serious right away. You understood that before I did, while I dithered around being all sensitive and hands-off like an idiot."

"Well, not exactly hands-off, Doc, there was the way you..."

"Shhhh." He gave her a stern look, and her insides turned to mush. "Let me finish. The other night you were just being honest about what you wanted, and I feel like such a jerk for saying things that hurt you, made you feel cheap. Because you're right. We're both adults. We have this amazing chemistry. As long as we're healthy and being safe, there's no reason we shouldn't sleep together. If that's what you still want, I'm up for it. No strings attached."

Her heart raced. Tilting her chin down, she looked up at him beneath her lashes. "Tonight?"

"Let's say tomorrow night. I'll pick you up for dinner. Someplace nice. Wear one of those sexy outfits of yours. After dinner, I'll ask if you want to go back to my place. You'll still have time to change your mind. But..."

"But?"

"But I hope you don't. Change your mind, I mean." He released her hand, stood up and grabbed his book. "I'll pick you up at six-thirty tomorrow."

"Okay..."

She slumped back in her chair, dazed, and watched him walk out of the cafeteria. What just happened? It was as if she'd lobbed a friendly serve over the net, and he'd smashed a spinning shot back at her and walked off the court without a backward glance.

One of the staff members at the next table leaned toward her. "Congratulations, honey. Doctor Temple is one gorgeous specimen of a man." The staffer's companion looked over and nodded. "I wouldn't say no to that." They laughed and gave her two thumbs up.

A flush climbed into Liv's cheeks. She ran trembling hands over her face and looked out the window at the rain-soaked garden. She supposed the hospital gossip mill would be grinding away like mad by tomorrow.

Her phone vibrated. She reached into her bag to grab it. There was a text from Patrick Ledeau. "Got the manuscript and results. Available for a meeting?"

She stood up and dashed for the exit. No time to think about the incredibly hot and confusing Dr. Temple now. It would have to wait for later when she could concentrate.

She texted Ledeau from the car. "I'm not far from your office. Be there in ten."

Chapter Thirty-One

· · · · · · · · · · · · · · ·

"We finally received a copy of Falwell's manuscript from the publisher," Patrick Ledeau said, pushing two printed pieces of paper across his desk toward Liv. "I hired an expert to run it through both plagiarism and authorship recognition software along with Cooper's manuscript. The results, as you can see, are interesting."

Liv frowned and picked up the first paper. Beside her, Cooper fidgeted, his knee bouncing up and down. "What does this mean, exactly?" Liv asked Ledeau.

"Basically, the plagiarism software gives only a fifty-three percent chance that the two manuscripts—Cooper's draft and Falwell's completed manuscript—are the same."

"So that's bad news, right? Or wait. Is it good?"

"It's almost an even split. Not enough to convince the publisher or the board. Keep in mind that this software only matches words, not content." Seeing Liv's confusion, he explained. "Let's say you and I told the exact same story. As long as we didn't use the same words, in the same order, the software wouldn't be able to detect the similarity. If Falwell took Cooper's basic plot and characters and rewrote the novel in his own words, to the software it wouldn't look like a match."

"That doesn't sound interesting so much as discouraging. We're right back where we started, both claiming they wrote the story first."

"That's not the interesting part," said Ledeau. "We also used authorship software to compare the publisher manuscript against samples of both Falwell's and Cooper's writing. According to my expert, this kind of software has been used to figure out who wrote anonymous books. They've even used it to analyze Shakespeare's plays."

"Christopher Marlowe," Cooper said. "He..."

Liv shushed Cooper. "Not important right now. Go on, Patrick."

"Okay. The results indicate there's only a forty-four percent chance that Cooper wrote the manuscript that Falwell sold."

Liv's heart sank. She looked over at her client. "Cooper, you have to be absolutely honest with us right now..."

"But wait a minute," Ledeau interrupted. "It gets better."

"Okay."

"There's only a *thirty-five* percent chance that Falwell wrote it." The lawyer gave her a smug look as Liv's mouth dropped open. "Told ya it was interesting."

"Can that be right?" She looked from Ledeau to Cooper. "Did you read the manuscript the publisher sent? Is it the same one you wrote or not?"

Cooper's knee jiggled up and down even faster. "I did read it," he said. He looked a little panicked around the eyes. "It's my story. I swear it is. The plot is exactly the same and so are most of the characters. But all the names have been changed, and Falwell reworked the physical descriptions. He even changed genders of a few of the minor characters. It's my book, but not exactly. It's been rewritten, sentence by sentence, page by page, so that it looks like I wasn't the author. Falwell was too smart to get caught submitting the story just as I wrote it, but I swear it's mine."

"But that doesn't make any sense because according to the author recognition software, there's only a thirty-five percent chance that the person who wrote the contracted manuscript was Mason Falwell."

Liv thought for a moment and asked Ledeau. "You used one of

Falwell's old books for comparison, I assume. Is it possible that his writing style changed significantly in the last five years? Enough to confuse the software?"

Ledeau shook his head. "Not according to my expert witness. I thought of that, too. She says an author's style may change to a certain extent over time, using words with more or fewer syllables or different combinations of words, but the author's use of function words—words like prepositions and conjunctions that give relational meanings between content words—remains relatively stable over time."

Liv thought about the rumors regarding Falwell's alcoholism. "Would cognitive impairment, say through substance abuse, change the author's use of function words?"

"Possibly. We can look into it."

She looked at Ledeau. "What about a third option. Could someone at the publishing company, a trusted editor, for instance, have rewritten it? I mean, if they thought it didn't sound enough like a Falwell novel?"

"Why would they do that?"

"Well, for one thing they stand to make a bundle on a new Mason Falwell book."

"The publisher's adamant that this is an exact copy of Falwell's manuscript. I suppose they could be lying. How about things on your end? Do you have anything solid yet?"

"I have a few new leads that may tie Falwell to the computer glitch that wiped out the files. There are also rumors that Falwell has an alcohol problem." Liv crossed her legs. "As far as motives go, I'd say money is a big possibility. There was a significant divorce settlement with the former wife, and Falwell and Karie purchased a new home together after they were married. There's a second home in South Carolina, and the kids from the first marriage must be getting toward college age. With no new royalties coming in, and a drinking problem affecting his output, he could have been desperate."

Cooper interjected again. "The decrepit old sot can't be that impaired. He was able to rewrite my entire manuscript so that plagiarism software wouldn't pick up on it. I just can't believe he's going to get away with this!" Cooper's knee continued to bounce.

Ledeau threw his friend a disgusted look. "Relax, Cooper. The expert we employed will point out all the similarities in character, plot, theme, and overall structure. My feeling is that we will be able to work out a deal with the publishers and Falwell, regardless of what Ms. Lively does or does not find out. We'll ask for a sizable remuneration."

Cooper paced the room. "That doesn't mean the college will reinstate me, though. I need proof that I was right to accuse Falwell, that I didn't provide false evidence to the honor code committee. I want more than money. My degree is important. My book is important. Writing is what I want to do with my life. This was supposed to be the start of my literary career."

Liv and Ledeau exchanged glances. Liv tried to soothe Cooper. "I promise you, I'm doing everything I can to find out what really happened with your thesis and the Long/Space accounts. This new information is, as Patrick says, interesting. I'll send you an updated report in a few days along with a breakdown of the hours I've logged."

The attorney said, "You do remember that you only get paid if we win this case?"

Liv gave him a tight smile. "I remember. And don't worry. If Falwell deliberately stole Cooper's story, I'll find out about it. There's no such thing as a secret, and I have someone in my crosshairs. Sit tight, boys. I'll be in touch."

Liv exited the building. She had just unlocked the door to her car when inspiration struck. She ran back to Ledeau's office, knocked on the door.

"Forget something?" Ledeau said.

"I was wondering. If I brought you another writing sample would your expert be able to run it through the author recognition software to check for a match? I have a hunch I'd like to test out."

"Sure," Ledeau shrugged. "Want to tell me where you're going with this?"

"Not yet," Liv said. "Like I said, it's just a hunch. Let's wait and see what happens when we run the sample, okay? I should get it to you by five."

"If you say so. I'll give my expert a head's up." Ledeau propped his arm against the door frame and leaned toward her. He had removed his suit jacket. She could see a large sweat-stain under his armpit. "By the way, have you made contact with that boyfriend of yours, Mickelson? I hear the Feds are still looking for him."

"Let's just put it this way, even if I had heard from Rob Mickelson, you wouldn't be on my list of to-calls. Okay?" Liv hitched her bag higher on her arm. "I'll be in touch later about that writing sample."

Ledeau just grinned. "I'll be waiting."

Chapter Thirty-Two

• • • • • • • • • • • • •

Trying to put Ledeau's comment about Rob out of her mind, Liv made a quick call to Professor Orin Calder at the English department and was relieved when he told her he had office hours scheduled for the next hour and a half.

"Listen, do you think you could get me Karie Falwell's MFA program application? No questions asked?"

Calder coughed. "Can you tell me why you want it?"

"No."

"I assume this is to help young Tedeschi."

She said nothing, just tapped her fingers on the steering wheel and waited.

"Okay, I'll do it. Give me half an hour and meet me in my office. That will give me time to get the file from Barbara's cabinet."

"Thanks, professor." Liv pointed her car in the direction of Longfellow College.

She turned on some Puccini, let the music wash away some of the tension in her shoulders. It was hard to believe it was only this morning she'd been having coffee with Ashleigh. In one day she'd discovered a possible connection between Karie Falwell and Justin Pfiester, attempted to speak to Jeremy Crete, argued with her mother, made up with Jasper, and met with Cooper and his lawyer.

No wonder she was exhausted. She needed a glass of wine and a long bubble bath before going to bed early. She'd pick up this file from Calder, drop it off with Ledeau, and head home.

Since she had thirty minutes to spare, she decided to drive past Mason and Karie Falwell's house. Windshield wipers slapping, she signaled right toward Park Street and cut across through Deering Oaks toward the college.

She turned left off Forest Avenue and found the Falwells' residential street. The houses here were late 19th-century, painted in heritage colors, overhung with mature oaks and maples. Wide front porches and white gingerbread trim matched well-kept, if small, fenced lawns.

In the rainy afternoon gloom, the lighted windows and streetlamps cast a golden warmth. Liv pulled the car to the curb a few houses down from the Falwell's quaint, blue Victorian home. The black Jag was parked in the driveway. She switched off the music, slumped lower in her seat, and watched the house for signs of activity.

Liv stared through the rain splattering and running down the windshield. Who really wrote *Hours of the Crossing*? Cooper admitted that the manuscript sent from the publisher was not his original writing. He claimed Falwell took his plot and characters and rewrote the story. On the other hand, the university believed Cooper typed Falwell's novel from handwritten drafts and then claimed the story was his, casting serious aspersions on a respected and important faculty member.

But recognition software didn't lie. It had no ulterior motives. The software should have matched the writing style to either the famous author or his student. Instead, the results were inconclusive on both counts.

Liv stared at the house. Two green, plastic trash cans sat beside the curb waiting to be picked up the following morning, and daffodils and tulips graced a small garden area at the side of the house. A small, red-handled spade leaned casually against the heritage blue siding as if someone had dashed for cover when the rain started.

Liv could think of only one other person who might have

rewritten Cooper's novel. Someone who had read all of Falwell's work. Someone who knew his voice as well or better than her own. Someone with writing ability and focus and editorial skills. Someone who also stood to gain from the sale of another Mason Falwell book.

Karie Falwell.

Liv watched the house, calculating. She didn't have time to confront the second Mrs. Falwell today, but the sight of the trash cans gave her another idea. You could find out so much about a person by looking through their trash. Notes, letters, statements, receipts. Telephone bills, prescription bottles, alcohol containers. If Falwell was drinking as much as people said, the evidence might be in those trash cans.

Pulling away from the curb, Liv drove around the block to the nearby Hannaford supermarket. She parked at the back of the lot and popped the trunk.

From her emergency clothing stash, Liv gathered a ratty, oversized plaid shirt, a knit cap, and worn-out sneakers. She pulled the shirt over her tee, changed shoes, drew the cap low over her ears. Grabbing a shopping cart left between parking spaces by someone too lazy to wheel it to the nearest carrell, Liv crumpled her emergency blanket, a gallon of water, a tarp, and several reusable shopping bags into the cart to look like a pile of personal belongings.

She pushed the cart to the end of the lot, turned onto the sidewalk, and headed back toward the Falwell house through the rain. She hoped no one would give more than a cursory, embarrassed glance at what appeared to be just one of Portland's homeless making her way down the street.

Keeping her head low and her shoulders stooped, Liv approached the trashcans at the end of Mason and Karie Falwell's driveway. A woman holding a large umbrella and walking two chihuahuas spotted her, gave a wide-eyed, panicked stare, and crossed the street to avoid contact. Liv stopped, knelt down to fumble with the lace on one of her ragged sneakers.

This was risky as hell, she thought, but the thrill seeker in her loved this part of her job. Perspiration prickled her scalp beneath the knit hat. She shuffled along the sidewalk and rolled her cart to some nearby recycling containers belonging to the Falwell's neighbors. Mumbling loudly, she grabbed a cardboard cereal box and shook it before placing it in her cart.

She glanced over her shoulder. The woman with the dogs scurried to the end of the street and disappeared. Liv ducked her head and grinned. The street was empty once again. She was good to go.

Reaching the Falwell's driveway and their trash containers, Liv took another surreptitious look around and popped the tops off the plastic bins. She grabbed the two bags, threw them into the cart, and skedaddled down the street as quickly as she could, adrenaline making her fingertips tingle.

She half expected Karie or Mason to come running out the door, demanding to know what she thought she was doing with their trash bags. There was also the possibility they had spotted her from inside the house and called the police. It wasn't a felony to pick up trash, but she didn't have time to deal with answering a bunch of uncomfortable questions. She'd told Calder she'd be at his office at four o'clock, and it was already three forty-five.

She wheeled the cart back to the Hannaford parking lot. Only after depositing the bags into the trunk of her car, tossing the old clothes on top of them, and getting back into the driver's seat did her heart-rate return to normal. She turned the key in the ignition, put the car into drive, and pulled out of the lot.

● ● ● ● ●

Calder looked up from some papers, a smile glinting beneath his Papa Hemingway mustache. He reached into a drawer and waved a file folder. "Olivia Lively. Here you are. I was able to procure what you needed, though there were some very pointed questions asked.

Barbara Kimble was extremely suspicious, and I had to promise her that this folder would be returned first thing in the morning." He held out the folder and widened his smile. "You owe me one."

"I do indeed." She raised her eyebrows. "Can I use that photocopier?"

"Oh. Yeah, I guess that makes sense." He let out an embarrassed laugh.

"Thanks. I owe you one. As soon as everything's settled with this case, I'll buy you a beer at the Arrow & Song."

She made the copy, handed the manila folder back to Calder, and went back to her car. With the rain pattering on the windshield, she flipped through the stack of papers. She glanced at Karie Bishop Falwell's MFA application and put it aside. Beneath the application were letters of recommendation from undergraduate professors and a thin manuscript whose original had been held together with a metal paper clip.

She looked at the title page. It was a short story by Karie L. Bishop entitled "Skyline Dreams." Liv lifted the cover sheet and skimmed the body of the piece. She put the stack of papers onto the passenger seat and shifted her car into gear.

Ledeau needed to get this to his expert right away. She called him from the road. "Hey, it's me. I got it. I'm on my way to you. Don't go anywhere."

· · · · ·

Ledeau scanned the short story and let out a low whistle. "Really? You think this will match the manuscript?"

Liv nodded. "I think so. Have your expert run it through the software and let me know how it turns out."

"This doesn't help us prove that Falwell stole Cooper's novel. It would only prove that Karie wrote Mason's book."

"That's true. But Cooper himself admits that the manuscript sent from the publisher is not his original." She paced around the room. "Someone with access to Mason's Long/Space account copied Cooper's manuscript files and rewrote the pages in their own words, changing things here and there. Karie Bishop is a writer. She writes and edits for a living. Let's say she's the one who stole Cooper's original story and edited it enough to fool authorship and plagiarism software."

"Go on."

"It all kinda fits. Mason's too impaired because of his drinking to understand what she's doing. He thinks the new book is a collection of odds and ends, not a brand-new novel. Expecting Cooper will have an understandably poor reaction, Karie realizes she must destroy Mason's notes and emails. I found out today that Karie has old connections to the IT department."

"How did she destroy the files without getting caught?"

"Inside help, for sure. I don't have details yet, but it's probably connected with a malware program called Red Eye. This guy by the name of Jeremy Crete knows something, but he's hiding from me." Liv bit at her thumbnail as she paced.

Ledeau sat on a corner of his desk. "What has you worried, Lively?"

"Something's bugging me. It's still possible that Karie actually wrote the original novel. Maybe she used some of Falwell's notes, or maybe she wrote it all on her own. Either way, Cooper had access to Karie's computer while he was working at the Falwell home. None of his MFA cohorts admits to seeing this manuscript or anything else he was working on all year. Maybe he had writer's block. Maybe he was going through a mental break."

"That's stone-cold, Lively. Cooper's your client!"

"I'm just covering all the bases. He could have found the manuscript while working at the Falwell house, retyped it and printed it out, and then arranged with someone in the IT department to sabotage the files. Again, Crete comes to mind. They were both in the MFA program. Maybe they had a deal to split the royalties or something."

"You don't really think that, do you?"

Liv shrugged. "I'm keeping an open mind. Once we find out who arranged to have those computer accounts deleted, we'll know for sure."

"The novel is set for publication in a few months. We don't have a lot of time."

"I'll keep digging. How are things going on the legal end with the publisher and the college, by the way?"

Ledeau shrugged. "Let's just say they're both concerned about a possible scandal. They aren't producing any longhand manuscript of Falwell's, which leads me to believe they don't have it. Which is saying something."

"Again. Cooper could have stolen Mason's notebooks, destroyed them."

"If I were their legal counsel, that's the tack I'd take. As it is, I think we can get them to the negotiating table if you can find me some proof, any proof, that Cooper was the original creator of this story."

Liv nodded. "Okay, counselor. I won't take up any more of your time. I have things to do and people to spy on."

"Want to get a quick drink before you do your Nancy Drew act? It's five post meridiem, and on my clock, that's martini hour. I know a bartender who makes them ice-cold, smooth, and three-olived."

Liv grinned. "When this thing is over, I'll take you up on that offer, but right now I'm beat. Goodnight, counselor."

Chapter Thirty-Three

• • • • • • • • • • • •

L iv woke the next morning refreshed. She'd followed through on her plans for a quiet evening, opted for chamomile tea instead of wine, and fell asleep as soon as she closed her eyes.

After a satisfying seven-mile run, she showered, drank a cup of coffee, and read that morning's *Press Herald*, scanning the headlines for any news about Rob. She hadn't noticed Agent Snow's SUV in a couple of days. Her involvement with Rob and now this knowledge about his criminal activities gnawed at her. She wanted him behind bars or out of the country where she never had to think about him again.

Pushing her ex from her mind, she folded the paper. Better keep her mind on her work, she thought. She toyed with the handle of her mug, stared out the window, planned her next moves regarding Jeremy Crete.

Fifteen minutes later, she prepared for a morning of surveillance work. She dressed in black leggings, a black hoodie, and a pair of sturdy, black leather Doc Martens. She packed granola bars, cheese sticks, and a couple of apples into a black, leather bag. Snacks staved off hunger and boredom in equal measure. She also brought a Thermos of water, her binoculars, and a camera with a zoom lens.

Surveillance gear organized, she drove to her office. She popped the trunk of her car, grabbed the trash she'd liberated from Falwell's house, and dropped them into her office. The odor of ripe banana and curdling milk seeped from the plastic.

If anyone thought her job was glamorous, Liv thought, making a face, they should see her now.

At least the weather was decent. The sun played hide and seek behind puffy clouds, and temps were forecasted to be in the low sixties. Liv made good time to Crete's sad-looking rental house and was happy to see his car in the driveway. She parked diagonally across the street where she could keep an eye on both the front and side doors of the brown cape.

Someone had raked the lawn, she noticed, and there were no newspapers or piles of mail cluttering the steps. Must have been Crete, she thought. Certainly not Lizard-Boy. She adjusted the rearview mirror, popped some gum into her mouth, and plugged her phone into the sound system. Choosing a recording of Mozart concertos, she slouched down to wait.

An hour and a half went by. Liv yawned, stretched her arms, took a swig of water, and chomped on an apple. Surveillance was not all it was cracked up to be. It's not like the movies where you only saw the exciting bits when the targets actually left the house and did something.

She decided to give herself another two hours and then call it a day.

Just before noon, a side door opened. Jeremy Crete stepped out and headed toward his car. Liv started her car, pulled up to the opposite curb, and blocked him in the driveway.

Jeremy looked startled, his face blank, but he didn't run back to the house.

"Hello, Jeremy," Liv said. "It's time we had another talk."

"I have nothing to say to you," Crete said, face stony. "Get away from my driveway, or I'll call the police."

Liv crossed her arms. "Okay. Call the police. We'll have a nice little discussion about Red Eye."

Jeremy's face went pale. "What do you know about that?"

"I know enough. The feds will know more. I'm acquainted with an FBI agent who will be most interested to hear about you and Dustin's little IT project."

Jeremy swallowed, his large Adam's apple bobbing in his long, thin neck. "Right now, you and Pfiester would be equally under suspicion, but if you cooperate, tell me what you know..."

She let the implication for immunity dangle there like a rope thrown to a man who had broken through the ice on a frozen, deep-water lake in January. *Grab it, Jeremy,* she thought. *Grab that rope.*

Jeremy bowed his head, took a deep breath, and put his hands in the front pockets of his faded blue jeans. When he looked up, his eyes were resigned. "Okay," he said. "I'm tired of this crap. What do you want to know?"

· · · · ·

"I knew there was something fishy going on with Tedeschi's and Falwell's Long/Space accounts from the beginning, and the stink that was radiating off Dustin Pfiester reeked of week-old trout, if you get my drift." Jeremy took a pull on his cigarette and blew the smoke over his head where it hung, fog-like, near the glowing fluorescent coil of the overhead kitchen light.

With her index finger, Liv pushed her digital recorder closer to Jeremy. "That's very poetic, Mr. Crete, but for our purposes can you be a little more specific? What made you think Pfiester was involved in those accounts?"

"The weekend the system crashed, I drove over to campus. Early. Like around two in the morning early. No one was scheduled to work in IT until noon, and Gus—my roommate-—had his bandmates here at the house and some chicks that like to hang around the band, a few groupies. They were partying. I couldn't sleep, so I thought I'd go over to campus and type up some of my new poems and send them to my advisor. I write poetry longhand, but the work needs to be submitted as a document. I guess you probably know that."

"Yes, I gathered as much. Keep on talking."

Jeremy sighed. "So it was two in the morning, two-fifteen maybe, when I pulled into the Danforth parking lot. I noticed Dustin's car there and a black Jaguar I didn't recognize. I thought that was weird because no one parks in that lot overnight. I let myself into the building with my key and headed downstairs. The door to the IT department was open, but the main room was dark. I slipped in. Dustin's office was the only space lit, and I was surprised to see him with Karie Falwell."

"Did you know who she was?"

"All of us in the writing program know who Karie Falwell is. Anyway, Dustin was pointing to something on the computer. Karie was leaning against the back of his chair. Her hands were on his shoulders. They looked intimate, I guess you'd say."

Liv nodded. "What did you do?"

"I tried to get out of there without attracting their attention." Jeremy's pale, lashless eyes blinked behind his glasses. "I'm not the most graceful person in the world. I tried backing out of the room and ended up tripping over my own feet. I fell against the door, slamming it shut. Dustin and Karie heard the door, looked up, and saw me sprawled on the floor. I stood up. I turned on the main lights and waved at them. They looked at each other, I saw their lips moving, and then Karie picked up her purse, left Dustin's office, brushed past me with a snotty look on her face, and left."

"Did you ask Dustin why they were there so late at night?"

Jeremy took another long drag on his cigarette. "Dustin called me into the office. He told me that the Long/Space system had crashed. When I asked him when he found out about it, he told me this bullshit story about how he and Mason and Karie were dining together at the Falwell house, enjoying after-dinner brandies or whatever, like I'm supposed to believe he and Mason Falwell are friends, when calls started coming in on his work cell. Dustin said that he headed over here to the department to take a look and asked Karie to come along because she used to work in IT back in the day and thought she could help."

Tilting on the back legs of his kitchen chair, Jeremy gave a short, scoffing laugh. "It was b.s., of course, but I went along with it. What do I care if the boss is making it with some faculty wife at the office in the wee hours of the morning? He was telling the truth about the system crash, though. I stuck around for a while, working on getting things rebooted. Went home around six. I came back in that afternoon along with several other staff members. By Tuesday morning most of the accounts were recovered, the system was working properly, and I figured that was that.

"But?"

"But on Tuesday afternoon I got a call from Cooper Tedeschi saying his email was still down. We knew each other from the program, so it made sense that he would contact me. I told him that the problem was fixed, and he started going off on me about how he still couldn't get into his files. I told him to relax, and that I'd look into it. That's when I discovered his account had been hit with encryption malware called Red Eye."

Liv nodded. "When did you start to suspect Dustin and Karie had something to do with Falwell and Tedeschi's files being infected with this virus?"

Crete flicked his cigarette ash into a small, floral dish on the table. "When I found out Mason Falwell's account was also infected. By this time, Tedeschi had already accused Falwell of stealing his manuscript. The encryption on both their accounts ensured the files shared between Tedeschi and Mason could not be used to prove original authorship. I also knew that Tedeschi was telling the truth about his manuscript."

"How?"

Crete hesitated.

"Come on, Jeremy. I need the whole story, or I can't promise you'll be protected when this whole thing goes down." Liv leaned forward. "I want to help you, but I can't do that unless you tell me everything you know."

Hand shaking slightly as he lifted the cigarette to his mouth, Jeremy caved. "Okay, okay. I read the files before they were infected."

"For the record, you're saying you hacked into Tedeschi and Falwell's files prior to the crash? Why?"

"It was just something to do to pass the time, all right?" Jeremy blew a stream of smoke above his head. "I read the work of most of the MFA candidates, checking out the competition. Anyone would do that, given the opportunity. Tedeschi's novel was pretty good. A page-turner. Decent literary quality. Probably good commercial fiction quality. The kind that makes money. Anyway, Falwell was tough on him, but encouraging, gave him a lot of notes."

"What did you do when you heard about Cooper's accusations?"

Crete blew streams of smoke through his nose. "Right, so I'm thinking Tedeschi will have this bright future in front of him while I toil away in poetic obscurity when Falwell suddenly announces a new book that sounds suspiciously like Tedeschi's. Cooper, naturally, claims the work is his. I knew he was telling the truth, but I didn't want to get involved. I figured Cooper would produce his manuscript with Falwell's edits and that would be that."

"But when the accounts were encrypted…"

Crete nodded. "I put two and two together. Karie and Dustin in here the night of the crash. Tedeschi and Falwell's files the only accounts affected by this Red Eye virus on the same night." He took another long drag on his cigarette before stubbing it out in the dish. "Anyway, it seemed pretty obvious to me that Mason Falwell had much to gain from that malware infection. And Tedeschi much to lose."

"You think Karie Falwell and Dustin Pfiester deliberately infected Cooper and Mason's files in order to cover up evidence that would prove Cooper wrote the manuscript being published as *Hours of the Crossing*. Are you willing to testify to that?"

"I just did." He nodded at the recorder. "Yes."

"Thank you." Liv inclined her head. "So, once you suspected the Falwells and Dustin of sabotaging the account, did you confront Pfiester?"

Jeremy shook his head. "No way. I wanted to finish my degree and get out of here. I felt bad for Tedeschi, but this was way out of my league. Pfiester was already suspicious of me. He started acting weird, and then he brought me on board to try to 'fix' the Falwell and Tedeschi accounts, saying he'd pay me extra. Basically, I knew it was a buy-out for my silence."

"And you agreed?"

"Yes. Look, Pfiester knows stuff. About me. About everyone who works in IT. There was always the implied threat that if I said anything, anything at all, Pfiester would make sure I'd regret it. And then he said, 'If I go down for this, you're going to go with me.' I asked him what he meant. He just shrugged and said not to talk to anyone about Red Eye."

Liv squinted. "Do you think he purchased the malware somehow and installed it on Falwell and Tedeschi's accounts?"

Jeremy caught her gaze and looked like he was going to be sick. "It goes deeper than that."

"How deep?"

"A year ago he asked me for some help with coding. Said he was working on a security program for the system. When I was looking at Falwell and Tedeschi's accounts, I recognized some of that coding." Jeremy reached for another cigarette. "I think Pfiester is the creator of Red Eye."

Chapter Thirty-Four

• • • • • • • • • • • • • •

After thanking Jeremy for sharing the truth and getting him to promise to go with her to the police within the next couple of days to tell them what he knew about the Red Eye malware, Liv called Cooper and Ledeau and asked to meet with them at her office.

They arrived at Liv's office just after noon, meeting in the parking lot. Liv led them into the building and unlocked the door to her office. A blast of noxious fumes hit them as the door swung open.

"What is that god-awful stench?" Ledeau said, taking a chair across from Liv's desk. "Smells like a waste treatment plant in here!"

Liv's face flushed with embarrassment. The Falwell's trash. After more than three hours in a room warmed by the sun streaming through the window, the breakdown of the garbage inside the bags had accelerated. The stench was almost unbearable.

"Sorry about that," Liv said, crossing the room. Let me open the window." She was beginning to regret her impulsive decision to pilfer Mason Falwell's weekly garbage. Chances were, there was nothing to be found in those bags, and now that Jeremy Crete had verified Cooper's story, going through them was probably not necessary.

All she'd managed to do was stink up her office.

She pushed the sash up as far as it would go, strode behind

her desk, and hefted the two bags of trash in either hand. "I'll be right back."

"Don't you have a scented candle you can light or something?" Ledeau waved a hand around in front of his scrunched-up nose.

"Just hang your head out the window if you are such a wuss. I'll see if there's any deodorizer spray in the restroom."

Ledeau ignored the head-out-the-window idea, and instead crossed one ankle over his knee. "Do what you have to do," he grinned at Liv. "We'll just sit here and wait with bated breath—literally—for your return."

"Stuff it, Ledeau," Liv said, her voice cheerful. She jogged outside with the bags, and tossed them beside the metal trash container situated in the back of the long, industrial building. Accumulated pieces of newspapers, soda bottles, and other debris had been snagged in the dead remains of last year's weeds which managed to grow in a strip of thin, poor soil next to the parking lot.

The waste management company that serviced the building was not scheduled to pick up the garbage today, she knew. The bags would be perfectly safe—and less noxious—outside until she found time to sift through them. If she decided to sift through them.

Liv returned to her office, sat down behind her desk, and crossed her legs. They looked at her, attentive and hopeful. This was definitely one of the better parts of her job.

"So," she said. "Let me share with you what I uncovered today."

By the time she was done telling her story, Cooper, who had been under considerable strain the past few months, was crying. He covered his face with his hands. "I can't believe it. I can't believe it."

Patrick passed Cooper a handkerchief and thumped him on the back. "Pull yourself together, Coop." He scrunched his eyebrows together and looked at Liv. "Crete's testimony's recorded?"

"Yes. I will type up a full report for you. If this goes to court, Crete will be able to testify that Cooper wrote the novel. There's no physical evidence, but his version of the events fits what Cooper's claiming."

"Crete said that Karie was there the night the files were encrypted? He thinks they were working together to cover up Mason's plagiarism?"

"Right. But that's just conjecture. All we know for sure is that Pfiester messed with the accounts. For your purposes, Crete can verify that Cooper wrote the original manuscript and Mason acknowledged that authorship by posting a critique on the work. It follows that Mason, through Karie, hired Pfiester to destroy the edited manuscript and email files, but we can't be sure at this point. I'll talk to Dustin again, see if he's a little more willing to talk now that Crete has implicated him.

She didn't say that it was probably only a matter of time before Dustin Pfiester was in custody for creating the Red Eye encryption malware. Liv wondered if Pfiester merely created the code and sold it to another party or if he was actively blackmailing victims for his own financial gain. Either way, he was in deep legal trouble.

Cooper took a deep breath. "Thank you so much, Olivia, for taking my case, for believing my story—or believing it enough to follow through. I… I can't tell you how much this means to me."

He turned to Ledeau. "So now we can go to the college and the publisher, right? They'll have to see I was telling the truth now."

Ledeau nodded. "I'll get on the horn and set up some meetings. We have your copy of your original manuscript and the Falwell manuscript from the publisher. Our expert will outline the similarities in tone, character, plot, theme, and structure. And now with Crete's testimony, it's clear from Falwell's emails that he knew full well that you were the creator of that story. I'm confident that you will be compensated by the publisher. Getting the college to reinstate you might be a bit trickier, but perhaps the threat of a lawsuit—and the publicity that would go along with it—might swing things in your favor."

Cooper's eyes watered again. "It's been such a nightmare."

Liv looked at the time. It was already two o'clock. She had a mani/pedi appointment in twenty minutes and then her big dinner date with Jasper.

"Okay, boys," she said, standing. "I hate to cut the celebration short, but we all have more work to do on this. I'll call you with any new developments. And, oh!" Liv let out a startled gasp as Cooper came around the desk and gave her a fierce hug. "Thank you," he mumbled into her shoulder.

Panic engulfing her, she resisted maneuvering him into a choke-hold and instead patted his back. "You're welcome. Now get out of here." She grabbed him by the shoulders, turned him around, and gave him a little push toward the door.

"I'll talk to you later," she said to Ledeau. "And stop smiling at me like that."

He tilted his head. "I wouldn't have taken you for a woman who was afraid of a little physical affection. Tedeschi's a good guy. He's just impulsive and passionate. Nothing to be nervous about."

She scowled. "Who says I'm nervous? I just don't like people invading my personal space, that's all."

"Touchy, touchy." He headed toward the door. "Keep me posted about Pfiester, though, and Lively? Impressive work today."

"Thanks, counselor. Just remember that when you get my bill."

Chapter Thirty-Five

• • • • • • • • • • • • • •

Her date with Jasper could not be going better.
"That dinner was incredible." Liv looked back at him as he helped her with her coat. "Thank you."

He ran his hands down her arms swathed now in luscious, antique gold and brown brocade against the chilly evening air coming off the waterfront. "You're incredible," he said. "I couldn't keep my eyes off you all night."

Wow, he was playing this night by the book. She grinned at him. "Aren't you the charmer?"

"I've been told." They stepped together along a brick sidewalk, bumped with frost heaves. Rustic streetlamps cast cones of golden light onto the narrow, cobblestone street, one of several in Portland's historic Old Port district.

Liv tiptoed along the uneven bricks, careful in her designer shoes. She didn't want to break a heel. Her coat was vintage, mid-calf with large embroidered peonies along the hem and a fox collar. While she didn't exactly approve of fur, the coat was 1920s, passed down from her grandmother. It had been Nanna's mother's coat, impeccably preserved, and she enjoyed the sensual tickle against her chin.

"I'll have to write a five-star review on Yelp," she said. "I mean, that salmon was excellent. And those little fingerling potatoes. Yummy!" She jabbered on about the meal as they walked toward his car, a long three blocks away. He let her talk, just kept that steady hand on her arm, giving her balance, something to hold onto. "Do you think we should have had dessert? I'm so full, but we could have shared."

She was nervous, she realized. A good kind of nervous.

They'd talked about their workdays—a successful quadruple bypass for him, and the latest developments in the case. She'd enjoyed the way he looked at her, the confident gestures, the flirtatious smiles.

Laughing at some silly thing he said over glasses of champagne and lovely, briny oysters, she realized how elegant and desirable she felt. At one point, he held her hand across the table and looked into her eyes. His pupils opened, darkened, making her breath catch and her cheek flush. That look held an unmistakable promise. She'd nearly fallen out of her seat.

She'd forgotten real dating could be like this. In fact, had it ever been like this? She couldn't remember.

With Rob, she'd grown used to sneaking off to a hotel room for clandestine sex and room service. That had been fun, too, but she understood what her mother and Ashleigh had been trying to tell her. Nice didn't necessarily mean boring. Steady didn't spell dull. On Jasper, steady looked very, very sexy.

The navy suit, white shirt, and fancy tie gave him a refined elegance. The two of them looked good together, she thought. Like they matched. Damn her mother for being right.

A block from his car, Jasper smiled down at her. "Ready for a nightcap?"

She looked at him from beneath her lashes. "I'm ready for everything."

He scanned the quiet street, lasered in on something to their left. "Well, in that case…"

She gasped when he pulled her into a narrow alleyway between two buildings.

The shadows partially hid them as he backed her against the rough, brick wall, pinned her hips with his strong hands. She

212 · SHELLEY BURBANK

opened her mouth to speak, but he kissed her and there were no words.

"Oh my!" A shocked female cry from the street interrupted their dalliance.

Liv and Jasper looked over. An older man and women, well-dressed and embarrassed, hustled away. Jasper looked at Liv, and they both laughed.

"I think you better take me to your place and show me your high school basketball trophies," Liv said. She ran her hand down his shirt, felt his chest rise and fall. She felt his heart pounding fast beneath her palm. "I hear you were a star or something."

His hand fell away from her, and her gauzy skirt settled back into place. "Give me a second," he said. She let out a knowing laugh, let her hand graze. He grabbed her wrist, growled, "Stop that or we'll never get out of this alley."

"Hey, it was your idea, Doc." She laughed softly again and stepped away, felt to make sure grandmother's emeralds were still safe in her ears. They were. She began walking up the street, squealed when he ran up behind her and grabbed her around the waist.

"I can't wait to get you home," he whispered in her ear before taking her hand and walking fast toward the car.

She trotted, breathless, in her heels. "Hey, watch out for the shoes!"

He bent down, put an arm under her knees, swung her up. "Here we go," he said. "Can't have you twisting an ankle. Why do you women wear those things?"

"Because men like how our legs look in them."

"True. Keep them on later."

•   •   •   •   •

Sweaty and sated, Liv flung an arm across Jasper's stomach and kissed his chest. She'd lost the shoes—and everything else—somewhere between the door and the bed.

She rolled away from him and onto her back. Eyes closed and arms flung over his head, Jasper muttered, "Where'd you go?"

"Nowhere. I'm right here."

"Mmmm, not close enough." He turned, nuzzled into her neck, put his arm around her waist.

She looked at the window across from his bed. Long, white curtains fluttered in the slight current seeping through the bottom of the window. The sleeping loft was spare, masculine, with its gray walls, reclaimed wood bedframe, blankets and coverlet in grays and taupe. A large oceanscape was the only art on the wall, and the loft overlooked the downstairs living and kitchen space. It showed a designer's touch in the granite countertop, glass tiles in the bathroom, the modern fixtures.

He really did have a trophy case in the living room—along with a wall of books and Horace, the skeleton, propped up in the corner wearing a bow-tie around his neckbone.

She turned so they were face to face. His eyes opened, half-lidded. "Hi, he said. He reached up and touched her cheek, ran his fingers along her jaw.

"Hi." She looked into his eyes as his fingers followed the curve of her ear, ran though the short layers of her hair, skimmed down the length of her neck.

"What are you thinking?"

"Not much when you do that." She grabbed his wandering hand. "Can I ask you something?"

"Sure," he said. "Anything."

"Were you really going to call me? When I came to see you at the hospital yesterday, you said you were going to call me. Is that true?"

He brushed his lips against hers. "Yes. Are you surprised? I'd be an idiot to let you go just because you aren't looking for a serious relationship right now. We'll wait and see how it goes. We'll date each other. Date other people. Play it by ear."

"And if we do get serious with someone else?"

"We'll talk about it. We'll keep things simple and open and honest."

"Okay." She played with his fingers. "Have you ever been married?"

"No. I came close once. Right after med school. She was a medical librarian. Older. Divorced."

"What happened?"

He rolled over on his back again, looked up at the ceiling. "She went back to her former husband. There were kids involved."

"That must have been difficult." She took a deep breath, jumped in. "I sort of know what that's like, to be the person on the outside of a marriage. Of course, in my case, the guy was still married."

She waited, wondering how he'd react to this confession.

He kept looking at the ceiling. A second went by. Two. "Are you still involved with him? Is that why you didn't want to get into a relationship with me?"

Even though his voice was even, nonchalant, she didn't buy it.

"No. We're done. He wasn't a good guy, and I was foolish to trust him. He told me he was getting a divorce. She'd been cheating on him, so I believed him, but after a few months I should have known."

She rolled over on her back, too. "It gets worse. I found out he's under investigation for mortgage fraud. The FBI is looking for him, and it's likely he left the country. I broke things off right before I met you. And then he disappeared. My parents don't know anything about him, so please don't blame them for setting you up with me."

He turned his head. "Don't worry, Olivia. I'm not going to judge you." He popped out of bed. "Do you want some water? I'm feeling a little dehydrated."

"No. I'm fine."

He bent down and gave her a quick kiss. "Okay, I'll be right back."

She smiled at him. "Sure."

Her smile faded. She got out of bed, pulled the coverlet around her like a shroud, padded over to the window. It overlooked some old brick warehouses and across the channel to South Portland. She heard him open the refrigerator door downstairs, the clink of glassware, the faucet running. Pensive, she hugged herself and looked out at the quarter moon just skimming the top of the nearest building. She thought about the confession she'd gotten out of Jeremy Crete that afternoon, about Cooper's happiness and Ledeau's compliment on her work.

Being with Jasper tonight felt like a reward for her hard work, a redirection of a relationship that had veered off-course into something too confining for her peace of mind. She needed her independence and her space. She needed to be able to come and go as she pleased without worrying about a man's expectations, social obligations, needs. Her work was her focus. Her sex life was secondary to that. Love? An unnecessary complication.

She pulled the coverlet closer. Jasper wanted honesty, so why did she feel ashamed telling him about her past? It was good that he knew, she told herself. She wasn't doctor's wife material. Sooner or later he'd find someone who was. In the meantime, there was this. Good food, flirtatious banter, hot and sweaty sex.

She heard Jasper coming back up the stairs, so she went back to his bed. She propped herself up on her elbow, trailed a hand down her hip and to her thigh. "Hey, Doc," she said, giving him a seductive smile. "Ready for round three?"

His eyes, intent and smoldering, traveled the length of her. He took a long drink, head tipped back, throat working. A few drops of water fell to his chest. He set the water glass on his bedside, got onto his knees on the mattress, flipped her over on her belly.

"Now I am," he said, hands gliding over her skin, warm lips placing perfectly-spaced kisses down her spine.

Chapter Thirty-Six

• • • • • • • • • • • • •

"Hey, gorgeous."

Liv opened one eye as Jasper bent over the bed and kissed the side of her neck. She smelled cologne and toothpaste and the starch from his shirt. "Hey, Doc." She pulled the sheet with her as she rolled onto her back, languid from sex and sleep. "What time is it? Feels early."

He placed a kiss on her mouth. She kept her lips clamped shut. Some people might be okay with morning breath, but she thought it was gross. Plus unfair because he'd already brushed his teeth.

"It's seven-forty-five. I'm supposed to be at the hospital at eight. Can I give you a ride home?"

"No, I don't want to make you late. I'll just call a cab."

He sat down, and the mattress tilted. "All day I'm going to be thinking about the way you look right now, rumpled and sleepy and sexy." He ran a hand up her arm, raising goosebumps. "I had a really good time last night."

He kissed her again. "You don't need to hurry home. Hang out here as long as you want. Take a shower. There's plenty of clean towels. Have some coffee. Toast. Eggs. Feel free to snoop in all my drawers. I have nothing to hide. Wouldn't be able to from a crack investigator like yourself."

She laughed and slapped his arm. "I wouldn't do that. Go save some lives."

When he was gone, she picked up his shirt from the night before and put it on. It smelled like him and hung halfway to her knees. She buttoned it, rolled up the sleeves, and walked down the stairs noticing the way tiny muscles in her legs ached after the previous night's romp.

Humming Vivaldi, she rooted around in his cupboard for coffee pods and a cup, pressed the button on the machine to get the water heated. The kitchen, tucked under the loft bedroom, gleamed with stainless steel, white cabinetry, and reclaimed hardwood flooring, teak maybe. She set the cup under the machine's dispenser, pressed another button, and watched the coffee spurt and pour.

Bringing the mug to her lips, she inhaled the steam, sipped, and wandered to the living room area. The ceiling, crossed with exposed beams and pipes, soared two stories. Tall windows in the exposed brick wall attested to the building's former life as some kind of factory. A large, gray sectional couch curved around a glass coffee table.

She walked along the bookshelf, trailing her hand across the spines. Many of the books were old, leatherbound and cloth, in very good condition. She wondered if the decorator had bought them by the pound or if Jasper had commissioned certain volumes. There was a set of old anatomy books, she noticed, and the Time-Life Books *Mysteries of the Unknown*, a series of slim, dark-spined hardcovers.

She pulled out the UFO volume, sat down at the island in the kitchen, flipped through the pages while she drank her coffee. Her phone buzzed in the pocket of her coat. It had been thrown carelessly over the back of the couch the night before, her dress next to it. Her shoes, however, were still upstairs next to Jasper's bed along with her silk stockings.

Setting the cup on the counter, she walked to the couch, pulled the phone from the pocket. Looking at the caller, she grinned. "Hi, Ashleigh. You'll never believe where I am right now."

"Turn on the news." Ashleigh's voice was tight, tense.

The smile faded from Liv's face. "What's going on?"

"Just turn it on. Channel Eleven. Call me back."

Liv looked around for the remote, pushed the power button, growled in frustration as she figured out how the controls worked. Finally she was able to get the local channel and pressed the volume button. A commercial ended, and the familiar face of the morning newscaster looked up and stared into the camera. Behind her, a woman's image popped up in a square, floating in the upper right corner of the screen.

"Federal authorities have arrested Gina Mickelson of Portland on charges related to mortgage fraud," the newscaster read from her teleprompter, her plum lipsticked mouth upturned at the corners. "The Federal Bureau of Investigation made the announcement of Mickelson's arrest at a press conference just minutes ago."

Liv thought, *what about Rob?* She leaned forward gripping the remote which shook in her hand.

The screen changed, showing FBI Agent Colin Snow speaking into microphones at a podium set up outside the Portland courthouse. "We have apprehended several suspects in this case," he said. "But we are still looking for Robert Mickelson who may be armed and dangerous. If anyone has any information regarding his whereabouts, we have set up a confidential tip line for listeners and viewers to share information." A number appeared on the bottom of the screen.

Liv bit her thumbnail as the video switched back to the news studio.

"Robert Mickelson is the husband of Gina Mickelson. Both individuals are charged with twelve counts of mortgage fraud. The FBI alleges that over the past year, Robert and Gina Mickelson and their accomplices knowingly participated in a scheme to defraud the Island Bay Savings & Loan bank where Robert Mickelson is employed as the commercial loan manager."

The newscaster swung in her seat to look into a different camera, a wider angle this time revealing her male counterpart sitting beside her. "Tom, from what we know, Gina Mickelson is affiliated with Germaine & Marks Realty, a company which specializes in commercial properties. Allegedly, loan applications were completed by Gina Mickelson on behalf of several fictitious businesses. Robert Mickelson approved the loans, and when the loans closed, the couple benefited financially from checks made out to Germaine & Marks Realty, Pewter Mortgage Company, and several dummy businesses."

"Hard to believe something like this was happening right here in Portland, Neva. Do we have any idea of the exact charges they are facing?"

"Yes, Tom. From what we've learned the couple is being charged with fraud associated with stolen identities, fictitious bank accounts, and multiple counts of wire fraud, each of which carries a maximum penalty of a $200,000 fine and twenty years imprisonment."

The camera zoomed in on Neva who talked to the viewers again. "Robert Mickelson is still at large. Anyone with information regarding his whereabouts should contact local police or call the FBI hotline. And now, let's go to Stefan to talk about this spring weather!"

Liv pointed the remote and pressed the power button. The television screen went black. Liv stared at the dark screen. So, Snow had arrested Gina.

She'd known it would only be a matter of time, but still, hearing it on the news came as a shock. Rob hadn't been caught yet. The FBI must be getting desperate since they were appealing to the public and setting up hotlines.

She threw the remote onto the couch, grabbed her phone, pressed Ashleigh's number.

"Omigod, Liv. How are you doing?"

"I'm shaken." She went back to the kitchen, picked up her coffee, stuck it in the microwave. "I just want this to be over. You'd think they would have captured him by now. I can't believe they are saying he's armed and dangerous. That doesn't sound like Rob. Is it awful that I don't even care if he gets away? If he ends up living the life somewhere in the Caribbean? I just want him gone."

"It's not awful. It's an authentic human reaction to stress. Are you worried that your name will get dragged into this somehow?"

"No. I don't know. Maybe? I've spoken to the FBI a couple of times, and I know they are keeping an eye on me, which is okay. I had a relationship with him, but I didn't know anything about his criminal activities. I gave him his files, and I never let him use my identification or bank account numbers or anything. The only connection with him that I have left is a box of momentos, notes and cards and stuff like that." She bit her lip. "And the Lakshmi."

"Lakshmi? What's that?"

"Oh, just this statue he brought back with him from some business trip. It's a Hindu goddess. Very pretty. The last time I saw Rob he asked me to send it to him. I did, but the courier service returned it to me as undeliverable, so I put it away. It's not valuable or anything. I think he was just being a jerk about it."

"Sounds like he has bigger things to worry about than a souvenir."

"Yeah." The microwave dinged. Liv opened the door and pulled out the mug of coffee. "So, on a more positive note, guess where I am standing right now?" She waited a beat. "Dr. Hottie's kitchen. Practically naked."

She pulled the phone away from her ear as Ashleigh let out a piercing shriek. "I knew it! I want to hear all the details. But not now. I have a parent-teacher conference in ten minutes. You're going to be at the auxiliary's Spring Fling tonight, right? I'll see you then."

"Okay, but…"

"This is excellent news, Livs." She heard voices in the background. "Gotta go. Love you. Talk later. Byeeeee!"

Chapter Thirty-Seven

• • • • • • • • • • • • • •

The Mowat-Seavey Mansion, built in the 1840s for a wealthy Portland businessman, Frederick Mowat, swarmed with the city's well-heeled citizens attending the Sharon Medical Center Women's Auxiliary Spring-Fling, a fundraising event that Liv's mother had chaired for the past six years.

The mansion, once a private residence, was now a favorite event venue. From the columned entrance overhung by a small balcony to the stunning ballroom with tall windows, flowing curtains, and tasteful ivory-paneled walls, the house called to mind a more gracious era.

Liv parked her car in the lot behind the building and made her way around the house via a brick walkway lined with hyacinths, tulips, and daffodils. To please her mother, she'd worn an embroidered silk organza sheath in bright yellow. It was form-fitting enough to make Liv feel sexy, but conservative enough to pass her mother's suitability radar. She'd paired the dress with navy sandals, sapphire earrings, and the cutest little navy clutch sprinkled with gold butterflies just big enough to hold her phone, her keys, and lipstick.

As she rounded the corner to the front entrance of the mansion, Liv heard shouting across the street. She glanced over. A small crowd of people had assembled. They carried cardboard signs protesting the hospital merger.

Someone had set up a flimsy barrier of orange cones and yellow tape, and Liv could see two bulky men keeping a sharp eye on the crowd. Security guards, Liv thought, turning her eyes from the protesters and making her way up the steps toward the heavy oak door of the mansion. Over the door, a beautiful stained-glass fan window glowed with light from inside the house, a contrast to the gathering dusk.

Liv was troubled by the protesters. Liv's father agonized over the negotiations with MainePatientCare, an integrated healthcare network that was absorbing and consolidating many small private and community hospitals, like Sharon Medical, around the state.

Staff, understandably, were worried about job cuts and the inevitable changes the network would demand. Patients voiced concern over the quality of care they were likely to receive, scared that their doctors would be let go or, if retained, would be so loaded up with patients that the individualized care they'd come to expect would be a thing of the past.

As a doorman hired for the evening's festivities opened the door for her, Liv glanced back at the protesters who were now chanting. Liv wasn't political. She did, however, worry about her father. He downplayed the controversy, but tonight she realized how much stress the merger was causing the community, the hospital staff, and by extension, her dad.

She turned and stepped through the door.

"Good evening," one of the mansion's staff greeted her as she checked her coat.

"Hello," Liv said. "How long have the protesters been out there?"

The young woman made a face. "Not long. Half an hour or so."

"Okay. Thank you." Liv wondered if anyone had alerted the police. There hadn't been more than fifty people in the crowd, and the security guards seemed to have things under control, but anything could happen.

Finding her place card on the table in the foyer, Liv entered the ballroom and looked around.

This year, Tiffany Lively decided to delight her guests with colorful paper lanterns hung from the ceiling. The rosy reds, jonquil yellows, and lily oranges of the lanterns created a playful atmosphere. Sprays of forsythia frothed out of blue and white vases were placed strategically around the room, while heavy tablecloths of taupe and gold anchored the round tables which were surrounded by delicate cane-backed chairs. There was a hint of the Orient to the decorating, Liv thought, that matched the house. Frederick Mowat had been an importer of goods from all over the world.

Liv spotted her table, wound her way through the guests—stopping now and again to say hello or air-kiss an acquaintance—and waved to her mother who was moving from one clump of people to another, working the room like the professional socialite she was. Tiffany smiled and nodded at her daughter, swiftly appraising and approving Liv's choice of attire.

"Thank god!" Liv huffed, as she sat down next to Ashleigh. "She approves. Hi, Trevor," she said, leaning forward to smile at her best friend's husband who, like Liv, had been dragged to these sorts of events his whole life.

"Nice to see you, Liv," Trevor said, putting a casual arm over Ashleigh's shoulders. "Your mother outdid herself this year. I think the band is playing a string-quartet version of George Michael's 'I Want Your Sex.'"

Liv burst out laughing, while Ashleigh smacked him with her purse. "Be good," she said in a fake-stern voice. "It's Haydn."

Liv looked up at the ceiling. "I have to hand it to Tiffany, though, the lanterns are fun. And you know the food will be divine. My mother agonized over the menu for weeks. Thank you for coming tonight. It really does mean a lot to both my parents. The backlash over this merger has been a strain on both of them."

"Was your mother expecting protesters?" Ashleigh said,

"Neither of my parents mentioned it. All I heard was spring pea soup, lamb chops, and how the florist wasn't sure about forcing enough forsythia to blossom in time," Liv answered. She glanced toward the bar. "I need a drink. Can I get either of you anything?"

"Let me go," said Trevor, standing up. "Champagne, right?"

Ashleigh and Liv watched him as he made his way toward the bar in the corner of the room. "He seems happy," Liv said, turning to her friend. "And you look tired. Are you feeling okay?"

Ashleigh nodded. "Rough week at school," she said. "And all this conception business." She leaned closer. "I'm a couple days late. Trevor is sure I'm pregnant..."

Liv put a hand on her friend's arm and squeezed gently. "Maybe you are. You are never late. Twenty-eight days every single time. Remember how irritated that used to make me? That's great. No wonder he looks so happy!"

"I'm not sure. I don't feel anything except worn out. And, frankly, crampy. But this isn't the time or place to talk about this. We have an appointment in Boston with a specialist tomorrow."

"Well, call me as soon as you know something, okay?"

Ashleigh cast her a grateful smile and nodded. "Okay." Her eyes went beyond Liv, and her smile faded. "Uh-oh. Just to warn you. I think your Dr. Hottie might have just walked in. He's not alone."

"What?" Liv swiveled around. Sure enough, there was Jasper Temple heading her way. Behind him trailed a petite, brown-haired woman Liv recognized. "What's he doing with Wren Osborne?" she whispered, turning back to Ashleigh.

"Who?" Ashleigh whispered, and then looked up at the couple approaching their table.

Jasper and Wren consulted their cards and stopped. "Good evening, Olivia," Jasper said, looking embarrassed. "It looks as if we'll be at the same table tonight."

Tiffany strikes again.

"Hello, Jasper," Liv said, pretending the two of them hadn't set the sheets on fire the previous night. "Hi, Wren. It's nice to see you. It's been ages and ages." Liv beamed at the couple, faking it all the way. "Ashleigh, I don't believe you've met Wren Osborne and Jasper Temple. Jasper and Wren, this is my good friend Ashleigh

Bancroft... oh, and her husband, Trevor, who is arriving with drinks."

Liv repeated the introductions for Trevor's benefit, and everyone smiled and nodded and pretended they didn't feel awkward. "I've known Wren since we took sailing lessons, oh, when was it, Wren? Fourth grade? Fifth?"

"You were in fourth, I was in fifth," Wren said, clasping her tiny hands together and shuddering. "I hated it. Still won't go anywhere near Daddy's boat, no matter how many times he tries to bully me into it." She laughed a little trill of a giggle. "Jasper, have I told you I'm afraid of the water?"

Jasper looked as if he'd rather be working the emergency room graveyard shift rather than sit at the table with Wren on one side and Liv on the other. Liv speared a look at him, raised her eyebrows. He flushed. "I'll get us some drinks, Wren."

Liv picked up her glass of champagne and took a large gulp. She had no reason to be angry. Jealous? Maybe. Angry? No. He'd been clear with her from the start about looking for someone to settle down with. She was the one who insisted on a casual relationship. They'd *both* agreed to date each other and other people, to keep things casual.

She gulped her champagne again. He could have warned her about the dinner tonight, though. He must have known she'd be there.

Jasper returned to the table with two of the evening's signature cocktails, a seasonal concoction called the Bee Sting garnished with a sprig of lavender.

"Thank you, Jassy," Wren said, taking the proffered glass and batting her eyelashes. She turned back to the rest of the group. "Did I tell you? Jassy's agreed to join the board of our darling little museum, as well. He's very interested in promoting the arts. He's agreed to join me on some jaunts to the most special, out-of-the-way galleries along the coast this summer."

Liv choked on her mouthful of champagne. Jassy? He shot Liv

a glance and had the grace to appear embarrassed. Ashleigh gave Liv a sympathetic look. Liv shook her head.

It was going to be a long, long night.

Chapter Thirty-Eight

· · · · · · · · · · · · · ·

A shleigh and Trevor introduced the topic of summer travel, and soon three others joined their table: a couple new to the Portland area and an older man who was a good friend of the Livelys and recently widowed.

Tiffany had placed the widower next to Liv, and she spent most of the evening chatting with him about his horses, his recent trip to Italy, and the new development in downtown Portland that the city council was negotiating.

By the time the dessert plates were cleared and the evening's speaker had finished her presentation on the global water crisis and its effects on health care around the world, Liv was more than ready to get home to the sanctuary of her apartment where she wouldn't have to watch Wren flirt with Jasper.

"Thank you all for spending your evening with us tonight," Tiffany Lively said into the microphone at the end of the evening. "Your continued support of the Sharon Medical Center Women's Auxiliary means we can bring innovative and exciting new programs that enhance the physical and mental well-being of our patients. Recent initiatives include a macrobiotics cooking series, a new weight-loss program for both men and women, one-on-one counseling with a staff nutritionist, and a support group for families of teens who are struggling with depression and self-harm behaviors. On behalf of the Sharon Medical Center Women's Auxiliary, I offer you my sincere appreciation and a wish for your continued health and well-being. Good-night."

Short and sweet, Liv thought, nodding approvingly at her mother who caught her eye as she stepped away from the podium and back to the head table where she and Liv's father were sitting with the guest speaker and some of the bigwigs from the hospital and MainePatientCare.

Liv followed Ashleigh and Trevor to the coat check, said her goodbyes, and stepped out the door of the mansion.

"Ms. Lively! Over here!" she heard a woman's voice say, and then she was blinded by a bright light.

"Move to the left," the woman's voice commanded, and the light shifted off to Liv's side so at least she could see. Liv recognized the speaker now as a correspondent from one of the local news channels. Before she could shield her face and escape back into the building, the correspondent shoved a microphone toward her. Liv grew aware that the light was for the benefit of a cameraman.

"I'm here in Portland with Olivia Lively," the correspondent said, "A few questions. How well do you know FBI suspect Robert Mickelson?"

"Not that well," Liv said, as someone behind her bumped the small of her back, causing her to lurch forward slightly.

The woman shot her a sly look. "We've been told you do know him. Are you aware that Mickelson's wife Gina was arrested yesterday and that he is under suspicion for mortgage fraud and is being sought by federal authorities?"

"Yes," Liv said. "I saw it on the news this morning like everyone else." Liv suddenly had more compassion for celebrities who were routinely hounded by the paparazzi. She attempted to move away from the camera and microphone. "Excuse me, I'm heading home."

"Just a moment," the woman said, blocking her way. Behind her, the protesters breached the makeshift barrier and crossed the street to see what was going on. "Gina Mickelson was released on bail this evening. She indicated to our news crew that you were romantically and professionally involved with her husband just prior to his disappearance, and she suggested that if anyone knew where he was, it would be you. Do you care to comment?"

Liv's heart pounded as the camera swung back in her direction. She tried to catch her breath, to gather her thoughts, but her mind went blank and she couldn't seem to exhale. "No. No comment," she managed to say. She was aware of protesters crowding in, holding up their cell phones and snapping photos. Probably videos as well. Liv wished she could shrink, disappear, anything to get her out of the spotlight and away from the cameras.

The crowd, assuming the news crew was there to cover the protest, began to yell and wave their signs around. Behind Liv, attendees of the fundraiser found their exit blocked by the commotion with the protesters, the news crew, and Liv. She looked around, feeling a wild panic tightening her chest. Everywhere she looked, eyes were on her. People crowded and jostled. She almost lost her footing and stumbled, but somehow remained upright. She spotted neither Gilbert nor Tiffany Lively in the fundraiser group.

Thank god, she thought. Her parents did not have to witness their only daughter's social humiliation.

"Ms. Lively. Did you or did you not have a relationship with Robert Mickelson?" the pushy journalist asked.

"No comment."

"Do you have any idea where Robert Mickelson is now?"

She leaned toward the microphone. "If I knew where he was I would, of course, share that information with the authorities. Now, please. Let. Me. Through."

Liv tried to get away from the news crew, but once again the reporter blocked her way. "But what about…"

The woman's voice stopped abruptly as a tall figure stepped between the correspondent and Liv. Jasper clasped Liv around the shoulders in a strong, supportive grip with one hand, and he covered the camera lens with the other.

"She asked you to let her pass." Jasper shoved his shoulder

against the pushy woman. "Come on, Liv," Jasper said. "Let's get you out of here."

He pushed his way past the journalists, holding Liv in the steady circle of his arm. Liv was aware of Ashleigh and Trevor falling into place behind them, preventing the crew from following. In the mansion's doorway, the curious faces of the partygoers peered out, frightened and appalled. The protesters, taking advantage of their moment, raised their voices in an even louder chant. "Bedpans not balance sheets! Bedpans, not balance sheets!"

Liv cast a backward glance over Jasper's arm as they ran along the pathway to the parking lot. "Who was the genius who thought up that slogan?"

Jasper laughed, guided her toward his car. "I'm glad to see you're unscarred by that experience," he said, opening the passenger door.

She settled into the seat while he reached over her to secure the safety buckle in place. She took a shaky breath. "I wouldn't say I'm exactly unscarred. I have a feeling there will be a few recurring nightmares."

He smiled at her, and her heart flipped. She might need to schedule an electrocardiogram if this kept up. "Thanks for helping me."

"It's the least I could do, Liv. Let's get you out of here."

He went around to the driver's seat, slid behind the wheel, started the engine. Avoiding the mob, Jasper rolled out of the lot and cut across town toward Munjoy Hill. Liv looked out the windows at Deering Oaks Park, the shadowy trees mere dark outlines against a charcoal gray evening sky. She turned her head on the headrest and looked over at Jasper whose face was calm and devastatingly handsome.

He glanced over at her. "All right?" he asked before turning his attention back to the traffic.

"Yeah," she said. "What happened to Wren?"

"Your parents offered to give her a ride home."

Liv let the implications of that sink in. "So, my parents knew what was happening." She rolled her head back, took a deep breath. "I was hoping they'd missed it. I bet they are mortified."

"I think they are more concerned about you. Are you okay?"

"I'm fine." She stared straight ahead. "That's not true. I really want to punch somebody, preferably that skanky news correspondent. Wipe that sly expression from her face. Do you know how hard I try to stay low-profile in this city? Notoriety isn't the best thing for a private investigator. This is not going to be good for my business."

"I'm sorry, Liv. Look at it this way. The worst is probably behind you."

"Maybe not." She looked over at him again. "That all depends on whether or not we're going to talk about you and me and last night. And about Wren Osborne."

Chapter Thirty-Nine

● ● ● ● ● ● ● ● ● ● ● ● ● ●

Jasper walked her to the door of her building. Liv had left a small lamp on in the living room, and the warm light signaled to her like a beacon. *Home*, she thought as exhaustion rolled over her, tugging at her like the tide.

With some effort, she raised her eyes to meet Jasper's. His rueful grin matched the one she managed to summon. "Fabulous party," she said. "Protesters and a news crew. Not to mention the outstanding lemon mousse dessert. Should make the society column for sure."

She tried to laugh, but instead, a strangled sound caught in her throat.

"Hey," Jasper said, putting a warm hand just above her elbow and giving her arm a comforting squeeze. "You don't have to be tough with me. Not tonight. You didn't deserve to be accosted like that."

Liv rolled her eyes. "Yeah. Well."

Jasper squeezed her arm again. "Are you okay now? Do you want me to walk you up? Stay with you for a while?"

"No, that's okay," she said. She met his eyes again, and this time they held. Sudden tension sparked in the air between them. "It probably wouldn't be a good idea. I mean, you were with Wren tonight."

Jasper's hand dropped from her arm. He nodded, his face wary. "I'm sorry if that bothered you."

"We slept together last night. Of course it bothered me. Did you just see her today and think, 'Oh, she's cute. Guess I'll invite her to Liv's mother's fundraiser?'"

"No. I dated her for a couple of weeks before I met you. When you said you weren't interested in a serious relationship, I thought it would be okay to accept Wren's invitation. After last night, I thought about bailing, but I didn't think that was fair to her."

"You could have warned me at least."

"I wasn't even sure you were going to be there."

"We both have phones."

Jasper nodded his head. "You're right. I messed that up. This is just weird for me. I'm basically a one-girl-at-a-time guy. I don't know what the hell I'm doing. Wren and I are dating casually. Not sleeping together, if you're wondering."

"And she didn't mind you driving me home like this?"

"Not at all. Wren's a nice woman. She tells me the two of you were childhood friends. Said she was always in awe of you, that you were daring and clever and what did she say?" He rubbed his chin. "Impetuous, I believe was the word she used."

"Isn't that sweet?" Liv clutched her bag. Jasper looked troubled and unhappy, and she hated that it was her fault. She put a hand on his arm. "I'm sorry. This isn't fair to you. I'm the one who said I didn't want a commitment. You have every right to date whoever you want. I was just surprised, that's all. It's perfectly fine. We'll have plenty of time to be together."

He gave her a skeptical look. She thought she read disappointment behind his eyes. "I should go then, I guess."

"Do you want to stay?"

"I told Wren I'd call and make sure she got home all right."

She clenched her fingers around her bag. "Okay, well, thank you for the ride and for rescuing me from that reporter."

He bent down to kiss her cheek. "My pleasure. I'm sorry this is so weird and that I'm so awkward. I'll call you tomorrow." To end things, she thought. He didn't know it yet, but he'd call her tomorrow to say he couldn't handle this kind of relationship.

234 · SHELLEY BURBANK

That it wasn't her, it was him. Yada, yada. She didn't blame him. Everything about her personal life was an utter mess.

"Goodbye, Jasper."

She opened her door and slipped inside. The night's events had really taken a toll on her, she thought, sliding one shoe and then the other from her feet. She carried them by the straps, swinging them wearily as she climbed the stairs.

She'd certainly hear from her mother tomorrow, if not later on tonight. That was a conversation she would love to avoid. And she didn't, couldn't think any more about Jasper. It was too painful, and she was feeling too lonely.

The doorbell rang before she reached the third floor. It had to be Jasper, changing his mind. Smiling, she ran down the steps, shoes in her hand.

She swung the door open wide. "Back already?"

She froze. Not Jasper. Someone else.

An unfamiliar man with a scruffy beard, longish brown hair, and glasses stood in front of her door. Liv glanced past him and saw Jasper's car turning the corner at the end of the street.

Uneasy, she swung her attention back to the strange man. Out of habit, she took note of his dirty jeans, oversized plaid shirt, and nondescript, dark-colored windbreaker. A battered bicycle was propped against the side of her building; next to it was a large backpack. She didn't recognize either the bike or the man from her neighborhood.

"Can I help you?" she said. "It's a little late to be knocking on doors."

"It's a little late for lots of things," the man said. His voice was low, gravelly. He reached out and pushed her away from the door and into the building. He plowed in after her, slamming the door behind him.

Liv let out a startled cry as she stumbled backward and fell against the steps. Adrenaline pumped through her, and instinctively she kicked out at her assailant with her bare feet. He didn't seem to feel the blows. He hauled her up by one arm, swiftly reached for her other and pulled both behind her back, holding her hands together with one of his. He clapped another rough hand over her mouth as she tried to scream.

"What's the matter, Livy, don't you recognize me?" The familiar voice in her ear was like a punch to the stomach.

Rob, she thought. Of course. It was just that kind of night. She moaned against the hand clasped over her mouth.

"The renters are out," he said, conversationally, "so there's no one to hear you yelling for help in here. But don't worry. If you cooperate, I'll be on my way, and you'll be no worse for wear. You understand?"

She nodded.

He took his hand away from her mouth. "See, not so bad, but hold on."

He produced a white plastic restraint from the pocket of his coat, secured her hands together behind her back. He reached down to pick up her small clutch purse which she'd dropped when he'd attacked. "Walk up the stairs, Liv," he said. "Nice and easy. Let's go."

"What do you want?" He didn't answer, just pressed close behind her and marched her up the stairs. When they got to the top, he pushed her again, knocking her head against the door so hard that she saw white sparks behind her eyes.

"I said quiet," he said, his voice conversational. "No talking unless I ask you a question. Now, let's see. Where are those keys?"

"Is that a question?" she smirked.

He smacked her across the mouth.

Tasting blood, Liv realized he'd cut her lip open. It didn't hurt. Not yet. But it would.

She watched as he fished around in her purse and came up with her keys. "Here we are," he said, shaking them. He found the one that fit her apartment door and nudged her into the apartment. "In we go."

Once inside, she turned to face him. "Is this absolutely necessary?" she said, glaring at him, daring him to hit her again. Her heart thumped so hard, her chest hurt. "Take this restraint off me, we'll sit down, have a glass of wine, and we can talk. I'm not your enemy, Rob, no matter what you think. Let me help you out. What have you done to yourself, anyway? You look like shit."

He gave her a mirthless grin, and suddenly she could see her lover behind the beard and the dorky glasses. "Pretty good disguise, huh?" he said, spreading his arms wide. "Guess I learned a thing or two from you, Liv."

"Guess you did." Liv tried to sound ironic and unconcerned, even though inside she was a quaking mess. Rob was desperate, otherwise, he never would have attacked her so viciously. The worst thing she could do now was show her fear. "So, what do you want?"

"I want the Lakshmi. Tell me where it is."

She squinted her eyes at him as her mind made the connection. "It was you, wasn't it? The office break-in. The attack on me here? You sent one of your thugs, the one with the scar on his eyebrow, to take the statue."

He hit her again, and she cried out.

"Where is it?" he demanded.

She licked the blood on her lip. "It's in the closet. In a shoebox. Under the ottoman. Where you'll notice the courier slip. I did try to send it to you. Not my fault you were running from the feds."

"Think you're pretty clever, don't you."

He marched her down the hall, opened her closet door, flipped on the light inside. He peeked under the ottoman, and then he shoved her onto it. "Sit down."

"Whatever you say," Liv said. Behind her back, she worked her wrists back and forth, checking to see if there was any possibility of slipping out of the restraint. The plastic bit into her skin, pinching painfully. She couldn't even turn her hands.

Rob swayed on his feet for a moment. She studied him with

narrowed eyes. He looked bad. His face was thin behind the beard. His eyes were bloodshot, sunken into shadows. He was breathing heavily, noisily. Like he had a cold, or possibly allergies, she thought.

She jumped up, went at him, butted her head against his nose, and kicked the inside of his knee. He screamed and fell down. Hands still tied behind her, she went for the door.

Chapter Forty

• • • • • • • • • • • • •

He was too quick.

She felt his hand wrap around her ankle, and then she fell forward, twisting at the last second so she ended up on her arm, not her face. Pain raced through her arm and shoulder. He grunted, grabbed her feet, and dragged her back to the center of the room. For a moment they just looked at each other.

Liv felt like she might throw up. Anything could happen. He could torture her. Rape her. Kill her. She was almost too terrified to think. She could feel her brain starting to shut down, her thought processes going fuzzy.

He limped over to her collection of scarves hanging from a thin rod suspended over a set of built-in lingerie drawers. Watching him run his hand across the silks, the dreamy gauzes, the soft cashmeres, Liv's stomach lurched.

Rob considered and then selected a silk Hermes print, one her grandmother had given her for her twenty-first birthday. "Ah, always one of my favorites," he said, running it over her cheek. "I liked it especially with your black dress. Or out of your black dress," he said, leering at her.

She scowled. "Don't."

Without warning, Rob dropped down next to her feet, grabbed her ankles, and tied them together with the scarf. Reaching for another one, he bound her ankles to one of the bench legs. She twisted in vain, glared at him. "Why can't we deal with this situation rationally, Rob?" she said. "I can help you. Just untie me, and we'll work something out."

Ignoring her plea, Rob smiled and shook his head slowly from side to side. He reached under the bench and pulled out the shoe box before standing and surveying his work.

"There! Beautiful and stylish, if I do say so. Very nice."

Liv just looked at him.

He grinned, and her stomach lurched again. He ripped open the box, unwrapped the statue, threw the wrapping and box to the floor. "If you'd just done as I'd asked, we could have avoided all this unpleasantness." He twisted one of the statue's hands. Liv heard a click. Eyes wide, she stared as Rob slid the bottom off the statue and a small golden key fell into his hand.

Rob sighed. "Gina sang like a bird as soon as the feds moved on us. Lucky for me, I thought ahead. Nobody knows about this, and by the time anyone finds you, I'll be long gone. Which reminds me," he held up her keys and rattled them. "I need to borrow your car."

"It's not here."

"Yeah, it threw me a little when someone else drove you home from that hospital shindig tonight." He made a shocked face, mocking her. "What? You think I haven't been watching you? Your car's still at the Mowatt-Seavey I bet. Did you drink a little too much of the champagne tonight? Needed a ride home? Or were you just hoping to get laid?"

He laughed when she turned her head away. "What, you think I don't know you? Who was he? I was surprised he didn't come upstairs. It's not like you to be coy."

Because she was tired of feeling scared, Liv called up some anger. "Screw you," she said between her teeth.

Rob laughed. "Oops! Sore subject, I guess. But we can't have you talking like that. Very unladylike, Ms. Lively."

He reached over and grabbed a third scarf, a yellow-striped silk, and even as she struggled, he stuffed it in her mouth, gagging her. "In fact, we can't have you talking at all."

When he was finished, he gazed down at her, a touch of malignant lust in his eyes. "Too bad I'm in such a hurry. You, that yellow bench, the restraint, the gag? Whew. Gotta admit I'm getting a little turned on." He winked. "Unfortunately, I've got to run."

Rob touched her cheek, and she moved her head away, glaring at him. "I'll keep this image in my head for some time to come. Pun intended, of course. Goodbye, Liv. And thanks for the car keys and for holding on to this for me." He waved the safe deposit key—-at least she assumed that's what it was—around. "Sorry to leave you all tied up in knots, but I can't risk you getting out and calling the police, can I?"

He stepped out of the closet, held the door open for a moment with his head stuck through the crack. "I'm sure someone will come along and find you pretty soon." With that, he flipped off the light, slamming the door shut and leaving her in the dark, immobile and mute. A second or two later, she heard the apartment door shut.

Liv struggled as the darkness closed in on her and her claustrophobia began to spiral, at first just a lazy coil of panic but then gathering intensity as the minutes ticked by and she helplessly worked against the fabric holding her feet to the bench. She tried to scream but the scarf in her mouth muffled the sound. No one would hear her outside the building.

It was no use. She was stuck. In the dark.

Alone.

•　•　•　•　•

Being locked in a closet, tied up with her own scarves, had only one advantage as far as Liv could tell. The forced sensory deprivation gave her plenty of opportunity to think. Alone in the dark with no possibility of escape, her thoughts turned from a fruitless "How can I get myself out of this?" to a more philosophical "How did I get here in the first place?"

After the first, frantic minutes ticked by, she willed herself to relax. She closed her eyes and remembered her yoga training, tried to still her mind as she had been instructed while lying limp and impatient on her mat next to Ashleigh during their Wednesday night class.

Breathe, she told herself. Picture yourself in a safe and happy place. Warm granules of sand beneath the soles of your feet. Fronds of palm trees waving overhead in the tropical breeze. The surf breaking in gentle waves against the beach.

Liv's bladder, heavy from two glasses of champagne, protested. She snapped back to reality in a hurry. Better not think about waves. The thought of someone finding her dead, fouled, gagged, and tied in the middle of her luxurious walk-in sent her mind back to the edge of panic.

If only Jasper had come up.

Another sickening punch of humiliation hit her gut. He'd gone from sleeping with her one night to attending a society function with Wren Osborne the next.

Her mind flashed to the sight of him and Wren walking into the event that evening, and her throat closed around the gag. Wren represented everything Liv had given up. Social status, traditional gender roles, a big society wedding, charity work, lunching with the ladies, children, luxury homes, cars, and boats.

Liv, craving a more authentic life, had rejected all that, determined to make her own way. She was proud of Lively Investigations and what she'd managed to create there. She liked online shopping, yoga with Ashleigh, and living in a space she'd decorated herself. She enjoyed driving a not-so-flashy car and helping people with their problems, digging into the underbelly of life, and exposing those who stole, lied, cheated, and abused.

She'd managed to create a less conservative lifestyle, but she hadn't always made good choices, especially when it came to men. They'd all been unattainable, irresponsible, selfish, emotionally unavailable, and in Rob's case, married. In a word, they were all as averse to commitment as she was.

And then she'd met Jasper. Handsome, suitable, someone her parents liked and respected. A man not only with good taste in food and cult television, but also well-educated, and caring, and fun to be with... He was a good man. Why had she pushed him away? Was she afraid to be happy or something?

Alone in the dark with nothing but her thoughts, Liv faced the situation honestly.

She had been afraid of getting tied down, she realized, and she'd gotten herself tied up instead.

Liv struggled against the restraints holding her wrists and ankles, grunting with frustration through the scarf stuffed in her mouth. Her bad choices and aversion to commitment were what got her into this mess. She might get out of this situation, she thought, but if she didn't mend her ways, she might end up dying alone at the end of a lonely life anyway.

That thought struck her as squarely and painfully as Rob's fist.

Scared, alone, brutally bound, and possibly facing a humiliating death, Liv's thoughts snapped into a startling, brilliant clarity. If, *when*, she got out of this, she was going to change.

For long enough, she'd kept people at arm's length, pretending to be so tough and independent and in control. All around her in the walk-in hung beautiful clothes, disguises that kept people from getting to know the real Olivia Lively, the one who cried when she watched romantic comedies. The one who felt awed and awkward when asked to hold a baby so she pretended to be disgusted. The one who attacked first and asked questions later, not just because she was tough, but because she was afraid of being vulnerable. The woman who, deep down, wanted to love and be loved with passion and intensity and loyalty, if she could only allow herself to accept it.

Liv felt her eyelids start to close as panic and despair gave way to exhaustion. She would sleep. Maybe when she woke up, she'd think of some solution, some way of wriggling out of her restraints.

She just needed a little rest.

Chapter Forty-One

• • • • • • • • • • • • • •

The sound of her doorbell startled her awake. She had no idea how long she'd been out. It could have been minutes or an hour. She tried to move her arms and legs, but her tendons felt as if they were being ripped apart. She couldn't feel anything at all in her feet and hands. Her neck was stiff and sore from how she'd slept.

The doorbell rang again. She was able to produce a scream, but the sound was muffled by the scarf in her mouth. Could anyone hear her through the scarf and the closet and the apartment and the building door, she wondered? Hardly likely. Whoever it was would probably give up and go away. She steeled herself for disappointment.

But then hope washed over her. She heard a crash and footsteps pounding up the stairs. There was a knock at the apartment door. A pause. The buzzer sounded. Another pause.

Liv closed her eyes, hoping, praying that whoever was out there would try to get in. She heard the door to her apartment open with a quiet click. Ah! Rob had forgotten to lock the door.

There were steps in the kitchen. Liv took a deep breath, managing to produce another muffled scream.

"Olivia? Liv? Are you here?" a man's voice called out. "Say something if you can hear me? Liv?"

She pulled at the restraints binding her wrists and ankles. Damn the solid construction of her precious walk-in closet. Damn all the clothes acting as sound-absorbers when she really, really needed to be heard.

"In here!" she tried to yell around the fabric. She heard the creak of shoes against her hardwood floor. A second later, wondrously, miraculously, the door swung open.

She slumped in relief. As tears sprouted in the corners of her eyes, she blinked at the dark silhouette of the man outlined against the brilliance of the electric lights flooding into the gloom.

The dark figure reached to flip the switch inside the closet, and Liv cringed as the light hit her dilated pupils. She squinted through narrowed eyelids as the man folded his arms, leaned against the doorway, and chuckled.

"I told you this closet was dangerous, didn't I?"

Colin Snow's sarcastic voice sent a warm rush of relief through Liv's entire body. She began to cry and laugh at the same time, choking and struggling to breathe. Her eyes widened, pleading for help.

"Shoot." Agent Colin Snow quickly unfolded his arms, strode over to Liv, and removed the gag from her mouth. "That was a bad joke," he said. "I'm sorry."

Liv moaned and slumped forward. He held her shoulders so she wouldn't topple onto the floor. "'hank you," she tried to tell him. "It's as 'unny", but her tongue felt thick and unresponsive.

"Shhh, don't talk yet. Can you sit up? Good girl. That's it. Hold still," Colin said, pulling a jack-knife from the pocket of his FBI jacket.

In quick, decisive movements, he cut through the Hermes scarf around her ankles and released her wrists from the plastic restraints that had been holding her arms behind her back for hours. She tried to move but found it was impossible. Every tendon in her body protested, and she cried out in extreme pain. Her arms and legs felt like dead, cold meat.

Colin caught her when she tried to stand. She was trembling so hard with shock and exhaustion, she let him take her in his arms and hold her close. Even if she'd wanted to protest, she couldn't speak.

"I've got you," he said, standing, holding her upright. "Don't be scared anymore, Olivia. You're going to be fine. I've got you."

Snow picked her up, one arm around her waist, another under her knees, and carried her out of the closet toward her bed. "I'm calling an ambulance," he told her.

"Not necessary," Liv said, gasping as the circulation began to return to her legs and arms in painful prickles. "But I am in desperate need of the loo. Would you mind a detour in that direction?"

"You were in dire straits, weren't you?" he said, swerving out of the bedroom and down the hall to the bathroom. He assisted her with a practical efficiency, making sure she was stable before leaving the room and making a call to 911 just outside the door. "Okay in there?" He tapped on the doorframe after giving the dispatcher Liv's address and disconnecting the call.

"Define okay," Liv grumbled. Feeling returning to her arms, she still struggled with her dress. She hobbled to the sink and peered at her reflection. Her face was pale and splotchy, and mascara rimmed her eyes in gray smudges. A cut was beginning to bruise on her forehead.

She ran some cold water, splashed her face, and wiped the mascara off as best she could with a hand towel. "I look like something the cat dragged in."

"A cat with good taste, then." She could hear the smile in Snow's voice. "If all you're worried about is your lip gloss, I guess you'll be all right."

Dizzy and a little wobbly on her feet, she lurched her way to the living room with Snow's hand holding her elbow. He settled her on the couch, and she said again, "I really don't need an ambulance. I'm fine now."

He sat down beside her, took both her hands in his, and lifted them, palms up. "These need to be looked at." She glanced down to see both her wrists cut and bleeding from the restraints that had sliced into her skin. She shivered. Snow elaborated. "I'd feel better if a medical professional examined the rest of you, okay? We need to make sure you haven't sustained any serious injuries."

"I'm really fine. Nothing wrong with me besides injured pride. When Rob knocked, I opened the door like a complete idiot. Didn't even look out the peephole. You know it was him, right? I'm assuming that's why you're here checking on me?"

"Yes. We've arrested him. Did he hurt you, Liv? I mean besides the tying up. Did he assault you?"

She shook her head slowly as a headache began to build up behind her eyes. "No. Not beyond pushing me. Knocked my head against the wall. Nothing sexual."

"Good. I'm going to get you a glass of water and wait for the EMS crew to arrive. You just sit here and relax." He jumped up off the couch and went into the kitchen.

"Water sounds good," she admitted as she watched him open cupboards looking for the glassware. "But I've been 'relaxing' in that closet with nothing to do but think for what feels like hours." She sat forward to glance at the clock in the kitchen. It had only been two hours since Jasper dropped her off. It felt like twice that. At least. "Colin? I need to know how you got that s.o.b."

He returned to the couch with a glass of water in his hand. "You are one tough cookie, you know that?"

"That's what you love about me, right?"

"Let's not go overboard. Just because I saved you from that lethal closet of yours doesn't mean I like you or anything."

"Thank you, Colin," she said, keeping her eyes locked on his. "I mean it. Thank you for being here."

"No problem. It's my job." He handed her the water, and he didn't say anything about her hand shaking, just wrapped his fingers around hers and helped bring the glass to her mouth. "Be a good girl and drink your water. And then you need to tell me everything you and Rob talked about."

Chapter Forty-Two

• • • • • • • • • • • • • •

"Okay, Agent, I've dutifully quaffed some water, and I have to warn you. I'm feeling much better. If you don't tell me right now how you nabbed Rob Mickelson, I might have to resort to desperate measures." Liv drew up her knees and tucked her feet against the back of the couch. Her body still hurt, but at least the circulation had returned.

Snow took a seat on the chair opposite and gave her a mocking smile. "What kind of desperate measures are we talking about here, Lively? I'm kinda tempted to sit here and find out just how far you'll go when your curiosity is all, what's the word? Aroused?"

"Ha! Don't flatter yourself, Snow." Liv relaxed against the cushions. She was enjoying the banter. "If you must know, I was thinking less along the line of seduction and more along the line of bribery. There's a bottle of Glenfarclas scotch in the cupboard beneath the sink. I could use a drop. How about you?"

"Tempting, but no thanks." Snow looked at his watch. "And I don't think you need any hard stuff either. Stick with the water. The medics should be here soon, and you don't need to ply me with alcohol to get what you want. I won't keep you in suspense any longer. You've been through enough torture already."

"Thanks for reminding me."

"Sorry." Snow leaned forward in his chair. "Okay, this really isn't an exciting story, but since you insist. As you know, I've been watching your building for a few weeks. I was pretty sure that Mickelson would show up here if he was going to surface anywhere."

"What made you so sure?"

"It made sense. He'd already contacted you once, at your office, remember? I figured he might come to you again. Also, you were right about the boat. The only snag was, he never tried to take possession of it. I guess Mickelson figured out we were waiting for him.

"So I had to think: where else would he go? Maybe to Gina, but he knew we were watching her. He didn't seem to have any close friends, and most of his colleagues are pretty pissed about what he's done to the company. When we took Gina into custody and charged her, he knew the net was closing in. He's smart enough to know he'd never get a plane ticket without fresh identification papers. He needed to get out of state and then out of the country. He needed some help. I figured he'd come to you for old time's sake."

"But why would he think I'd help him? More to the point, why did *you* think I'd help him? Am I under suspicion?"

Snow's eyes were intent, searching. "We were hoping to arrest Mickelson getting his boat. For some reason, he never showed up to claim it. We thought someone might have tipped him off."

"You thought I told him?" Liv stared at the agent. "That doesn't make any sense. Did you ever stop to think that maybe he spotted some of your guys lurking around? Up the coast, a federal-style haircut would stick out like a sore thumb. I told you about the boat in the first place!"

"Relax. I believe you. But you understand I had to cover everything. You'd do the same, right?"

She gave a grudging shrug.

"So, a couple days ago, we get a couple of calls reporting that someone who fit Mickelson's description was hanging around the bus terminal. According to employees there, he never attempted to buy a ticket. He must have figured we'd flagged his name and posted his photo. I kept checking here at your apartment just in case he showed up. I saw you arrive home with the doc, figured you were in for the night. So I went to get a coffee and checked in with my partner. He told me you'd been on the news."

"Yeah, it's been a swell night all around." Liv shifted, winced.

"I passed by here again, saw the doc's car was gone, and noticed a scruffy-looking guy on a bicycle heading downhill. Seemed like an odd time to be riding around on a bike, so I tailed him thinking it might be one of Mickelson's mules acting as a go-between for you and Rob."

"Still with the distrust."

Snow ignored her cynical tone. "Sure enough, the guy went straight to your car. He ditched the bike and unlocked the driver's side door. I apprehended him and realized it wasn't some lowlife mule. It was Mickelson himself. I cuffed him. I called dispatch. The police arrived to take him into custody. The end."

Liv blinked. "That's it? He didn't try to run away? You didn't have to shoot him in the leg? Didn't have to bash his head in even just a teeny, tiny bit?"

"It wasn't that dramatic," Snow said, his voice dry. "Mickelson seemed almost resigned when I approached the car and told him to step back. I thought for a split second that he might try to escape, but he just hung his head and did what I told him. As I cuffed him, he said something about you getting what you deserved and called you a name I don't feel like repeating."

"I assume he's at the police station?"

"Yup. He refused to speak without a lawyer present, so he'll be cooling his heels at Portland PD overnight. We'll question him tomorrow. Anyway, once he was all squared away, I started wondering what he meant about you getting what you deserved. I tried calling you, but you didn't answer, so I decided to come back up here and check on you."

"You mean, you decided to come back here and see if I'd aided and abetted a wanted criminal. What if I'd been with the doctor?

He could have come back you know. That would have explained my not answering the phone."

Snow's mouth quirked. "I guess we have something in common, you and I. We're both impatient. I didn't want to wait until morning."

"And for that, I am forever grateful, Agent Snow," Liv said, shifting on the couch.

The paramedics arrived. They bandaged her wrists, asked her questions about aches and pains, took a look at the bump on her head, and told her she was probably fine but to make an appointment with her primary care physician for a more thorough check-up. In the meantime, they said to take aspirin for the pain and to get plenty of sleep and fluids.

Snow talked to the officers on the scene and kept a general eye out to make sure nothing was overlooked. She gave her statement and told Snow about the Lakshmi statue and the key. He said they'd look into it. It was after three a.m. by the time the medics and police were finished, leaving Liv and Snow alone again.

"Are you going to feel safe here tonight?" the agent asked Liv as he prepared to go back to his hotel. "Is there someone I can call to come and stay with you? Or somewhere you'd like to go? What about your parents?"

"No," Liv said, yawning and barely able to keep her eyes open. She felt as if she'd been run over by a truck. "No need to worry them. I'll be fine. The deadbolt to the apartment door still works. I just want to crawl into bed and sleep for twelve hours."

"Okay, then. I'll see you at the station tomorrow." Snow reached out and gently brushed hair from the bandage on her forehead. "Get some sleep. You look like the walking dead."

"You're such a sweet talker, Agent Snow. With lines like that, I can't imagine why you're still single."

"My name's Colin. Once this case is wrapped up, maybe you can let me practice my pick-up lines on you. See if I can get you to go out to dinner with me."

She bit her lip. "That sounds nice. Um, before you go, could you do me one little favor?"

"Sure. What?"

She turned around and looked over her shoulder. "This zipper? There's no way my arms are going to manage that tonight."

"If I didn't know better, I'd think you were trying to seduce me after all."

"Don't flatter yourself. I can't even move."

His fingers brushed her skin as he lowered the zipper of her dress. "There. All set. I'll just head out. Don't forget to bolt the door behind me."

She followed him to the door, slid the bolt over after he'd gone, and shuffled into her bedroom. She didn't look at the closet. She couldn't think about all that now. She was too tired. Instead, she let the dress fall, slipped into bed, and was asleep as soon as her eyes closed.

Chapter Forty-Three

● ● ● ● ● ● ● ● ● ● ● ● ●

The next day, Liv texted Ashleigh and told her Rob had been arrested. Ashleigh rang her on the phone right away, and Liv told her about the attack, about being stuck in the closet, about the FBI agent who'd rescued her, much to her chagrin. "Do you need me to come over?" Ash sounded worried if slightly preoccupied. "We're still in Boston, but we can be home in two hours."

"No," Liv assured her. "I'm fine. Really. You and Trevor enjoy your weekend in the city. How did it go with the doctor?" She wanted to ask if Ash was pregnant, but didn't want to upset her friend.

"It went fine," Ashleigh said, her voice full of excitement simmering beneath the calm surface. "I'll talk to you when we get back Sunday night. It's pretty big news."

"Don't keep me in suspense. You're pregnant, right?"

Ashleigh paused a second, then squealed. "Yes! The fertility treatments worked. We're so excited. Trevor's so happy he won't leave me alone. I've locked myself in the hotel bathroom right now with the water running in the tub. He offered to take a bath with me, and I told him I could manage just fine without his help. It's sweet, but I need some time to process."

"I'm so, so happy for you, Ash! When you do allow Trevor in, tell him I say congratulations."

"I will. But what about you? You could have died. I want to throttle that weasel, Rob Mickelson. It's a good thing he's in custody or else I'd hunt him down and… and…"

"That's not very centered of you, Ash," Liv said, laughing. "I thought forgiveness was the answer."

"No one messes with my best friend, or else."

"Or else what? You'll analyze him to death?"

"Are you making fun of me?"

"Just a little. Thank you for calling though, and offering to come home."

"Are you sure you're okay?"

"I was a little sore yesterday, but now I'm fine. I seem to be having some residual panic attacks, but Tiffany's coming over to keep me company tonight. She'll be here soon, so you don't need to worry about me being alone and panicky."

"You're going to hang out with your mother? Are you sure you're all right?" The sound of the water stopped. Liv heard a splash, and then Ashleigh let out a contented sigh. "Ah, that's so lovely and steamy. This is a really nice hotel. We'll have to come down here sometime for a girl's weekend. We can go baby shopping! But wait, we were talking about you and your mother."

"That's okay. Being stuck in that closet gave me a different perspective on things, one of them being the realization that my parents won't be around forever. Tiffany drives me insane, but she's my mother. I'd like to have a relationship with her, a good relationship if I can, while I can, you know?" Liv paused. "Plus, I figure it will be impossible to worry about panic attacks when I'm busy sparring with Tiffany about what to throw out of that closet. I'm doing a major clean-out. If there's anything you want, tell me now or forever hold your peace."

There was silence on the other end of the phone. Then sniffling.

"Ash, are you crying?" Liv's voice was incredulous.

"Sorry," Ashleigh said, blowing her nose so that Liv held the phone away from her ear. "It's the hormones."

"Well stop it before I start crying, too."

"Listen, I'm glad you're okay. I'm glad Rob's in custody. I still want to hear all about what you and Dr. Hottie talked about when he drove you home. Right now I just want to relax in this bath before Trevor starts knocking on the door and reminding me about not missing our tee time."

"What do you mean 'our' tee time? Golfing? As in the both of you?"

"I've been taking a few lessons so I don't embarrass Trev on the links. I have to go. Take care of yourself, Liv, and call me later if you need to talk or if your mom is driving you crazy. Sometimes these things take a while to hit you emotionally."

Liv didn't know if she meant assault and battery or her mother's passive-aggressive comments.

Smiling, Liv assured Ashleigh that she would be fine and hung up the phone. Good for Ashleigh, she thought. Playing golf with her handsome hubby. Boston for the weekend. Pregnant after months of disappointment and fertility treatments. She was happy for her friend, but somehow felt deflated herself.

The feeling lasted all evening as she and Tiffany went through Liv's closet and weeded out any of the pieces that no longer fit or felt right, including anything that reminded her of Rob and their ill-fated affair. Out went the pink raincoat, the silk Japanese kimono, the Manolo sandals, and all the scarves. She'd never wear a scarf again. In fact, she was considering a complete change of wardrobe. A new style to fit her new outlook on life.

Whatever that was. She knew she wanted to change, had to change. But how exactly?

"Don't be hasty," Tiffany said when Liv tried to throw all her dresses into the donation pile. "Some of these you'll regret discarding. Why don't you send them home with me? I'll store them for a while, and if you want any of them back, you only have to ask. If in a year you don't miss them, well then I'll take them to the consignment store myself."

"You'd do that for me?" The day after Liv graduated from college and said she was moving to an apartment on the other side of the city, Tiffany had her childhood room packed up into boxes and delivered to Liv's new address.

When Liv called to demand why, Tiffany had calmly said, "Since you no longer live here, your possessions belong with you."

Now Tiffany pursed her lips for a second and then snapped, "Why wouldn't I do that for you? Goodness, Olivia, can't you just accept my help and be happy about it?"

"Sorry. You're right. It's probably a good idea to make sure before I give these all away. Some of them are really beautiful, aren't they?" Liv reached out to feel the skirt on a brown wool Prada dress with a daring plunging neckline. She'd found it online for a good price back when she'd first opened Lively Investigations. "Maybe I'll keep this one."

Tiffany nodded, her eyes gleaming. "Well, maybe you should. It's darling."

Tiffany spent the night, and they stayed up watching Audrey Hepburn movies and eating popcorn from giant bowls. It was fun. But when Tiffany went home on Saturday morning, the fog of depression threatened to descend.

"What are you going to do with yourself today, Olivia?" Her mother gave her a hug when all the clothes were piled in Tiffany's Lexus. "I don't like to leave you."

"It's okay, Mom. I'll take it easy. I'll go for a run, take a bath and maybe a nap, and read a book."

"Not one of those horrible true crime stories. Why don't you try a romance novel? They're so wonderful and uplifting. Or maybe Jane Austen…"

Liv rolled her eyes. "I've been picking out my own reading material since I was seven, Mom. Thank you for staying over. It was fun. I'll see you and Dad tomorrow at brunch." She gave Tiffany a kiss. Tiffany got in her car and drove away, arm out the window, gold bracelets jangling, ostentatious diamond flashing in the sunlight.

Thinking about her half-marathon ambitions, Liv went for a long-overdue run, ending up at Back Cove. She caught her breath in the park and watched the young parents chatting together while their kids chased after the ducks. A few people jogged or walked their dogs along the path.

She stretched, working out the kinks in her shoulders which were still sore after her ordeal in the closet. Overhead, a few white clouds scudded, and the grass was greener than it had been the day before. It was all so pretty and peaceful—the kids, the dogs, the scenery— but a gray fog of doubt and depression crowded the edges of her heart. She shook her arms and legs, impatient with herself.

Coffee, she thought. She needed coffee and music and people and art. Life and light. Anything to keep the gray fog at bay.

"Olivia!"

A tall, dark-haired figure, panting and sweaty, jogged toward her. She blinked, hardly believing her eyes. "Jasper?"

He came to a stop beside her, huffing and puffing. He put his hands on his thighs and bent at the waist. He tried to talk, held up a hand. "Wait just a sec. I just have to... catch... my breath."

She laughed. "Are you going to be all right?"

He stood up, let out a short, wheezy laugh, and shook his head. "You up to date on your CPR?"

"I think so. What are you doing here?"

"Jogging, obviously."

"Yeah, but why?"

He looked at her face, let his eyes drop to the bandages on her wrists, and looked back up with a question in his eyes. "I heard about Rob Mickelson's arrest. Are you okay? Can we go somewhere to talk? Get some coffee?"

She held out her hands. "It's not what you think... the bandages. Something happened after you left Thursday night."

"I know. Your mother called me an hour ago. I'm so sorry I left you there alone. If I'd had any idea..."

"How could you have known? Rob Mickelson's a scumbag. I can't believe I ever found him attractive. My radar was every kind of screwed up." She shook her head as if to clear the troubling thoughts away. "Anyway, in addition to fraud, he's now facing charges of kidnapping and assault."

"Why did he attack you?"

"I had something of his, but I didn't realize what it was or why he was so desperate to get it. Turns out it was Rob who organized the break-in to my office and the attempted robbery at my apartment. He wanted to get his hands on a safe deposit key he'd hidden in a souvenir statue he'd given me after one of his trips. Turns out he'd squirreled away hundreds of thousands of dollars in cash and some false identity papers along with art and jewels. He could have disappeared out of the country." She looked down at her feet. "I really know how to pick them."

"You can't blame yourself." Jasper stretched his calf muscles and groaned. "I'm going to be sore tomorrow. Why do you like this exercise stuff again?"

"It's good for the heart, Dr. Fancy Cardiologist. Anyway, I can blame myself a little. I've messed up a lot of things lately." She gave him a rueful smile. "So let me get this right. My mother called you, and then you just happened to get in the mood for a run around Back Cove, huh? Pretty coincidental."

"There's nothing coincidental about it. I really wanted to see you, and you weren't answering my calls."

She raised her eyebrows, turned, and began to jog away. "I wasn't ready to talk to you," she laughed over her shoulder.

He called out, "That's it, huh?"

She turned again, jogging backwards, and smiled. "I thought you said something about coffee. Come on."

He groaned, shook his head, and took off after her. "Okay, but first one there has to pay."

"You're on."

He caught up with her, and his voice huffed in between breaths. "Gonna tell me where we're headed?"

"Someplace awesome." Time to introduce him to Coffee By Design. He was going to love it. "Just try to keep up, Doc."

Chapter Forty-Four

• • • • • • • • • • • • • •

It wasn't until early Monday morning that Liv remembered the trash.

At seven a.m. the street was quiet and the sun was peeking out from behind some wispy white clouds. Hauling a trash bag and her recycling bin out at the curb, Liv's mind flashed back to the Falwell's trash that she'd stashed outside the dumpster at work in the hopes of finding clues about the couple's motives for stealing Cooper Tedeschi's manuscript.

Even though she'd been able to find enough evidence for Cooper to prove he was the originator of Mason Falwell's latest story, there were still questions left dangling like strings of Christmas lights on porches well after the holiday season ended. Most bothersome was the question of why Karie Falwell had rewritten Cooper's manuscript and submitted it under Mason's name. Did she want the money? Did she want recognition for her husband? Had Mason asked her to do it?

It was time to take down those dangling questions, roll them up, and put them away.

Liv had just finished a short run and was still wearing a sweaty T-shirt and jogging pants. Figuring there was no sense in getting into clean clothes before digging through garbage, she grabbed a pair of yellow rubber gloves from under the kitchen sink and a blue tarp from the storage space in the basement before heading down the hill to her office. Getting into her car, she thought about Rob

and his desperate attempt to use her sedan as his getaway vehicle.
"Time to go car shopping," she muttered to herself as she turned
the key in the ignition and pulled onto the street. Out of habit, she
looked around for Snow's SUV, but it was nowhere to be seen.
Why would he be there, she chided herself. He'd caught his
target and was probably busy right now working on a report so
they could prosecute Rob and Gina Mickelson and put them away
for a good long time. Just because he'd rescued her from her own
stupid closet didn't mean anything. He was just doing his job.
She'd probably never see him again.

Liv drove to her office and pulled up near the back of the
building. The trash bags were right where she'd left them beside the
dumpster, a little damp and a lot smellier but intact. Relieved, she
hopped out of the car, gathered the tarp and gloves, and grabbed
the bags. Minutes later, she was inside the empty building. She
spread the tarp on the floor of her outer office, put on the yellow
plastic gloves, and ripped the bags open, remembering to breathe
through her mouth instead of her nose.

She wasn't sure what she was hoping to find. Jeremy's testimony
proved that Cooper had originally written the story later submitted
by Mason Falwell to a publisher, via his agent. Plagiarism software
indicated that Karie, Mason's wife, actually rewrote the manuscript
prior to submission. She'd also worked with Dustin Pfiester to
permanently delete any and all digital proof that Mason had seen
and commented on Cooper's original story. The facts all pointed
to Karie Falwell as the perpetrator of this very unethical action of
stealing Cooper Tedeschi's work.

Why had she done it? Financial gain was the most obvious
answer. If Mason and Karie needed money, why didn't Mason
write his own novel? Was it a case of writer's block? Or did it have
something to do with his alleged drinking problem?

As she spread the detritus out on the tarp and stirred through
it with her gloved fingers, Liv thought back to the day she'd taken
the bag. There had been no recycling bin, she realized. If there had

been, she could have counted the empty liquor bottles. There were no empties in the trash, either. Just coffee grounds, eggshells, a milk carton, the heel of a loaf of bread with green mold growing over it. The plastic wrapping and styrofoam tray that once contained chicken breasts purchased from the supermarket according to the ripped label. A used-up pen. Wadded up tissues and paper towels. Nothing exciting.

A smaller, plastic shopping bag was knotted up and placed inside one of the larger ones. Liv ripped it open. More tissues, these with black and red smudges that indicated they'd been used for makeup removal. The wrapper from a bar of soap. This was obviously the bathroom trash. A pink disposable razor. An orange medication bottle with a white cap. Strings of dental floss. An empty cardboard toilet paper roll.

Liv picked up the medication bottle and studied the label. It was from a local pharmacy. She set it aside, picked up the rest of the trash. Tying the bags closed again, she took them and the tarp to the metal trash container and tossed everything.

Liv re-entered the empty Fiber Foxx building and let the door shut behind her. In the dead quiet and dim lighting, she felt a shiver of fear. What if someone came in and found her alone?

Her heart began to race, so she took a deep breath to steady herself. She couldn't do her job if she was afraid. That thing with Rob was a one-time assault, she reminded herself. She hadn't been paying attention, and it had cost her.

She'd kept her wits about her, for the most part, and she'd learned her lesson. From now on, she'd be super-vigilant. She took another deep breath and hurried into her office.

Holding the prescription bottle, she sat down behind her computer. The Donepezil prescription had been filled for Mason Falwell at a small business that advertised itself as a locally-owned, customer-oriented pharmacy. Liv didn't recognize the drug. Instead of waiting to boot up her computer, she pulled out her phone and did a search.

Donepezil was a drug used to treat Alzheimer's Disease. It was prescribed for patients with mild to moderate dementia.

Liv sat back against her chair. Her mind whirled as a few pieces of the puzzle fell into place.

Mason Falwell had Alzheimer's or some other form of dementia. This most likely explained why he was irritable, forgetful, confused, moody, and unable to perform his job. Teaching and writing demanded facility with language and analytical skills–all potentially impacted by the disease. The way he wandered into Ruth's bagel shop that morning? The antisocial behavior his colleagues had reported? All pointed to cognitive impairment and the ravages of Alzheimer's disease.

Feeling excited about this discovery, Liv pondered the timing. Five years earlier, Mason had announced he was done writing. Had he been diagnosed at that time? If so, did he inform the college? Or were Mason and Karie keeping his condition a secret?

She turned the Rx bottle over and over in her hand. Falwell had been a prolific and commercially-successful author. He'd made plenty of money over the course of his long writing career. He'd always been generous with donations and scholarships. So why hadn't he simply retired instead of playing out some charade that he was still competent to write and teach? What had motivated Karie to rewrite Cooper's book and submit it to Mason's publisher? Greed? Pride? Status? They must have known the consequences of getting caught would be devastating. Why not just let Falwell retire in peace and dignity rather than risk this kind of public humiliation?

There was still a mystery to be solved, a piece of information she hadn't yet uncovered, the key to the entire case. And one person held the answer.

Liv put the bottle into her bag and headed home to shower off the stench of the Falwell's trash. She had a visit to make.

Chapter Forty-Five

● ● ● ● ● ● ● ● ● ● ● ● ● ●

Liv pulled up at the curb in front of the Falwell's house and turned off the ignition. It was near noon, and most people in this well-to-do neighborhood were at work. Karie's black Jaguar was in the driveway, however, and the street was quiet. Liv had called the writing department, and Barbara had told her Mason was in class until twelve-thirty.

Liv would have Karie all to herself.

Stepping from her car, Liv tugged the long hem of her white blouse over her blue jeans and adjusted a new pair of tortoiseshell sunglasses over her eyes. She checked to make sure she had her recording app running and tucked her phone into her back pocket. Finally, she slung the handles of her red leather bag over her shoulder and trotted up to the front door of the house.

Just before ringing the bell, she glanced into the sideyard and spotted a lone figure stabbing at a patch of garden with a garden spade. Perfect.

Liv crossed the lawn, her spiked heels sinking into the soft ground beneath the spring grass. "Hello, Ms. Falwell? Karie? Could I have a word with you?"

Karie looked up. Her blonde hair was pulled back into a scalp-tugging ponytail, and in her baggy jeans, green rain boots, and oversized knit sweater, she looked more like a graduate student than the wife of one of the country's best-selling novelists. She wore a pair of worn leather gloves on her hands with which she gripped the red handle of the garden spade. She turned another clump of dirt before jabbing the blade into the ground.

"What can I do for you?" Karie's voice was hard, suspicious, and as Liv drew closer, she noticed fine lines around the woman's eyes and mouth. Karie Falwell looked haggard, prematurely aged, exhausted. She squinted at Liv and said, "Have we met? You look familiar."

"My name's Olivia Lively, remember? We met when you were with Mason at the library café. I was wondering if you could answer a few questions for me regarding Cooper Tedeschi and his claim that your husband stole his manuscript."

"Now I know who you are," Karie said, her eyes as flat and emotionless as her tone. "You're the private investigator who's been snooping around campus and trying to discredit Mason. I'd like you to leave. Now."

Liv nodded. "Okay, but let me ask you one question first. How long ago was Mason diagnosed with Alzheimer's?"

Karie stared for a moment, and blotches of red appeared on her pale, high cheekbones. "I don't know what you're talking about." She pulled the spade from the dirt, turned her back, and began to carve out another block of the trench she was double-digging.

"Of course you do," Liv said, her voice crisp. "You're probably the one to pick up the Donepezil at the pharmacy, the one to make sure he takes it on time, the one who calls in the refills. Judging from our previous encounter, I'd say you also stand guard for him around campus—deflecting attention, talking for him when necessary, and running interference at lunches and other social occasions. Maybe even doing some of his online work?"

Karie stared, her eyes wide and unblinking, stunned.

Liv tilted her head. "How long have you known? A year? Two? It must have been very disappointing. You break up the guy's marriage. You even get him to marry you. But then you find out the man you married is sick, his mind deteriorating, and soon he'll only be a shell of his former self."

Karie stiffened. She drove the spade into the ground with impressive power. The sharp edge of the heavy blade cut through the dirt, leaving only the wooden shaft and handle exposed.

"Mason's fine, and I couldn't be happier."

And your voice couldn't be more snooty, Liv thought. *But you won't be on your high horse for long.* She reached into her purse and held out the orange prescription bottle.

"I have the bottle, Karie. I know what this drug is for and who the prescription is made out to. Mason has dementia. And you're trying to hide it."

The woman glanced at the bottle and snorted. "So that was you with the trash bags. I should have known." She went back to digging. The scent of earth and crushed grass rose from the ground at her feet. "My neighbor dropped by last week, concerned because she saw a homeless woman lurking around our house, rooting through the trash. My, what a glamorous life you lead."

"So you do admit that Mason has Alzheimer's?"

Karie shrugged. "It's in the very early stages. We are doing what we can to slow the disease, and the drugs are working. It isn't yet affecting his ability to work, if that's what you're implying."

"Five years ago, Mason announced he was done with publishing."

"Just because Mason hasn't published anything in five years doesn't mean he's impaired or that he hasn't been writing." Karie's eyes flickered for a second. "In fact, Mason never stopped writing. He's been working nonstop on *Hours of the Crossing* for the past several years. It was to be the culmination of the series. He didn't want to be pestered by the public, so he told reporters he was through with publishing. This December, he completed the work and sent it to his editor. It's that simple. Think what you want."

Liv stepped closer. "Here's what I think. I think you're lying. I think Mason's brain has degenerated to where he can barely make it to classes, let alone write. I think the two of you kept it hushed up. I think you wanted Mason to write another novel, but he wasn't able to pull it off this one last time. He should have retired, but instead of telling the truth, he kept going, hoping for a miracle. A new drug or some other therapy."

Karie stood, stone-faced, unresponsive. A blue jay screeched overhead.

Feeling confident, Liv slid the bottle back into her bag. "But the miracle came in a different form, didn't it? Cooper Tedeschi, a brilliant, young, unrecognized writer eager to please his hero and mentor, shows up at Longfellow. By sheer luck, it turns out he's writing a novel very much in the vein of your husband's old work."

Karie looked sideways, but she stayed silent.

Liv pressed on. "As the semester progressed, you hatched the plan to steal Cooper's manuscript as soon as it was finished. Mason got him the work-study job typing here at your home. Mason encouraged Cooper to continue until the entire novel was complete, and when it was, Mason submitted it to his agent. Meanwhile, you arranged with the IT department to erase the original files and emails so there would be no proof of who wrote the book. That," Liv said, "is what I think."

Karie gave her a cold smile. "That's quite a wild story. It's total fiction, of course."

Liv shifted her weight, and her heels sank a little deeper into the mud beneath the grass. She made a face. "This ground is soft, isn't it? I should have worn boots. Yours are nice. Reny's?" She mentioned the famous Maine store in hopes of throwing her opponent off balance.

Karie just glared at her. Liv wondered how much longer she could push it before Karie got fed up and marched inside the house.

"Anyway," Liv cleared her throat. "We both know it's not fiction. I may have missed a few details here and there, but the basic plot is solid. Of course, there are a few questions that still need to be answered."

She pulled her phone from her back pocket and showed Karie the recording app. "If you admit what happened, tell the whole truth, maybe things will go easier for you in court. Karie, I promise you, I've already gathered enough evidence to prove Cooper wrote the original manuscript, not Mason. But if you help us out, we can end this whole thing."

Karie leaned toward the phone. When she spoke, her voice was flat. "You're trespassing. Get out of here or I'll call the police."

Despite the threat, Liv decided to push a little harder. "I'll leave in a minute. I'm curious about something. Why would Mason risk his reputation and legacy for one more novel? He's sold like a zillion copies of his books over the years. He's earned millions in advances and royalties. He's one of the top-paid writers in the world. He couldn't possibly have done it for the cash. So what was it? Did he miss the adulation, the fame?"

Karie was agitated now, her eyes wide and her mouth angry. "Mason doesn't care about fame. He's always written because he loves the art, the act of creating, the language, the story. You have no idea what he's like!"

Liv was pleased. Finally, she'd broken through that icy barrier. "Then it was you who came up with the scheme. Makes sense. It must have been disappointing, getting your claws into this famous, brilliant writer and finally marrying him, only to realize he's a dud. Washed up. Losing his marbles. And you'd end up taking care of him. When he was diagnosed, you must have wanted to run screaming in the other direction—or back into the arms of your lover, Dustin Pfiester."

Karie's face registered shock, but she glanced at Liv's phone and clamped her mouth shut. Liv smiled. "But you couldn't do that, could you? How would it look if you abandoned your husband when he was ill? And besides that, you'd lose all the money and prestige, wouldn't you?"

Overhead, a blue jay swooped and let out a harsh cry. Karie gripped the handle of the spade. Her tone was low, her words slow, spoken through clenched teeth. "Shut up. You know nothing about me, either."

"You must really hate your life now. How much fun can it be, babysitting an old, addled, dying man? I bet you resent Mason for getting you into this mess. You're stuck. You can't walk away. As the saying goes, you've made your bed. You can't do anything except wait for him to die so you can get your hands on his money and the rights to his work. In fact, Mason's eventual death will set you up for life, won't it?"

With that, Karie was done. She shook with anger, but her expression remained cold and immobile as stone. "I don't have to listen to this." She started to walk toward the house.

"Actually," Liv called out, playing her last card. "I'm pretty sure Mason didn't rewrite Cooper's manuscript at all. You did."

Karie's back stiffened. She twirled around. Bright spots of color bloomed on her pale cheeks. She held the spade like a trident. "I wish I were a good enough writer to pull that off, but if you were a better investigator, you would have found out that I couldn't even get into the graduate writing program here. I wasn't good enough to make the cut, and I'm certainly not talented enough to fake a Mason Falwell. Maybe you should consider a writing career yourself, Ms. Lively, because this story of yours would make a good whodunnit. Conniving wife. Illicit love affair. A taste for fame. A fortune in the balance. The plot is thin, of course, but the story has potential. As fiction."

She smiled, but her eyes were dead and threatening. She turned the spade toward the ground and drove it in. "However entertaining your theory, the truth is Cooper Tedeschi is delusional. I should have seen it the first time he came around here, offering to work as Mason's assistant. That boy is obsessed with my husband, and he followed him around campus like a lost puppy from the very first day he stepped on the Longfellow campus. Mason couldn't shake him. Every day, there Cooper would be, sitting in front of his office door, waiting to talk to him after class, stalking him at lunch, begging for attention. It was pathetic. Finally, Mason took pity on him and agreed to let him type his manuscripts. I was against the idea, but once Mason decides on something, that's it. Cooper was here at our house seven days a week practically, transcribing Mason's handwritten pages to the computer. Somewhere along the way, the boy convinced himself that he'd written the novel."

"The evidence paints a very different picture."

Karie shrugged "What evidence? Cooper had plenty of opportunity to validate his story, but there's no evidence."

"Thanks to you and Dustin Pfiester." Liv smiled. "You see, Karie. I know about Red Eye."

Chapter Forty-Six

• • • • • • • • • • • • • • •

Karie's calm faltered. "I—I had nothing to do with that."

"I have a witness who says otherwise. You were there the night the Long/Space system crashed. Even though the entire system went down over the weekend, only two accounts were infected with the Red Eye virus—Cooper's and your husband's. Coincidence? I don't think so. You worked in IT with Pfiester when you were both undergrads at Longfellow. Is that when you became lovers? He must have been devastated when you dropped him for the oh-so-famous Mason Falwell."

Liv stepped a little closer to Karie. "But when Mason was diagnosed with Alzheimer's, you hooked up with ol' Dustin again. Did he play hard to get? Or was he just grateful to be back in the fold, so to speak?"

She gave a short laugh, taunting the other woman, trying to goad her into telling the truth. "Once you were back together, I suppose it was easy to sweet-talk him into sabotaging the accounts, especially if you promised to share the enormous profits from the sale of the book with him. So tell me something, Karie. Did you ever stop sleeping with Dustin while you were married? Or did you keep him dangling as a boy toy on the side the entire time? Did poor Mason even know you never loved him but only married him for his connections and his bank account? It must have been hard to sleep with an old man when you had young, virile Pfiester waiting for you across town."

The last of Karie's composure evaporated. Her eyes narrowed, her lips pressed together, opened, and pressed together again. "Did I do it for the money? Yes! But not for the reasons you think!"

A deep flush spread up her neck and across her cheeks. She lifted the spade with both hands as if to swing. She cast a murderous look at Liv who took an involuntary step backward and prepared to defend herself.

Instead of swinging, Karie let out a scream and threw the spade to the ground. She stepped toward Liv, her face a mask of fury, and spit out the words she'd been holding back. "You stand here wearing your oh-so-perfect designer shoes and carrying a leather bag that costs what normal people spend on groceries in a month, maybe two, and you think you know everything? Well, you don't! You don't!"

"Explain it to me."

Karie's eyes lasered Liv with contempt and fury. "I came from nothing. Literally, nothing. Did you look into my background? I grew up in a trailer park out in the sticks with a mother who drank herself into oblivion every night, and who brought home men who thought I was there as a consolation prize when Mom passed out. I spent my high-school years mostly on friends' couches and spare mattresses. I never had money for basics like underwear and deodorant, let alone designer jeans and sparkly makeup. My friends' parents helped me when they could, but it wasn't the same as having my own parents. There was a guidance counselor who took me under her wing, who told me if I worked hard, she'd make sure I got to college. So I did, and she did. I worked my way through school on scholarships and part-time jobs, and I told myself I'd never be back in that trailer park, no matter what."

Liv felt a stab of pity. "Okay, so you were poor, and you took one look at Mason Falwell and thought, 'There's my meal ticket for life?' You didn't care that he was already married, already had a couple of kids, and that he'd be jeopardizing his career and his reputation to be with you?"

"You are so dense!" Karie brushed a gloved hand over her face, leaving a streak of mud. "You don't understand. Mason Falwell's books got me through those awful years. When I was cold and shivering beneath an old sleeping bag in a trailer with no heat because my mother forgot to pay the electric bill that month, I could escape into this fantasy world that Mason created. On holidays, when I was crashing at a friend's house and all their family came over for dinner and I heard the whispered questions, 'Who is that girl?' and 'Why is she here?' and 'Wouldn't she be better off in foster care?' I could go into some corner and read his books and forget that my mother never once tried to find me, never once made sure I was doing okay."

Shocked by what she was hearing, Liv nodded in sympathy.

Karie paced. "Mason's books saved me. When I went to college, the only thing I wanted to do was to write just like he did, to create stories and live in that semi-real world of fiction that had been my escape for so many years. When I found out Mason was going to be teaching here, I couldn't believe it. He'd been my childhood savior. The thought of being in the same room with him, well, that was a dream come true."

Karie stopped. She rubbed absently at her cheek, leaving more dirt streaks. Her eyes were lost, looking right through Liv for a moment and then focusing again. Her mouth had softened for a moment, but then tightened as she glared at Liv. "At first, I just wanted to see him, to hear him speak, to just hang around anywhere he was, but then we started talking. He was kind, too, so kind to me. He must have thought I was a moron, but still, he encouraged me to keep writing. Even though I hadn't been accepted to the MFA program, he told me I had talent and to keep writing." Karie took a breath. "Eventually, I began to tell him bits and pieces about my past, and as we got closer, he also began to confide in me. His marriage was falling apart. His kids barely talked to him anymore unless they needed money. He was lonely. I was lonely. Eventually, we fell in love."

Karie's eyes went wide and pleading. "Don't you see? I love him. I love him so much I'd do anything for him."

Liv sucked in a breath. The raw pain in Karie's voice pierced her usual professional calm. She felt sorry for Karie, but it was time to get to the truth, once and for all."Was it your idea or Mason's to steal Cooper's manuscript?"

Karie's shoulders dropped, and a defeated look crossed her features. "Mason didn't—and still doesn't—have any idea. When he is lucid about it at all, he thinks the book is a collection of old stories he wrote before his first novel and stuff he wrote before his diagnosis."

"When Mason announced five years ago that he wasn't going to publish anymore, was that when he was diagnosed?"

"No. We didn't know at that time, although he was already experiencing difficulty writing. He thought he was just in some sort of slump, but the writing was a mess. Storylines didn't make sense. He'd try to get a chapter onto paper and would lose his train of thought. Then he'd get frustrated and lash out. At me. At his ex-wife. At his kids even. She ended up moving down south to get away from him."

"That must have been scary for you."

Karie ignored that. "We didn't know it at the time, but his inability to write was the first sign of his diminishing capacity. Mason made the announcement that he was no longer going to publish and would instead focus on teaching. It changed expectations. After that, people left him alone and stopped pestering him about a new book."

"And then when you got the diagnosis?"

"When we got the diagnosis three years ago, it was like the end of the world. To me, it seemed impossible that this man, this giant, this hero who had lifted me up and protected me now would need me to protect him. We were advised by his doctor not to wait but to get his affairs in order as soon as possible. We went over timetables for the progression of the disease, medications that could help, and options for when Mason was no longer able to care for himself. At least there's plenty of money, I thought."

Karie continued, her voice wavery. "For the first time, Mason gave me access to his financial information. I looked into his bank accounts, his investments, and I thought I had to be missing something. There was almost nothing. It was a nightmare. I knew he'd lost a lot in the divorce. He'd felt guilty about his wife and kids. She got the big house here in Portland and then he bought her the place in South Carolina. She got half their savings.

"Then he paid for private school and Ivy League tuition for all four kids—two are still in graduate school now. On top of all that, people were always asking him for donations. One person he trusted got him to invest in a dot.com company that went bust."

Karie shook her head. "If I'd known about his dementia earlier, I could have done something, but Mason was generous. He never said no to anybody who came asking for money for this cause or that charity. I loved him for that, but by last year, one of the best-selling authors in the world was practically broke. I didn't know what we were going to do when he needed nursing care."

Liv nodded and tried to sound sympathetic. "All that time, you kept his diagnosis a secret from the college. That must have been difficult."

"Yes," Karie said, taking a deep breath and letting it out slowly. "We needed the insurance. Alzheimer's medicine isn't cheap. We needed the salary. It became harder and harder for Mason to critique student work. I began to help him. To make that easier, we asked students to submit electronic documents and corresponded through email rather than handwritten critiques the way he'd done in the past. It was sad but funny in a way. There I was, the girl who wasn't good enough to be accepted into the MFA program, basically teaching and advising students in the program."

More fraudulent than funny, Liv thought, but she refrained. For some reason, Karie had decided to tell her story, and Liv's recording device was getting it all. She felt a rush of triumph, the payoff for all the hard work that she'd put into the investigation so far. These were the moments she lived for. Celebrate later, she told herself. She didn't want to miss anything Karie was saying, just in case.

The other woman wiped her dirty gloves on her jeans, a nervous movement that left giant smudges on the faded fabric. "Mason could still run writing workshops, though he depended more and more on the students to critique each other in class while I crafted the deeper responses using Mason's Long/Space account. In the meantime, I was desperately trying to figure out what we were going to do once Mason got too ill to continue. By last fall, we knew it was going to have to be his last year. He'd have to retire. He hadn't been there long enough to build up much of a retirement nest egg, and like I said his past earnings from book sales were gone. I just kept thinking if only he could publish one last book, it would be enough to pay for nursing care until… well, just until."

"So you tried to write that book using Mason's old notes?"

Karie nodded, her eyes clouding over. "Yes. I tried, but there wasn't much to go on. I sent a few chapters to Mason's agent, and he wasn't enthusiastic. In the meantime, I was reading and working on Cooper Tedeschi's novel. This is what you have to understand. I liked Cooper. I didn't want to hurt him. But here was this kid blatantly copying my husband's style, writing a book that Mason himself could have written a few years earlier, and ripping off Mason's themes. Sometimes I'd think I was reading one of Mason's old books, the prose was that familiar.

"One morning I was reading Cooper's latest chapters, making notes and suggestions. I was exhausted. Mason had started getting restless at night, wandering around and falling down occasionally. I was afraid he was going to hurt himself. I was trying to do my own work plus my husband's. It was all too much."

Ah, Liv thought. That's what happened when Mason stumbled into Ruth's bagel shop too early in the morning. Despite trying to maintain a professional distance, she found herself feeling sorry for Karie Falwell.

Karie sighed. "So I was reading Cooper's book that morning and the thought popped into my head that I could send it to Mason's agent. At first, I thought I might talk to Cooper about a possible collaboration. I considered explaining the whole situation to see if he would be willing to work 'with Mason' on the novel. But Cooper's attitude scared me off. He was very full of himself. The more I thought about it, the more I doubted he'd be willing to collaborate, especially if he thought Mason considered the work good enough to be published. Why would he want to collaborate when he could submit it to publishers under his own name? And what if I was wrong? What if it wasn't good enough anyway? I rewrote it, changing names and places to fit Mason's made-up world, and sent it to Mason's agent to see what he thought."

"And the agent thought it was good."

"Yes, he loved it. Before I knew it, he'd sent it to the publisher who made a huge offer, and it was like an answer to my prayers. The only problem was Cooper and the electronic files that would prove he wrote the original story. I went to Dustin to ask, theoretically, how I might erase the electronic communications and files. Before he'd help me, Dustin insisted I tell him everything. He said if he was going to stick his neck out for me, he needed some leverage in case things went wrong. I had to implicate myself. And then…"

Karie's face hardened, and all at once, Liv could see the neglected and abused child who had managed to survive by using others and by being used as well. "We worked out an agreement."

Liv's voice was soft. "You mean, he said he'd help you if you slept with him."

"That's right," Karie hissed. "And don't you dare judge me for it. I did what he wanted and he encrypted the files. He crashed the Long/Space system as a cover."

"Did you know the program was Red Eye?"

"Not at first. Later, yes."

"And what about Cooper? Didn't you feel guilty for stealing his work?"

"Of course I did! But like I said, he was blatantly copying my husband's style and themes, anyway. I mean, I get it. I wanted to live in that world, too, and if Mason wasn't able to write it for us, I sort of understand why others would try to expand that world on their own. In a way I'm grateful to Cooper Tedeschi for being such a fan of my husband's work that he was able to do what I couldn't—write a Mason Falwell novel.

"If he'd just been sophisticated about it, if he'd come to me and Mason quietly, I could have offered him compensation. I would have recommended him to Mason's agents and publishers, once Mason officially retired. If he'd been a little savvier, he could have become Mason's literary heir, so to speak. But instead, he went public, stalking Mason everywhere, going to the school newspaper, throwing public hissy fits. I was afraid he'd find out about Mason's illness somehow and blow everything. I had to make sure he was kicked out of school, and the officials didn't like his behavior either. It reflected badly on the college and the program."

Karie shrugged. "He should have been smarter. Do you suppose the publisher would have even looked at a manuscript from an unknown, unpublished fantasy writer fresh out of college without any help? Without my editing? I doubt it. It was good, but maybe not good enough to get through the slush pile. Not without Mason's name attached to it, anyway."

Liv blinked. "That's a pretty cold way to look at it."

"That's publishing."

"You stole a kid's dream for your own personal gain."

Karie flushed, angry again. "Haven't you even been listening to me? Not for personal gain. For love."

The blonde woman began to pace around, clomping over the sod in her gardening boots. "Mason gave up everything for me—his marriage, his relationship with his kids, a beautiful home, half his money. He deserves better than to spend the last years of his life in some second-rate nursing home. He deserves a private nurse or a really good Alzheimer's facility, one where he would be comfortable and well-cared for. Don't you get it? I would have robbed a bank for him. I would have sold my body on the street for him. Anything."

Anger flushed deep red on her cheeks again as she came to stand in front of Liv and glared, hands fisted inside her gardening gloves. "And now you've ruined it, you shallow designer Barbie doll. I hope you're pleased with yourself, because your clothes and your shoes and your fancy bags are all you'll have at the end of the day. At least I loved someone. At least I was loved back. You know what I see when I look at you, poking your nose into other people's lives because yours is so devoid of anything? A spoiled, pampered, fashion plate with a credit card where her heart should be."

Karie stepped forward, tripping on the sod she'd dug up and falling onto her hands and knees in the mud. She crouched back, sitting with her knees underneath her, and pounded her fists into her thighs.

As she listened, Liv went cold from her scalp to her toes. She looked down at Karie with some expression between pity and scorn. "And you know what I see when I look at you? Someone who dug herself into a hole she won't be able to crawl out of. Thanks for your statement."

Karie scrambled to her feet and lunged for the spade. "What would you have done?" Karie screamed and threw the spade toward Liv. "I love him!"

Liv stepped out of the way, and the garden tool sailed harmlessly past her and clattered into the driveway. She spoke calmly. "You were right about one thing. I've never had a love like you describe. Maybe if I did love someone like that, I'd be willing to turn my life upside down and backwards to take care of him. Maybe I'd sacrifice myself before I'd let that person come to harm. Maybe I'd pawn all my possessions or even my body, as long as it was only me that was getting hurt. But you know what? I wouldn't hurt someone else, and I wouldn't steal someone else's work. That's where I'd draw the line. And that's the line between you and me.

Not my fancy clothes and my privileged background.

"Some people in your life tried to help you. Some people reached out and lifted you up. You could have asked for help this time, too. Instead, you took advantage of a struggling young person. You stole from him. You took the one thing that really mattered to him. That was how you repaid those people who helped you, including Mason Falwell. He wouldn't have wanted this, and you know it. At the end of the day, it all comes down to values, and yours are pitiful and you knew better. I'm sorry for you."

With that, she wheeled on her high-heeled pumps and walked away.

Chapter Forty-Seven

• • • • • • • • • • • • •

"I'd like to propose a toast." Cooper Tedeschi stood up fast, swaying and holding up the Longfellow College beer stein that Ethan, Marion, and some of the other MFA students had presented to him as a welcome back to the program and the school. Just that afternoon, he had been reinstated to the writing program. After spending the better part of the spring reconnecting with his cohorts, he was finally in. The group made it clear, however, that any obnoxious behavior on Cooper's part would be cause for a swift withdrawal of camaraderie.

Cooper had accepted the gift, and the warning, with good grace. He even apologized for the obnoxious attitude he'd displayed prior to his dismissal from the writing program. "I was a smug, self-important butthead. I deserved your scorn. But now you've allowed me to come back into the group, and I want you to know how much I appreciate this your friendship and this stein." He began to slur his words. "This beautiful, wonderful stein."

"Just say it, Tedeschi." Ethan sounded both irritated and indulgent. "It's just beer. Stop waxing poetic about it."

"Duly noted," Cooper said. "Thanks for the beer if not for the gratuitous literary advice, Muller."

"I'll show you the gratuitous end of a whup-ass stick," Ethan muttered, but no one paid him much attention.

It was Mid-June. A group had gathered at the Arrow & Song following the final negotiation meeting in the Tedeschi-Falwell case. That afternoon, all the parties had converged in the Longfellow College boardroom—Cooper, representatives from the college, Mason and Karie Falwell, Jeremy Crete, editors from the publishing company, the lawyers—and the details of the settlement had been ironed out once and for all.

It had been the last of several such meetings. Afterward, Liv joined Cooper and Patrick Ledeau and the students at the bar to celebrate. Liv wanted all the recent details. Her last task for the case had been sending Ledeau a copy of her recorded conversation with Karie Falwell along with a typed report and a bill for services rendered. After that, she'd closed the case file and moved on.

She looked at her watch. Speaking of moving on, she needed to get home. She was cooking for someone tonight at her place.

"To Olivia Lively," Cooper said, sloshing the steinful of beer in her direction. "She believed I might have been a delusional sot, but she took my case anyway, and she ferreted the clean and solid truth from the stinking, academic rot of Karie Falwell's garbage can. Literally. She saved my writing, my career, my life." His words were slurred and overwrought but nobody cared. They all raised their glasses and cheered, "To Liv!"

Cooper bent down and gave her a hug while everyone cheered. "Oh, yeah," Cooper said, raising his stein again. "I'm rich and famous, baby!"

Another cheer went up. Ethan threw Cooper a sour look. "Douche," he muttered under his breath. Marion nudged him with a sharp jab of her elbow.

Liv laughed and leaned over to click glasses with Patrick. "I'm glad it worked out, Ledeau. Keep me in mind the next time you need a private dick."

He gave her a broad wink. "Honey, you're no dick, but I have you on speed dial just the same. This case has pushed my career into overdrive, you know. The press alone would have been worth the time and effort I put in. The phone won't stop ringing. I've had to hire a legal assistant. All in all, it was a pleasure working with you."

"I'm glad to hear it. I enjoyed working with you, too." Orin Calder tapped Ledeau on the shoulder, and the lawyer turned to talk with the professor who asked if by any chance Patrick would be interested in joining a men's summer softball league. They were one guy short, and he looked like he could field a ball.

As the boisterous voices rose and fell around her, Liv turned her thoughts back to the unexpected outcome of the Falwell-Tedeschi debacle. Cooper, after several rounds of offers and counteroffers, had finally agreed to sell his manuscript to the original publisher for an undisclosed but sizable advance. In exchange, he'd agreed to officially share authorship with Mason Falwell, whose name on the cover would ensure mega sales and a spot on best-seller lists.

Karie was awaiting a federal trial, but because she'd agreed to work with the FBI in nailing Dustin Pfiester for cyber-crimes and fraud, it was expected that she would receive a light sentence, possibly only house-arrest which would allow her to care for her declining husband. The proceeds from the sale of *Hours of the Crossing* meant there would be enough money for long-term care in a facility when the time came.

Liv twirled her glass of wine and thought about the Falwells and what Karie said she'd done for love. She wondered what that kind of love felt like. Even though she'd told Karie she'd never stoop to that level, who really knew?

As for Mason, he had quietly retired from the college in May. He and Karie could be seen walking down to Buoy Bagels almost every morning, hand in hand, united in what would be a losing battle with a brutal disease that would suck memory and ability from a brilliant man's mind and body.

The college, eager to wrap up all loose ends, invited Cooper back into the writing program if he agreed to drop a threatened lawsuit.

"I'm surprised, Cooper," Liv said to him now, turning to the fledgling author.

"Surprised? About what?"

"That you were willing to compromise your principles and share authorship with Mason. I would have thought it would offend your artistic sensibilities or something like that."

"Well, you know, I guess I could have schlepped the 'script out to other publishers, but there was no guarantee anyone would have taken it. This way, I get a big advance, I can pay off you and Patrick, and my name will be connected with Falwell's. They've given me a three-book deal, and my agent's confident that once I'm established, they'll continue to buy my work. It's not a bad deal. Plus, the college reinstated me in the writing program, and I'll have my bona fides by September. They might even hire me to teach a couple of undergrad sessions in the fall since Mason is retiring. It's all good. It's better than good. It's amazing. The best part is I'm writing again." He looked at her with a sappy expression in his eyes. "And it's all because of you, Liv. Thank you for believing in me, for not calling security and getting me kicked out of the Glitterati Ball that night."

Liv's heart softened. "You're welcome, Cooper. I'm looking forward to reading that book of yours in its final version."

"Come to a reading here at the college and there will be a first edition with your name inscribed inside the flap. You'll want to hold onto it. It will be worth something someday."

Liv gave his arm an indulgent pat. "Great," she said. *Young men and their egos,* she thought. "Well, on that hopeful note, it's time for me to go."

"Don't leave yet! The night is young and so are we. Let me buy you another glass of wine. Come on. Just one more."

"Nope." Liv shook her head and stood up. "Bye, everyone. Good luck with all your endeavors."

"Where are you going, Lively?" Ledeau said.

"Keep on writing all of you." Liv waved at the table. "I have a date."

Chapter Forty-Eight

. . . .

At home, she changed into a pair of faded jean shorts and a simple T-shirt. She padded around her kitchen with her bare feet enjoying the cool floorboards. Consulting the open cookbook, she wiped her hands on her new apron, a design by one of the textile artists in the warehouse cooperative.

With the sound of a scratchy Maria Callas recording of the *Casta Diva* aria floating through her apartment, Liv checked the orzo steaming in a pot on the stove while stirring garlic, tomatoes, pitted Kalamata olives, and basil as they sauteed in a pan of good olive oil. Sniffing, she turned off the flame and dumped some fresh scallops and lemon juice into another pan to quickly cook. She was just about to mix everything together into a buttered casserole dish when the door buzzed.

A flush rose to her cheeks. He was early. She was a mess. She didn't care.

She ran lightly to the door, buzzed him in. "Come on up," she said. Her heart was pounding, so she put her hand to her chest. A piece of garlic fell from her finger onto the front of her apron. She threw open the door. A bouquet of orange daisies greeted her.

"Wow, for me?" she said, pushing the bouquet aside and wrapping her arms around the man behind the flowers.

Jasper's eyes gleamed. "These are for the table. You get something else."

"Ooh, what would that be?" Liv's voice went husky as she moved her face even closer to his, their lips a mere half-inch apart. She could feel his warm breath on her face, smell his pine and leather cologne, dizzying and distracting. She forgot about the casserole. All she could think about was his mouth.

"This," he said, closing the distance. As he kissed her, everything inside her lit up.

She pushed him away and stalked into the kitchen, leaving him standing in the doorway holding onto the daisies.

"This is all the thanks I get for bringing you flowers? I expected more."

"You're early. I have to pop this casserole into the oven," she said, tossing the words over her shoulder.

He followed her into the kitchen, rooted around for a vase, and placed the daisies on the table which was set with bold red and yellow linens that matched her apron. She glanced at him and noticed he was grinning at her. "What?"

"Nothing. Well, actually, you saying you have to pop a casserole into the oven and wearing, what, another new apron? How many do you have in your collection now?"

Liv shrugged, embarrassed. "I don't know. Five. Maybe six." She stirred the scallops and orzo and garlic together into a dish. "Hand me that feta, please?"

He did, and then he leaned against the counter and watched her, his eyes hungry. She pretended not to notice, but he was oh-so-sexy in his jeans and white button-down shirt rolled up above his wrists. She opened the feta and broke it into pieces to scatter over the top of the orzo.

"You're so domesticated now," he said, snagging a piece of cheese and popping it into his mouth. "Cooking classes. Homemade meals. Aprons up the wazoo. When I first met you, you told me you weren't the settling-down type."

"I remember."

"And you couldn't cook. You were so impressed by my *poulet au boursin*."

"I remember that, too." She slid the casserole into the oven and wiped her hands nervously on the apron. "I haven't changed that much. I'm still the feisty, independent private eye you fell in love with. I've just, uh, tweaked my modus operandi a little bit. Besides, I thought you wanted domesticated."

"I want you. Domesticated or free-range. Any which way. Actually, I can think of some pretty good which ways right now. How long is that casserole supposed to cook?"

She laughed. "Thirty minutes." Strong arms wrapped around her. His body pressed into hers from behind. One hand slid up, cupping her breast, and his breath tickled the back of her neck. He bit lightly on her earlobe, sending an arrow of desire straight down her belly. "I bet you have some champagne chilling in the fridge. Am I right?"

She leaned into him, twisted her face up for a kiss. "Mmmm, yes, there's some Veuve Clicquot in there," she murmured against his lips. "I've decided it's all I'm going to drink from now on. I hope I'm not getting too conventional for you, Doc." She moved in for another long, deep kiss. He spanned her hips with his big hands, held her still, just the way she liked.

He abruptly let go of her and turned to the refrigerator. She lost her balance a little, squeaked, and regained her footing. She leaned her hip against the counter. "What are you doing?"

He opened the refrigerator door, grabbed the champagne, and snagged two wine glasses from the table. Without answering, he stalked out of the kitchen, a man on a mission.

"Where are you going with that?"

He continued toward the bedroom. Without turning his head, he yelled, "Turn the oven to low, get naked, and get in here." He disappeared into the room, but then he stuck his head around the frame, blue eyes gleaming with mischief. "Oh, and bring the apron."

Liv's heart thudded, but she couldn't repress the smile on her face. "Okay," she said, turning the oven off and running down the hall to catch him. "But what are you going to wear?"

"Just get in here. I heard you have a big closet. We'll think of something."

She did. They did.

Acknowledgments

• • • • • • • • • • • • • • • •

This book would not exist without the expertise, investment, and encouragement of many talented people. Eddie Vincent and Cynthia Brackett-Vincent, publishers extraordinaire. Deirdre Wait, brilliant cover artist and book designer. Debbie Broderick, Georgette Carignan, and Wendy Farrand, members of the fabulous Advance Copies writing group, who listened, read, commented, corrected and believed through several drafts. Mary Ann Giasson, fellow writer, for all the craft talk over the years. Kevin St. Jarre, excellent writer and author friend, who introduced me to Encircle Publications. Kathy Lynn Emerson, and Cynthia Dagnal-Myron, talented writers and teachers who generously read and provided blurbs. And to other readers and friends, too many to name, who have inspired, believed, and pushed me to follow this crazy dream for so many years. Most of all to my husband, Craig Burbank, for believing in me, always, and supporting me in all the ways. Thank you.

About the Author

• • • • • • • • • • • • • • •

Shelley Burbank is a mystery and women's fiction author and journalist based in Maine and San Diego, California. She's a contributing writer to the *Waterboro Reporter* newspaper, and her short fiction has been published nationally in *True Story, True Love,* and *True Confessions* magazines. Regional and literary publications include *San Diego Woman Magazine* and *The Maine Review.* Shelley was also the co-writer of a full-length, nonfiction memoir, *THE LAST TEN DAYS: Academia, Dementia, and the Choice to Die* by Martha Risberg Brosio. For the latest news, find Shelley on Facebook and Instagram, and visit www.shelleyburbank.com.

If you enjoyed reading this book,
please consider writing your honest review
and sharing it with other readers.

Many of our Authors are happy to participate in
Book Club and Reader Group discussions.
For more information, contact us at info@encirclepub.com.

Thank you,
Encircle Publications

For news about more exciting new fiction, join us at:

Facebook: www.facebook.com/encirclepub

Instagram: www.instagram.com/encirclepublications

Twitter: twitter.com/encirclepub

Sign up for Encircle Publications newsletter and specials:
eepurl.com/cs8taP